Gringolandia

a novel

LYN MILLER-LACHMANN

Curbstone Press

First Edition, 2009
Copyright © 2009 by Lyn Miller-Lachmann
All rights reserved.

Cover design: Guillermo Prado
Printed in Canada by Transcontinental Printing

This book was published with the support of the National Endowment for the Arts, Connecticut Commission on Culture and Tourism and donations from many individuals. We are very grateful for this support.

Library of Congress Cataloging-in-Publication Data

Miller-Lachmann, Lyn
  Gringolandia / by Lyn Miller-Lachmann. -- 1st ed.
    p. cm.
  Summary: In 1986, when seventeen-year-old Daniel's father arrives in Madison, Wisconsin, after five years of torture as a political prisoner in Chile, Daniel and his eighteen-year-old "gringa" girlfriend, Courtney, use different methods to help this bitter, self-destructive stranger who yearns to return home and continue his work.
  ISBN 978-1-931896-49-8 (hardcover : alk. paper)
  [1. Fathers and sons--Fiction. 2. Political activists--Fiction. 3. Chile--Politics and government--1973-1988--Fiction. 4. Post-traumatic stress disorder--Fiction. 5. Journalists--Fiction. 6. Chilean Americans--Fiction. 7. People with disabilities--Fiction. 8. Madison (Wis.)--Fiction.] I. Title.

PZ7.M6392Gri 2009
[Fic]--dc22

2008036990

CURBSTONE PRESS   321 Jackson Street   Willimantic, CT 06226
phone: 860-423-5110   e-mail: info@curbstone.org
www.curbstone.org

Author's Note

In September 1970, the Chilean people elected as president the socialist physician and politician Salvador Allende. Allende moved to nationalize (place under state ownership) key industries and to redistribute the country's wealth in a more equitable manner. His actions provoked the United States government, which feared the rise of another Communist nation in the Americas. After a three-year destabilization effort, the United States, through the Central Intelligence Agency, backed a military coup led by Chilean Army commander General Augusto Pinochet.

The coup, which took place on September 11, 1973, led to the deaths of Allende and approximately 3,000 of his supporters, the imprisonment and torture of more than 30,000 others, and the exile or emigration of nearly a tenth of the country's population. The coup ended Chile's long history of stable democracy and rule of law—a source of pride for this South American nation—and ushered in seventeen years of violent repression. The Pinochet regime reversed not only Allende's policies but also earlier decades of social reforms, leaving the economy in the hands of free market policies that brought economic growth along with increasing misery for the poor. Today, Chile has one of the most unequal distributions of wealth in the Western Hemisphere.

In keeping with the provisions of the 1980 Constitution, which he wrote, Pinochet held a plebiscite on October 5, 1988. After years of living in fear, and despite press restrictions and other rules favoring his side, the Chilean people voted NO to continuing Pinochet's dictatorship. A civilian government took over in March 1990.

The characters in *Gringolandia* are invented but based on actual people who struggled against censorship, repression, and terror to bring democracy to their country. The musician Victor Jara and the young photographer Rodrigo Rojas Denegri (also spelled De Negri) were, unfortunately, real victims of the Pinochet regime's brutality.

For Further Reading:

Allende, Isabel. *My Invented Country*. New York: HarperCollins, 2003.

Arce, Luz. *Inferno: A Story of Terror and Survival in Chile*. Madison: Univ. of Wisconsin Press, 2004.

Constable, Pamela and Valenzuela, Arturo. *A Nation of Enemies: Chile Under Pinochet*. New York: W.W. Norton, 1991.

Dorfman, Ariel. *Other Septembers, Many Americas: Selected Provocations, 1980-2004*. New York: Seven Stories Press, 2004.

Jara, Joan. *Victor: An Unfinished Song*. London: Jonathan Cape, 1983.

In memory of Alexander "Sandy" Taylor
1931-2007

Part One
Then

Chapter One
October 23, 1980
Santiago, Chile

A crash, followed by a scream, jarred him from a deep sleep.

It was his mother's scream. Daniel threw back the covers and sat up straight.

She screamed again. Now fully awake, he heard strange voices. And footsteps that were neither hers nor his father's.

"Where is he?" the stranger demanded.

Where is who?

"He's not here," she said. "Please don't wake the children."

"Liar!" the man shouted. The sound of a slap made Daniel tremble. He didn't know whether to bury himself under the covers or get out of bed to defend his mother. Muffled sobbing rose from the living room. In the apartment on the other side of his bedroom wall, a baby began to wail.

Hugging himself to stop his shaking, he tiptoed to the door and opened it a crack.

The room seemed filled with soldiers, men dressed in khaki uniforms with black ski masks covering their faces. He counted four. Each wore a holster on his belt and carried a machine gun. A real gun, the kind that could kill. The men surrounded his mother, small and scared in her nightgown. Her cheek was bright red.

"Search the place," the tallest one commanded.

A fat soldier came toward Daniel's room. Daniel shrank against the wall behind the door. In an instant the door came apart, and a wood panel smacked his forehead. He yelped in pain.

"I got him!" the soldier shouted.

Rough hands seized Daniel by his pajamas and dragged him into the light.

"Damn! It's his kid!"

Daniel blinked rapidly and tried to cover his eyes with his right hand, but the tall soldier grabbed both his wrists and jerked them behind his back. His feet were kicked out, and he landed on the rug with a dull thud that knocked the breath from him. Wool bristles scraped his cheek. A small, cold, hard object pressed against the side of his head. He smelled grease mixed with garlic.

"You tell us where he is, or we blow the brat away."

For a long moment his mother said nothing.

Mamá, are they really going to kill me?

The baby wasn't crying anymore. In the total silence, Daniel heard a click.

"The...the window," she stammered.

The soldier removed the pistol from the side of Daniel's head and stood. Daniel lay on the floor, struggling to catch his breath. Without his glasses, he could not read the insignia on the man's shoulder patch, but he guessed CNI, the secret police. The man lifted his walkie-talkie from his belt and gave a rapid-fire command. "Close up all the exits to the courtyard. He climbed out the back window."

Daniel imagined the soldiers running swiftly and

silently to their posts, just like in the police shows on TV.

But they were after his father. And his father wasn't a criminal.

His father drove a taxi. That was all Daniel knew about his work. He took Daniel and his sister, Cristina, to school in the beat-up green *colectivo* every morning and came home every night by suppertime.

Lying on the living room rug, he visualized his father. Tall, with gold wire-rim glasses, wavy red-brown hair, and a mustache and beard. Large gentle hands and strong arms. Even now that Daniel was eleven, almost twelve, his father could still lift him onto his shoulders to watch a *fútbol* game.

Maybe he can get away from them. If I hadn't made noise…If I hadn't gotten out of bed… Tears filled Daniel's eyes, and he squeezed them shut.

The shattered door to the apartment swung open and slammed against the wall.

"He's ours, boss."

Daniel pulled himself up. In the seconds before one of the other soldiers pushed him down again, he saw three men with helmets and no masks drag his father inside. His father wore a rumpled white shirt and black pants. It looked as if he had put them on in a hurry.

"Marcelo!" Daniel's mother screamed.

Daniel heard the thud of a fist against a body, followed by a harsh grunt.

Someone grabbed Daniel by the hair and jerked his head back. He looked up into the covered face of the tall one. The boss. The man's eyes were black and terrifying in the shadow, and his mouth, a little round hole cut out of the mask, moved like the mouth of a robot.

"Boy, you watch this," he snarled. "This is what happens to communists."

The helmeted soldiers left. The tall man crouched and ground his knee into Daniel's shoulder blades. Rough hands in his hair twisted his head back. The other three masked men pounced on Daniel's father, aiming blows at his head and body. His glasses flew off and were crushed beneath a black boot. He fell to his knees. Blood ran down his face into his beard.

Daniel closed his eyes and tried to shut out the sound of his father coughing and choking, horrible gasps. *They're beating the life out of Papá. Someone... make them stop.* When Daniel opened his eyes again, his father was on his hands and knees. A soldier's boot struck the side of his head. He flopped onto his back and lay motionless.

"Let's get him out of here."

They had brought a giant canvas sack, like the equipment bag for the *fútbol* team, only bigger. Two soldiers rolled Daniel's father into a ball, and a third pushed him in.

Their hands bloody, the three soldiers hoisted the bag and carried it through the door. Daniel strained to see if there was any movement in the bag, or if his father was already dead. The leader stood, grabbed Daniel by the front of his pajama shirt, and dragged him to his knees.

"You learn your lesson, boy?"

Daniel said nothing.

The man shook him and shouted, "You answer me, you little bastard!"

Daniel nodded quickly.

"Good," the man said. "Because we live in a great

country. To keep it that way, we have to get rid of subversives. Or they'll take over and create chaos. Or another Cuba." He paused, lips pressed together in the hole cut out of the black mask. His arm dropped to his side. "Oh, what the hell. You're just some commie's stupid kid." He spat onto the carpet, shouldered his rifle, and followed the others out of the apartment.

Daniel thought he would never get up from the floor, but he found himself standing as soon as the soldiers were gone. He picked up the twisted wire frames of his father's glasses. His mother hugged him.

"I'm sorry, Mamá," he mumbled over and over.

"It wasn't you. They would have found him anyway."

"Will they kill him?"

"No, Danielito. They're just taking him to the police station to answer some questions. He'll be home soon."

Daniel knew she was lying. "Did he commit some kind of crime?"

She shook her head and answered, her voice steady, "No, he didn't. He wasn't the one who committed the crimes."

Daniel heard a whimper from his sister's bedroom. His mother went inside and came out clutching seven-year-old Cristina's hand. Tina sucked her other thumb, a ragged doll pressed to her chest.

Salty tears had dried on his mother's cheeks. She held him and his sister tightly. Her hair was rumpled, and her face seemed suddenly older.

Daniel thought as hard as he could. If he thought about it hard enough, maybe he could make the day go away. His father would be back with them as if nothing had happened.

Take this day away, he implored God. His father had told him there was no God, but he couldn't think of anyone else who had the authority to take back a day.

Chapter Two
The Hole
1980-1986

Marcelo knew only what the other prisoners told him. In the third year of a nineteen-year sentence, he awakened one day unable to move. Unable even to speak, his tongue a huge cotton plug in his mouth.

The *compañeros'* version too was sketchy, incomplete. Guards had taken him downstairs to the commander on a Sunday morning. The *compañeros* recalled it was Sunday, for the doctors, the ones who kept the prisoners alive so they could be tortured another day, were gone to church. He was dragged back to the cell the next day—naked, unconscious, covered in filth, bleeding from his nose and right ear.

Several hours later he had a seizure. Guards took him away again.

* * *

He awoke in a bed, under white sheets in a white room. A uniformed man with a machine gun stood over him.

Where am I? A question perfectly formed in his mind came out as a long, indistinct wail.

"Shut up, you," the armed man snarled.

Who are you?

"*Jué*, his eyes are open." The man disappeared from Marcelo's field of vision. After a few moments, Marcelo heard the dialing of a telephone, then, "Boss, you won't believe it. I think he's coming to."

A pause.

"Yeah, I thought we had a vegetable on our hands."

Another pause.

"So what do you want me to do?"

There was a click, like a cigarette lighter flicked open.

"And if he asks questions?"

* * *

"You stupid *huevón*, you fell down the stairs. Yeah, that's how it happened. Did you want to kill yourself?"

"Screw you," Marcelo mumbled.

"I bet that's it, Aguilar. You talk big, but you're a coward like the rest of them."

Light shone hot in his face. His vision blurred, and at the periphery of his left eye there was only darkness.

"Now tell us who took those letters out."

"I don't remember."

He sensed impact against his face, but on the numb left side. His right jaw started to ache in delayed reaction to the blow.

"Then tell us what you do remember."

* * *

His green taxi carried more than passengers. It carried the truth on slips of paper that he committed to memory, then swallowed. Leaflets blown by the wind through the *poblaciones* told the victims' stories and named their murderers and torturers. Word spread of the taxi's driver, a former journalist, who wrote the leaflets and dropped them off where the wind would take them to the places they needed to go.

Once in prison Marcelo had a way of seeing through blindfolds. And the last name he remembered before everything went blank was Commander Alberto Estrada.

* * *

"How low can those fascists go? Torturing a crippled man," the *compañero* named Jaime said.

Pain twisted Marcelo's body. This time, he was sure they'd cracked a couple of ribs. With each breath he almost passed out.

Jaime, who'd been a medical student on the outside, started to work Marcelo's paralyzed left leg. Marcelo's back muscles seized up and he screamed.

"Damn it, you're worse than the guards!" Marcelo could speak by now, but slurred his words as if drunk.

"I have to do this if you want to walk again. That hospital didn't do a thing, just threw you back here."

"Can you wait until tomorrow?"

"You'll be just as sore tomorrow."

* * *

Over time the *compañeros* brought him back. If it weren't for them moving his paralyzed limbs and teaching him to speak again, he might as well have thrown himself down the stairs like the guards said he'd done in the first place. When he finally began to walk, he swung his left leg out, foot dragging, and he often had to grab the wall, cell bars, or furniture for support. The arm remained weak and clumsy. If he didn't fall asleep holding something in his left hand, he would awaken with the fingers curled and digging into his palm. But from the day he regained consciousness forward, his memory remained intact, and he pledged never to forget those who saved him.

* * *

The interrogators wanted to know about Commander Estrada. The hole in Marcelo's memory cost him cracked ribs, a couple of broken teeth, a half-dozen encounters with the electrified metal bed frame, cigarette burns, and solitary confinement. Solitary was the worst.

After the beating, they dumped him into a box, one and a half meters long and less than a meter wide so he couldn't lie down. There was no one to help him stretch his paralyzed side, which contracted in agonizing spasms. The solitary cell had no windows; it was as if he lived in an endless night. He told time by the length of his matted, filthy hair and beard.

Three men took turns guarding the cells. He couldn't see them but their voices were distinct. The guards took bets on who would be the first of the solitary prisoners to die. One had his money on Marcelo, and every time Marcelo tried to sleep, the guard woke him and asked, "Aren't you dead yet, Aguilar?"

"No."

"Then will you hurry up and die? My daughter's birthday is coming up soon, and I want to collect my pesos so I can buy her a new skirt."

Another guard would warn him of the next interrogation. It took away the shock, but he spent the time until then shaking and sweating, reliving the last ordeal.

"Why don't you just tell Commander Gonzales what he wants? Then you'll be out of here."

"Even if I could I wouldn't."

"He's getting really mad, I tell you. If you don't confess this time, he's going to crack the other side of your head against the wall."

Marcelo ran his good hand along the side of his head, where the hair had once been shaved but was now just as long and tangled as the rest. He felt the part of his skull that had caved in, and the realization came to him that the guard was telling the truth. From his days as a journalist he knew the damage didn't come from a fall down the stairs, which would have left evidence of multiple impacts.

More than a year of confusion cleared. His stomach burned with rage. "Did you see it?"

"No. I heard about it. And I heard he's ready to do it again."

"Then I won't be able to confess, because I won't be able to speak at all."

"You know, Commander Estrada was a friend of mine. He used to invite us guards to his home for a picnic once a year. When my wife got sick and I had her hospital bills, he paid the school fees for my kids. Did it ever occur to any of you communist bastards that he had a wife and three kids and another one on the way?"

"Did it ever occur to you that the thousands of people you murdered had mothers or wives or children who wept for them, too?"

"I hope Commander Gonzales kills you so I don't have to listen to your crap."

It was the second time the guard had mentioned this commander's surname. Marcelo pushed on, as if programmed. "Carlos Gonzales?" He really had no idea, but the name Carlos came to him.

"Miguel Gonzales."

"And why are you telling me his name if you think I had anything to do with whatever happened to Commander Estrada?"

"Because I don't expect you to get out of here alive."

* * *

"We already have a confession from one of the other prisoners that you ordered the killing of Commander Estrada. Your pain will end if you plead guilty."

For a moment Marcelo considered who might have betrayed him. But that was their tactic, to claim that a *compañero* had betrayed a person to sow discord among the prisoners. And people often broke under torture or under the influence of truth serum.

"My pain will end because you'll execute me for a crime I didn't commit."

"Yes, it's a capital crime. You can choose to die with pain, or without pain."

Marcelo silently repeated the commander's name, so he wouldn't forget it even if the son of a whore bashed in the other side of his head.

"I'll die like a man."

* * *

They didn't torture him to death that day. And the next time a guard came to get him, it was to release him from solitary. When he returned to the cell he shared with the *compañeros*, a bundle of letters was waiting for him. Two years' worth of letters from Victoria, who after his arrest had taken their children to the United States. How ironic, he thought, that they would end up there, in the home of the CIA that had installed the dictatorship. The postmark read Madison, Wisconsin. She wrote about the children, her graduate studies in sociology, and her meetings with people to secure his release. Commander Gonzales sent down pens, paper, and instructions for him to write her back: "Write that you are in good health and being treated well."

"And if I don't?" he asked the guard.

The guard shrugged. "Just write what he said."

"I'm not going to write a lie."

The guard took the pens and paper away.

* * *

His time in solitary set back his rehabilitation, and when he returned to his cell he could no longer walk unaided. Another *compañero*, Pablo, rigged up a cane from a broken table leg he'd pilfered from the interrogation room. Even so, Marcelo stumbled often and in one fall broke the wrist of his weak arm. He still wore the plaster cast, which had turned yellowish gray from the filthy cell, the day Commander Gonzales arrived with three guards.

"Aguilar," the commander bellowed.

"Here." Marcelo remained on his back on the cement floor, pressing his feet to the wall, an exercise to strengthen his bad leg.

"Stand and salute."

Jaime and Pablo, who had been playing chess, helped him up. He gave Gonzales a half-assed salute.

Gonzales signaled to one of the guards, who unhooked his keys from his belt and unlocked the door. The guard slid the door open. The sound of metal against metal echoed in the cavernous space.

The commander beckoned Marcelo forward. "Let's go. Your sister has come to pick you up. You have seventy-two hours to leave the country."

Part Two

Now

CHAPTER THREE
February 8, 1986
Chicago

Papá's plane is late. Mamá steps up to the window in front of the empty jetway, her nose almost touching the glass. I run my finger along the edge of the leaflet I've stuffed in my coat pocket and stare beyond the runway to the shimmering snowbanks that cover the fields.

While Mamá's trying to teleport the plane to O'Hare, I slip the leaflet out and unfold it. I pulled it off a kiosk on the UW campus this afternoon so I can recognize Papá when he steps off the plane. "CHILEAN POLITICAL PRISONER," it reads. Below is the picture the way I remember him, with gold-rim glasses, wavy hair, and beard. In the picture, my father is smiling.

Every year they hand these things out. Mamá and the rest of the Latin America Solidarity Committee. They stand around campus, pushing them on people who only toss them out moments later. Then Professor and Mrs. Ballard, who arranged for us to move to the United States, come over for dinner and talk with Mamá in Spanish until late at night, mapping out a new letter-writing campaign or planning a concert to raise money. Their voices echo in our small apartment while I have to get Tina to sleep.

I stay away from campus when they're leafleting. I can't stand to look at the flyers with Papá's picture, like those milk cartons with the missing kids' faces plastered

18

all over them.

Have you seen him? Marcelo Aguilar Gaetani. Missing since October 23, 1980. Taken at age 32...

He'll be almost 38 now.

"Daniel?"

I glance up to see Mamá next to me.

"I told you not to bring it," she says in Spanish. "He doesn't look like that anymore."

"Sorry." I wad the blue paper into a tight ball and drop it into a nearby wastebasket. In a few minutes I won't need it anyway. He'll be here in person. No more pictures in the family album or on kiosks. My real father—the one I remember, the hero everyone else has been talking and writing about for years—will be back.

Mamá motions me toward the window and straightens my tie for what has to be the twentieth time. I push my long wavy hair out of my face. My hair looks dark in the window's reflection. In fact, it's brown with red streaks like Papá's, and lots of people say I don't look Hispanic. If I feel like enlightening them, I tell them Hispanics come from all over the Americas, and we don't always have brown skin and eyes and dark hair. I adjust my glasses and check the taxiway for a very late plane out of Miami. My foot taps the tile floor to the rhythm in my head: *apúrese, apúrese.*

"Do I look all right, *m'ijo*?"

Mamá fingers the single strand of pearls she's wearing over the navy wool dress she brought from Chile. The dress is too tight, but she hasn't gotten any clothes for herself since we arrived in Wisconsin almost five years ago. "You look fine."

The whine of engines shutting down bursts through

the window. I see the giant nose of a 747, the light in the cockpit, the green glow of the starboard wing. People crowd around us, but speaking Spanish with Mamá makes me feel like it's just her and me. Mamá puts her arm around my waist and pulls me to her.

I wish Tina could be here with us, but Mamá had her stay with the Ballards overnight. She said it was because of the length of the trip—Madison to Chicago and back—and the late hour. She was right about the hour. I stifle a yawn. I want to look alert for Papá. Make him proud. I stand up straight.

Passengers pour into the terminal. I watch Mamá for a cue. She lets all the bearded men go by, and all the young ones too. I notice the tourists, still dressed in brightly colored short-sleeved shirts, and three girls in tight jeans. Any other time I would have watched the show, but tonight my focus returns to the jetway. The flood of passengers turns to a trickle.

"*Mira*," Mamá whispers, holding my arm. "There he is."

"Where?"

"Coming up the ramp."

There's a thin man with gray hair long enough to cover his ears and the back of his neck. He walks slowly, swinging his left leg outward. His foot drags along the floor. "No way," I say to her in English.

She hesitates, as if she isn't so sure either. The man shows no sign of recognizing us. His gaunt face is clean shaven, though with a couple of days' stubble, and he wears no glasses. One eye looks smaller than the other. As he comes nearer, I see it's almost closed. He wears a faded, stretched-out blue turtleneck and black pants frayed at the cuffs. His clothes hang off him, scarecrow-style.

"It's him," Mamá says. "Ileana told me about the limp."

"Oh, no," I murmur. Then it hits me, right in the stomach. This is what I did, by getting out of bed when the soldiers came.

I step toward him. Mamá holds me back. "Give him a chance to see us first. He doesn't have his glasses, and we don't want to rush at him."

"Why not?"

"He's okay, but Ileana says he's a little nervous about being touched."

I nod, but inside my down coat I'm shaking. Sure, she told me about Papá being tortured, and it was on the leaflets, too. But that was just words. This guy is really messed up. Maybe he isn't Papá. Maybe this is some kind of sick joke, some way they have of torturing the family, killing Papá and sending this crippled guy to take his place.

"Victoria! Danielito!"

Six years and all doubts disappear with that voice. I'm eleven again, and Papá is calling me—his voice low, tight, and smooth like the radio announcer he once was.

My parents hug. Ignoring what my mother just said, I throw my arms around both of them. I feel Papá stiffen and pull away.

Did I hurt him? "*Bienvenidos*, Papá," I say, my voice choked up more than I expected. My father hesitates, then grabs me. His grip is weak, unbalanced. I wrap my arms around him and feel his bones, hard and sharp against my hands. I ease up, afraid of squashing him. He's no taller than I am—how did that happen? He hangs on to me as if I'm propping him up, and I don't want to let him fall.

"I hardly recognized you. You've gotten so big," he

says in Spanish.

But Papá is so much smaller. "How are you?" I ask, in our language. Soon enough, I think, he'll have to learn English.

"I survived. I'll be back to give the general and his friends a hard time. That's the most important thing." My father slurs his words a little. He lets me go and gives me a clenched-fist salute with his right hand. His eyes are bright. "Where's Cristina?" he asks Mamá.

"I had the Ballards keep her. I knew it would be—"

His grimace cuts her off. At that instant, I realize lateness had nothing to do with it. Tina would be seriously freaked out right now.

Papá squints in the direction of the main terminal. "Is there a way out of here?"

"*Sí, amor.*" Mamá takes his arm. Together they start down the corridor. I hang back and keep pace with them. I wish I could hurry them along, get them out of the airport. I want to talk to Papá alone. I tell myself it wasn't my fault, he's not as bad as he looks. After all, he gave me the same clenched-fist salute I'd seen in the old photos of him. The same salute people always give when they aren't afraid of standing up to their government.

"How was your trip?" Mamá asks. A glacier could get out of the airport faster than those two.

"Long. I've never seen a plane so big."

The only time I've ever flown was when Mamá, Tina, and I moved up here. Our plane was huge, too, which was kind of cool except that we were leaving the only home I'd ever known.

"Did you get something to eat?"

"I wasn't hungry."

"Was it a rough flight?" I sense the concern in her voice. I know she's afraid to fly, but it's more than that.

Papá shakes his head. "Rough was those old DC-3s I flew when I worked for the radio station. This was nothing." He shrugs one shoulder.

After a few seconds, Mamá asks, "Did you get our letters?"

"Censored and up to two years late, but I got them."

Then why did you hardly ever write us back?

As if to answer my silent question, he continues, "There was a long time when I couldn't write you. Then they tried to make me tell you I was okay and being treated well. I wasn't going to write a lie, so I didn't write at all. I'm sure you understand."

"Chelo…" Mamá's voice catches on his nickname. Papá whispers something to her. I dig the toe of my sneaker into the floor. *Wasn't that what the leaflet was all about?* I ask myself. *Wasn't that what Mamá told me all these years? How he'd refused to stop writing the truth even though his life was in danger?* They had a lot of nerve, putting him in prison and then making him write nice things about it.

Papá teeters when he steps on the escalator to the baggage claim. Mamá reaches out to steady him, but he waves her away. "I'm fine," he says sharply. He presses himself against the handrail, away from us.

The suitcases are already there by the time we get to the baggage area, and a few unclaimed ones are riding around in circles on the conveyor belt. The place is almost deserted. Papá points to a hard blue plastic case standing upright.

I lift the case off the conveyor belt and stagger

backward under its weight. I'm pretty average in size but solid. I work out to keep in shape for soccer season and playing my electric guitar, which can feel heavy after a few forty-minute sets. So I wonder how Papá got the suitcase this far with his limp and everything. "What do you have in there?"

"Books. Papers. I don't imagine they have too many books in Spanish up here."

Mamá cuts in. "Daniel's taking a Spanish class at the university."

Papá gives me a crooked smile that reveals broken and missing teeth. "That's super."

"He got an A last semester."

"I always knew my boy was smart." Papá looks at me straight on. "It's important that you keep up your Spanish."

Papá sits on the suitcase and pulls a crushed pack of cigarettes from his back pocket. "They don't let you smoke in here," my mother whispers.

"And I don't want the gringos arresting me on my first day." He taps the pack against the suitcase. "So where can I?"

"Outside. But it's freezing," I tell Papá. He woke up to summer in Chile, and I'm sure he has no idea how cold it can get in the Midwest.

He swears under his breath and shuffles toward an exit marked TAXIS AND LIMOS ONLY. Just inside the exit door he sticks a cigarette in his mouth and lights it with a disposable lighter. He blows out a mouthful of smoke.

"I'll get the van," I say to my mother.

I start toward the exit for the parking lot. Mamá grabs my arm. She's shaking her head. "I wasn't prepared for this," she says in English.

I lay my hand on her shoulder. A single tear rolls down her cheek. I focus on her strand of pearls to avoid having to look her in the face. She always wants to be strong for us, but a lot of times when I can't get to sleep I hear her in the next room crying.

"It's fine, Mamá."

"No. I knew about the accident."

"What accident?" I fight the sinking feeling in my chest.

She goes on like she didn't hear my question. "I knew he wasn't the same. But what those people did to him…" She takes a breath. "And I wasn't there. He was suffering, and I wasn't there."

"Really, he's all right," I tell her, trying to believe it myself. "He doesn't walk too well, but like you said, he's okay." I recall the soccer games—*fútbol*—that he used to play with the other men in the neighborhood. And with my friends and me. It didn't look like he'd ever play with us again.

"I could have done more."

"You did the best you could." Letters, meetings until late in the night, phone calls, leaflets on campus. Thick envelopes arriving in the mail from Amnesty International and from places all over the United States. At one point she even contacted a group in France. "And you were taking care of us, too."

"But I didn't bring your sister. He wanted to see her."

"She'll be home in the morning." I pull my shoulders back and toss the hair from my face. "Besides, she would have only gotten in the way. She's too young."

Mamá pulls a tissue from her purse and dabs at her face. The tissue comes away with brown and pink smudges from her makeup. "Please go ahead and get the van," she says, her voice now steady. "I'd like to stay here with your father."

Avoiding the sleeping airport policeman, I bring the van around to the TAXIS AND LIMOS ONLY exit, load the suitcase in the back, and help my father climb to the front passenger seat. I notice he can barely use his left arm. His wrist is stick-thin, and the skin is paler and smoother than that of his hand. I wonder if he'd hurt his wrist earlier and reinjured it lugging the heavy suitcase.

"You're driving?" he says to me.

"Yes."

"Unbelievable." He shakes his head.

"I got my license a year ago. I'm an experienced driver."

"And the last time I saw you, your feet didn't reach the pedals. Remember you tried to drive the taxi to your friend's house and ended up in a ditch?"

Embarrassing memory. I was really dumb once.

"Nice van, you two. Is it yours?"

I answer. "No, it's my friend Willie's. We're in this band together called Firezone, and he lets me use it sometimes."

Papá sits up straight. "A band? What kind of band?"

"Rock, mainly. And reggae. I play lead guitar, and Willie's the drummer. Another guy, Trevor, is the lead vocalist, and his brother Paul is on bass." Just talking about the band makes me excited. I want to tell him everything. I want him to come hear me perform. "We play in a teen club called the Jam, every Friday night." I jerk the van out of the parking space, almost popping the clutch.

"So you're a rock and roller now that you're in Gringolandia?"

The coldness of his tone shocks me, even more than him calling this country Gringolandia. I always knew the United States government had something to do with the coup and still supported the dictatorship, so it confused me when Mamá told me we were moving up here for her to go to graduate school. Even now, my whole body tightens up when I see a policeman. I rush to explain. "I play everything. On Sundays I play Latin American music at a church. A friend of mine, her father—"

"You play in a church?"

"It's a gig, Papá. They pay thirty dollars a week."

Papá lights another cigarette. "Okay, I used to work with the church too, when I was doing my newspaper. They're good people, as long as you don't start believing any of it. So do you have to play religious songs?"

I lie. "No. Only Latin American songs." As the smoke wafts over to my side, I open the window a crack and shiver at the icy wind. I get the point. He has no interest in my music.

Papá coughs and turns toward my mother in the back seat. "Has the other one adjusted this well?"

She hesitates as if she too is surprised by the way he's asked the question. I think he should be proud of how we've done. Except for poor Tina.

"It's been hard," Mamá says. "Daniel's helped a lot, especially with his sister. I thought he'd have the worst time, being older."

"It wasn't that bad," I mumble. I don't like to think about the first few months, when I couldn't understand what anyone was saying. I had no friends and sat alone in my bedroom playing the guitar my favorite uncle, *Tío* Claudio, had given me before I left Chile. My first soccer team changed all that. After a year or so, I learned enough English to avoid being a complete social and academic zero, and now I speak it with an accent that makes girls go wild.

"Well, don't get too comfortable," Papá says. "We're going back to our country."

My mouth drops open. "Marcelo," my mother says in a low voice, almost a growl.

"As soon as I convince the rest of you to come with me."

You're crazy, I want to say. *After all they did to you, you want to go back? And what about our lives here?* But I wait for Mamá to answer first, the way I've been raised to do.

"They gave you three days to leave. I assume you're banned from returning."

Papá takes a final puff of his cigarette, drops it on the floor of Willie's van, and grinds it out with his good foot. "I have my ways."

"Forget it. It's too dangerous."

Papá glares at her, like she's not supposed to backtalk him either. I press my lips together as tight as I can and ease the van onto the interstate. I can't go back to Chile. Not even Mamá knows this, but I've written for the papers to get my U.S. citizenship, and when I turn eighteen, it's going to be official. I glance at Mamá through the rear view mirror. She looks helpless, confused, and small.

I turn the radio on low while Mamá and Papá talk about the situation in their faraway country. On the sports station they're still rehashing the Bulls game that finished a couple of hours ago. I listen until the station begins to crackle and fade.

CHAPTER FOUR
February 9, 1986
Madison

Ten hours later I'm standing outside Courtney's Sunday school classroom, waiting for the bell to ring. There's a dull roar inside, and the teacher's begging the beasts to settle down for one more minute. I don't hear Courtney, who's just the aide, but who sometimes does a better job than the teacher of shutting them up. Sixth and seventh graders can be rough. My sister's that age, so I ought to know.

The bell sends a knot of preteens through the door. Holding my guitar case above my head to keep them from laying their paws on it, I squeeze inside. Courtney's cleaning a spill by one of the desks. Glue. Around us are the remnants of a Valentine's Day craft project gone bad—construction paper everywhere.

"Aren't they a little old for crafts?" I whisper to her.

She nods and grimaces. "They were supposed to be making valentines for their parents. You know, honor thy father and mother," she whispers back.

Across the room, the teacher's rearranging desks into neat rows. "I'll take care of it, Mrs. Roberts," Courtney says. The teacher thanks her and leaves.

As soon as Mrs. Roberts is out of the room, Courtney gets up from the floor and we kiss for a long time. She runs her fingers through my hair, and my entire body tingles. After we separate, I loosen my tie, and she smoothes her peasant skirt.

"I was thinking about you while we were doing the lesson. At least until Mrs. Roberts brought out the construction paper and the kids went wild."

"What were you thinking?" I pause and smile. "I mean, about me. Not that lame craft project."

Her laugh tinkles like wind chimes. She's braided a few strands of her blond hair in front, and I stroke the skinny braids.

"Your father getting back and all. How you hadn't seen him in so long, and here he is, returning in time for Valentine's Day."

Or sort of returning. I know I'm supposed to say something to make her think I'm really excited, but I feel confused and dull. I had to play at services on less than five hours' sleep. I want to get home. I'm thinking that Papá will be all right after he's had a good night's sleep, that the long trip and the heavy suitcase made him like that.

Courtney rummages through some papers on a table at the back of the room. "I bought something for you guys. Kind of a homecoming present," she says. "I hope the kids didn't find it."

I push aside a pile of scissors. There's a sampler-size box of chocolates with an envelope attached. "Is this it?"

"Yes." She hands the present to me. "Did your father get in on time last night?"

I pick at the envelope's flap. "The plane was hours late out of Miami. We didn't get home until after three this morning."

"And then you had to wake up for church." She gives

me a pitying look.

"I wanted to. I could have taken the day off."

"So how's he doing?"

"Okay. He was asleep when I left."

Courtney's face turns serious. "He must be exhausted, after all he's been through."

"Yeah, but he wants us to go back to Chile."

"Wow!" she says, mouth open.

"Courtney, that would suck. Talk about a long-distance relationship."

"Yeah, but that's incredible. After being in prison and all, he wants to go back and fight." She starts to stack the red pieces of construction paper. I work on the white ones. "Maybe later this year he can come and speak to the Spanish Club. You can play, and he can talk about his experiences."

I sigh. Ever since Courtney became president of the Spanish Club, she's been trying to get me to play South American music and to talk about growing up in Chile. I don't mind playing, but I can do without the political discussion. Chile's in the past, and I want to keep it that way.

"You know I'm much better at playing than talking. And I don't know about Papá. He doesn't speak any English."

"That's okay. I can translate. I have an A in AP."

"He speaks real fast. Not like me or your teacher."

"Then you can come and help." When I don't reply, she asks, "Why not?"

I set her present down. Courtney's been my girlfriend since last year, when she answered my sign offering Spanish tutoring. She'd started Spanish late and was trying to skip a year to get into AP. She's ten months older than I am, and she's graduating this year while I have another year to go. Last week she sent in her deposit for UW. She's sticking around for me even though she's smart enough to go to Harvard. And besides, she and her parents wrote letters to get Papá released. I owe her.

"I'll wait until he's rested a little. Then I'll ask him," I answer after a moment.

I need to return Willie's van. Courtney offers to drive me home afterward. I suspect ulterior motives. "I can get a ride from Willie," I tell her.

"No, you can't." She laughs. "After last night, he'll be out of commission until Wednesday."

"What happened?"

"An all-time record keg stand at Ryan's party."

"Okay, I'll take the ride," I say.

She tries one more time to get invited inside when she drops me off, but I put her off by promising her I'll talk to my father today about the Spanish Club. My mother's waiting for me when I come in the door.

"We have a problem," she whispers in English.

"What?"

"Your sister." She motions to the sofa, where we both sit, side by side. "When she got home, she saw your father, screamed, and ran into her room. She won't come out."

"Super. Where's Papá?"

"In our bedroom." Mamá sighs. "We need to talk. All of us."

"Now?" I have Courtney's present in my hand. I was hoping for a more pleasant reunion, one involving candy. I hand the box to my mother and tell her where it came from.

"That's so nice," she says. "I hope we can have her over soon. Reverend and Mrs. Larkin too."

"She asked me, like, a hundred times today already."

Now she picks at the envelope. At this rate, it's going to be pretty tattered by the time we ever get around to opening it. I start toward Tina's room. Mamá grabs my arm. "Please don't ask him what happened."

Exactly what I planned to do.

"And tell Tina not to ask him either. We need to let him decide when and what he wants to tell us."

I shrug helplessly. "Sure."

Tina's door is locked. I knock. A muffled "Go away" greets me.

"It's me. Daniel."

I hear footsteps, and the doorknob clicks.

Tina's room looks ransacked, but it's like this every day. Clothes on the floor, unmade bed, crookedly hung posters. The posters announce demonstrations for freedom in Chile, and there's even a poster for the literacy crusade in Nicaragua that the Ballards brought back from one of their trips. Mine's still rolled up in the back of my closet. Bruce Springsteen's got my only blank wall.

"I heard you saw Papá," I begin.

"That's not him." She shivers a little in her desk chair. Her legs are drawn up to her chest, and she's wrapped her arms around her knees. She's wearing her pajamas and an oversized shirt that makes her look even scrawnier and younger than she is.

I try the honest approach. "That's what I thought last night."

"Why didn't they bring me?"

I don't tell her it's because she's too young, whines

nonstop, and has been known to throw tantrums at age twelve. She would have been screaming in O'Hare Airport in front of three hundred people. "It wasn't my decision."

"Wimp," I hear her mutter.

That stings. Letting it go, I continue, "Anyway, they want to talk to us. You can't hide in your room forever. Papá's here to stay now." I'm supposed to tell her she's banned from asking him any questions, but I'm just happy to get her out of the room.

Mamá and Papá are sitting next to each other on the sofa. Tina takes the only armchair, so I bring over one of the metal kitchen chairs with the red vinyl seat cushions.

Mamá takes Papá's good hand. His other hand, with the pale, skinny wrist, is curled into a fist on his lap. He's wearing a black turtleneck today, but it's no less ragged than the blue one he wore last night. He glances at Mamá and starts to speak.

"I know it's been a long time, and I don't appear the way you remember me."

Tina shrinks back in the chair and draws her legs up again. I'm not sure she understands him that well, because her Spanish isn't as good as mine—she'd just turned eight when we left Chile—and Papá's speech isn't clear even though he's had all morning to sleep.

"A lot has happened, and I'm going to spare you the details. But I'm still your father, no matter what I look like or where we're living. I don't know how you did things for the past five years, but there will be no screaming and running away when I'm here." As he speaks, his voice gets louder until he's almost shouting. He glares at Tina, who hides her face between her knees and whimpers. Mamá looks shocked, like she didn't expect this to be the way he would tell us whatever he planned to tell us.

"Your father's going for rehabilitation," she says quietly. "The Ballards have arranged it. He's going to get better."

Papá takes a pack of cigarettes and a lighter from the back pocket of his jeans. He leans forward, sticks a cigarette in his mouth, and lights it. His back is hunched, and I can make out his spine under the turtleneck. "I've learned to live with how I've changed. You will too." He's talking out of one side of his mouth while the cigarette dangles from the other. It gives him a tough-guy look that's kind of cool until I realize that he's paralyzed on his entire left side.

I want to know how he got that way, but I don't dare ask. I promised Mamá I wouldn't. I wonder if Tina will figure it out and say something.

She doesn't. Her arms are now over her head, covering her ears. In an instant, Papá reaches over with his good arm and jerks one of her hands away. She yells.

"You listen to me!" he growls. The lighted cigarette falls from his mouth and drops to the floor.

"Marcelo!" Mamá touches him. He twists away from her. I grab the cigarette, but it's already burned a spot on the carpet.

He drops back to the sofa. I hand him the cigarette. He inhales, and flicks the tip into the copper ashtray on the coffee table.

"Maybe we should open the box," I say, reaching for Courtney's gift. "My friend bought it for you."

"*Sí. Sí.*" Papá seems to have calmed down. But while he and Mamá tear off the wrapping together, I glance to my side and notice that my sister has slipped away.

Chapter Five
February 14, 1986
Madison

Papá gets new glasses and starts rehabilitation therapy—five days a week, plus exercises to do at home. His version of classes and homework. On Wednesday, Tina gets into a fight with another girl and ends up with internal suspension for the rest of the week. Mamá, who's teaching two sociology classes at the university this semester, has to cancel her office hours on Friday to meet with the principal after school.

It has turned cold—really cold, below zero any way you measure it. The car won't start on Friday, and Papá has to get a ride to the clinic from Mrs. Ballard. Mamá has to take the bus to Tina's school. Nobody's happy. When I come home from school, Papá orders me to fix the car.

"The battery's dead because of the weather," I explain. "When it warms up, the car will start." I can call Courtney or Willie to stop by and help me jump it, but they'll want to come inside, and I'm not ready.

"Take a look at it. You might have corroded terminals."

He's probably right. The entire car is rusting out. And if I wait until it warms up, it could be the middle of March before our junk heap rolls again.

I snatch the keys from the coffee table. Papá grabs his coat from the back of the metal chair. "You don't have to go out there," I tell him.

"I don't send people out unless I'm willing to go myself." He struggles into the heavy down parka that the committee bought for him. He's already figured out that if he slides the parka over his head, he can simply yank the zipper up with his one good hand.

"You've never been in this kind of cold. You'll need a hat under that hood." I toss him my thick brown wool cap.

He can't quite get it onto his head. I go to help him. When I reach for the side of the cap, my fingers graze his head. He staggers backward.

"No!" he shrieks. The color drains from his face. His eyes are wide, terrified, and he's breathing hard. I step away from him. His chest still heaves, but now he's trembling, and I remember too late what my mother told me in the airport last week about not touching him. He stumbles along the wall to the kitchen and vomits into the sink. The sound makes me curl up inside. I look away, at the poster of the city of Valparaíso taped to the wall over the sofa.

"Don't you ... ever ... do that again!" he gasps. When I glance back at him, he's glaring at me, his mouth twisted.

"Sorry," I mumble. It's the least I can do for costing him his lunch. My face is hot, but the rest of me is ice-cold. I pick up the cap from the floor and tug it low, over my ears. I wish I could disappear completely under it. "I'll take care of the car if you want to lie down."

"No, I'm fine." He rinses his mouth and spits. "Let's go."

Outside, he pulls the hood of his parka over his head.

"You were right about this cold." He walks slowly along the path through the graduate student apartment complex, leaning on a wooden cane so he won't slip on the ice.

"I'm sorry about touching you. I forgot." I wonder how he manages to get through therapy.

He grunts. I guess he doesn't want to talk about it. I walk the rest of the way ahead of him.

Out by the car, we're like an operating-room team—all we need is rock music in the background. He hands me the tools. I whack the white sulfate deposits off with a wrench and file the terminals clean. I take off my gloves to reconnect the wires, and the cold bites all the way through to my bones.

"Try it," he says.

The ignition turns over a few times, then catches. The car jumps to life. The radio blasts Aerosmith. I turn it off and roll down the window. "I have to let it run for a while," I call out to Papá. "Do you want to come in the car or go back inside?" I'm kind of hoping he'll go back. I'm afraid of doing or saying something wrong again.

He leans his cane against the fender and climbs inside, with some difficulty because his bad foot catches on the frame. We sit there, mostly in silence, for the twenty minutes it takes for the battery to recharge. He smokes a cigarette. I ask him about therapy, and instead of answering, he asks me about school. I tell him that besides Spanish, math is my best subject, and I want to study engineering in college.

"Engineering? We've never had an engineer."

"What about *Tío* Claudio?"

He blows out a mouthful of smoke. "That's your mother's side. He's all right, but the less I see of her family, the better." After a few seconds, he asks, "What do you like about it?"

"Figuring out how things work." The math was also easier to understand when I didn't know any English. Besides, in math there are right answers, and once you get them, the problem doesn't go on and on.

While I'm talking, my mind is focused on Papá's head and how he became violently ill when my hand grazed it. I'm thinking he didn't freak out when Mamá and I hugged him at the airport, although he was a bit stiff. And she's held his hand a bunch of times since he got home. But there's nothing wrong with his head except for the fact that in a little more than five years his hair went from reddish brown to gray.

He grinds out his cigarette in the ashtray. It's time to go. I hold out his mittens for him to put back on. He turns to face me. In my mother's subcompact, it's the closest he's been to me, and it's daylight, too. Even with the hair covering it, I notice the other side of his head—the good side, where I touched him—is dented above the ear.

I swallow. Now I'm shaking. "Papá?"

"Yes?"

I don't understand how he can be paralyzed on his left side if he got injured on the right side of his head. I point to my head—the left side, like he's looking at himself in a mirror. "Is that what happened to you?"

He nods. "Congratulations, engineer."

* * *

Papá says the right side of the brain controls the left side of the body and vice versa, so his head injury on the right side means the left side of his body is paralyzed. Actually, only partially paralyzed, since he has some feeling and movement on that side and can sort of walk. He's getting a brace from the knee down so the leg will be more stable and able to take his full weight. He won't tell me how he got messed up in the first place. All he says is, "It wasn't an accident."

Somehow he's learned to get my wool cap onto his head with only one working hand, and now he won't take it off. Except when he showers, because I can see his wet hair sticking out from under it afterward. I think the cap makes him feel like his head is protected, and anyway, if he keeps it on all the time, he doesn't have to struggle with it when he goes outside in the cold. I consider the cap as my present to Papá for *el día de San Valentín*.

Chapter Six
February 23-25, 1986
Madison

Every day, Courtney asks when she can come over to meet Papá. Before he got here, she used to eat dinner with us at least twice a month. Tina asks when Courtney's coming, and I don't want to tell my sister she's part of the problem. At first, Tina tried to avoid Papá by taking her plate into her room for dinner. Then he yelled at Mamá about Tina's lack of manners, so now she sits at the table a grand total of ninety seconds, shoveling her food into her mouth. Then she flees to her room.

The week after Papá's return, Mrs. Roberts, the woman Courtney teaches with, quit. Reverend Larkin let Courtney take over the class for the rest of the year.

If it were me, I'd be nervous, but Courtney seems excited. She spends several afternoons in the church library in search of ideas. For her first class, she settles on a Bible *Jeopardy!* game that she's found at the back of the AV closet.

I tell her she can come over after class. I figure if the lesson flops she'll be bummed and won't want to stay long.

Courtney's lesson is a success. I hear it the minute I get to her classroom door. The kids are answering questions and cheering for one another. Courtney's cheering with them. In the end, she gives everyone a prize and tells them they're all winners.

When we get to the apartment, Tina runs to her first. "I finished my puzzle," she says, grabbing Courtney's hand. "The one you gave me of the subway map. Come see." She starts to drag Courtney to her bedroom.

Courtney gently pulls back. "Just a second. Let me talk to your mother." Courtney's a lot bigger than Tina, but she's not putting up much of a fight.

"Come on," Tina whines.

"Cool it," I say under my breath. Tina gives me a dirty look.

Mamá comes over from the kitchen, where she's been rolling dough for empanadas. On Sundays she sells them in our neighborhood to make extra money. When Papá first arrived, I was worried what he would think about her peddling empanadas like the poor people in Chile, but he hasn't said anything. Mamá's family would be horrified if they knew. Growing up, she had servants to take care of her, and now she's been taking care of us by herself.

Mamá and Courtney hug. They talk for a while in Spanish about Courtney's family and school and the Sunday school class, and then Courtney asks about Papá.

"I'll see if he's awake. He's in therapy all week, and it takes a lot out of him," my mother says.

"Either that or he's avoiding…" I wave my thumb in my sister's direction.

Mamá narrows her eyes at me and presses her lips together in a frown. She goes to the bedroom. "Marcelo! Come and meet Daniel's friend."

Papá limps into the kitchen. He's wearing oversized pajama bottoms and a T-shirt. And the cap. "What friend?"

"I told you she was coming this afternoon." Mamá appears as dismayed as I am at the way he looks. She introduces them and adds, "Courtney speaks Spanish."

Tina squeezes past us to her room.

"Say something, then," Papá says to Courtney.

Courtney blushes. "I'm in…four years Spanish at school," she sputters in Spanish. "I want to meet you much."

Papá nods. "And where did you learn to speak so well?"

"Daniel teach me."

"Yes. I see." Papá flashes me an amused smile. I really want to pull a Tina now and disappear into my room.

Mamá jumps in to save both Courtney and me. "Her father is the minister of the church where Daniel plays. She and her parents helped with the letters."

"I'm very grateful." Papá bows slightly.

"Perhaps you can come and speak…," Courtney squeaks. Her face is still flushed. I consider helping her out, but Papá will be around a long time, and so will school. Even so, I feel bad she's so tongue-tied. I know she speaks better than that.

Papá looks almost as uncomfortable as Courtney now. "I'm very grateful to you and your family," he repeats. "You'll have to excuse me. I'm working on an article." He turns to go.

Courtney's nervous smile fades. I have to say something, or I'm going to hear all week how disappointed she is that she hardly got to talk to him. "Courtney just got promoted to full teacher today at church. And her class went really well."

Mamá congratulates her and gives her another hug.

Papá hands me the car keys. "Go pick up some lemon juice. I think we still have some pisco left for a celebration."

"Marcelo, they're just kids."

"Daniel has a pretty gringa, and she's a teacher too. That is reason to celebrate."

"It's also against the law. Until they're twenty-one."

Papá grins. "Well, I sure don't want to break any laws."

Courtney stands there like she didn't quite understand. But that doesn't stop her from trying. "I'm president of the Spanish Club at school," she begins.

"That's good," Papá interrupts, his tone impatient. He rests his hand on my shoulder. "Daniel, I just got a call from the radio station. They want to interview me on Tuesday at noon. I'd like you to translate."

Noon. That's AP Physics. There's a unit test on Tuesday. I glance at Mamá. "Is there anyone else from the committee who can translate?"

"I can do it, Señor Aguilar," says Courtney.

"Courtney's a very good writer," I add. "She's won awards and had stories published."

Papá motions me to the bedroom. He sits in his desk chair. I remain standing.

"*M'ijo*, your gringa is beautiful, but I don't want her translating."

"Why not? She was only nervous because she's always wanted to meet you. And I have a big test that day."

"You can make it up. I'll write you a note." He pauses. "Let me see. 'Please excuse Daniel Aguilar from school so he can translate for his communist father on the radio.' No telling what kind of trouble I'll get you into."

"It's not like that here, Papá. The school doesn't care."

"No point in taking chances." He taps a pen on a blank piece of paper. "Think of something."

Instead of thinking of an excuse, I remember my grandparents back in Chile. Mamá's parents. The arguments after the soldiers took Papá away...

* * *

"Allende was a communist."

"He was a great leader," Mamá said. *"He believed in democracy for everyone—not just for the rich. Your people and the gringos had to kill him. So what do we have now? Murderers and torturers."*

My abuela's *face turned purple.* "Marcelo *put that nonsense into your head." She faced me, but her crooked finger pointed toward my mother.* "Daniel, *don't believe these communist lies."*

"Don't drag him into this. He's growing up without a father—thanks to your beloved generals."

Was my father really a communist, whatever that was? Were my grandparents fascists? Was the world going to be divided between them?

I thought so, at least until I arrived in Wisconsin. Here nobody talks about it, at least not outside social studies class. And when they do it in class, I make my mind go somewhere else.

* * *

"You should give Courtney a chance," I say to Papá. "It would mean a lot to her."

"I have an excuse for you. Eye doctor. You got my eyes."

He puts Tuesday's date on the paper, but the way we

do it in Chile, with the day before the month. 25.2.86.

"Now tell me how to write it in English."

* * *

One of the members of the committee picks me up from school and drives me to the radio station, where I meet my father. It's located in a one-story building on the scruffy edge of downtown. Papá's standing outside the building, smoking, even though it's freezing cold.

"Your education has been neglected," he says. "Today it officially begins."

A tall, bearded man meets us at the door and introduces himself as Mark Gunderson, the host of the program. He offers us something to drink. Papá takes coffee. Mr. Gunderson brings me a Coke from the machine in the corner of the lobby.

He gives us a tour of the station. I linger in the control room, examining the fancy equipment and thinking about the cool mixes I could do if I had stuff like that. In the studio there are three chairs arranged around a microphone and a set of headphones on the back of each chair. Mr. Gunderson takes a sound check and gives us last-minute instructions. A red light clicks on over the door. We're live.

His first question is about the history of the military dictatorship. Piece of cake. I know all this from listening to my mother. I repeat Papá's answer in English, staying three or four words behind him.

We're ten minutes into the interview, according to the digital clock next to the control board.

"What were the events that led to your own arrest?" Mr. Gunderson asks.

It takes me a few seconds before I realize I'm supposed to translate that question from English to Spanish. I do it quickly and glance over to my father, hoping he hasn't noticed my screw up.

Papá shifts in his chair. "I was a sportswriter and had my own radio show, too." He pauses. Mr. Gunderson smiles. "After the military coup in 1973, I was detained for several months and banned from publishing. I drove a taxi to support my family. But just because I was prohibited from politics, and from my profession, didn't mean I could close my eyes to the injustice and repression."

My mouth pronounces the words in English, but my mind is screaming, *Why? Why did he speak out when it was so dangerous? Why didn't he think of us, his own kids?* I fix my eyes on Mr. Gunderson, as if I could make him read my mind and ask the questions. But he doesn't, and Papá goes on speaking. I can't ask. I have to translate.

"I heard stories, people who lived in the slums, people whose relatives had been detained, beaten, tortured, killed. Some had simply disappeared, and no one knew if they were dead or alive. I heard of secret prisons where the worst abuses took place. A friend of mine, who was a printer…"

I wonder if I knew him. I quickly file through the memory of my childhood but come up blank.

"He and I started a newsletter, *Justicia*. It exposed the locations of secret prisons and what was going on there. It also named some individuals responsible. We shared our information with the church's human rights organization, which assisted the relatives of the victims. Some people used our information to take direct action against the dictatorship."

"In what way?"

For some reason, Papá hesitates before answering. "We revealed the location of one detention center, and some *compañeros* helped about a dozen prisoners to escape and go underground. But our goal was documentation, so that the torturers will one day be put on trial. Right now, that's not possible because there is no real system of justice. The courts, like everything else, are in the hands of the dictatorship."

He stops. I used to tell myself that if I ever found the soldiers who beat up Papá and took him that night, I would simply blow them away.

"How did you get your information?" Mr. Gunderson asks.

"I am not at liberty to say," Papá replies. "Some of those people are still in Chile, and their lives might be in danger. I'll just say I was an experienced investigative reporter, and I had my ways."

"What happened to your friend?"

Papá stiffens, and my muscles tense as well. "The torturers...killed him. They applied electric shocks to get him to confess, and he died of cardiac arrest on their table."

I suck in my breath. But there's no time to think about it, because Papá presses on.

"It's uncommon for someone to die under these circumstances, because the prison officials bring in doctors to calculate how much a person can stand."

Doctors? Like Willie's dad? I can't breathe. Papá's words swirl past me. His voice is calm, matter-of-fact. Almost cold.

"I received minimal attention for my injuries, except

for a few months I spent in a rehabilitation hospital for a head injury they gave me. But even there I was denied my rights to communicate with my family or the outside world."

"Were you ever able to see your family while in prison?"

I can answer this one. No.

"They had to leave the country less than a year after my arrest. I asked them to because of the work I was doing on the inside." He looks at me, his expression for a moment apologetic, and then he goes on. "Whole families were often tortured to extract a confession from one member. I couldn't put the *compañeros* at risk, nor could I do that to my wife and young children."

"That includes this fine young man sitting here," Mr. Gunderson says. He introduces me as if the whole thing has been planned, the way our band's lead singer, Trevor, introduces us during our concerts.

But this isn't some club gig. Papá's saying that all of us, little Tina included, could have been tortured just because of what he was doing. Suddenly it's hot under the studio lights, and I notice that both my fists are clenched.

Mr. Gunderson lifts a piece of paper from the top of the control board. The familiar leaflet. "It says here you were confined to solitary. What was that like?"

"The most important thing to keep in mind was survival. When my printer friend died, I realized it was up to me to continue the struggle. I had to bear witness to the conditions I had written about in *Justicia* and to the heroism of the men I met in prison."

"We have a caller on the line. It's Courtney, from Madison." Mr. Gunderson punches a button. "Hello,

Courtney, you're on the air."

I'm sweating for real. There's feedback on the line, and Mr. Gunderson tells her to turn the radio down. In the background, I hear the din of the hallway outside the cafeteria, where the pay phone is. I wonder how many kids she has listening. I wonder how many teachers have stopped to listen.

"I just want to say that the person you have on the show is really courageous, and I totally admire what he's done."

I just want to say that my life is now public knowledge at West High School, and nobody's going to let me forget it.

Papá looks at me for the translation, but Courtney says, "I'll translate." She delivers the sentence in perfect Spanish.

"Thank you, Courtney," Papá says.

"Do you have a question for our guest?" Mr. Gunderson asks.

"Yes. Do you plan to start a newspaper in the United States like *Justicia* to let people know what's going on in Chile?" Again, she repeats the question in Spanish.

"While I hope to raise awareness here in the next few months, I plan to return to my country. The opposition to Pinochet is growing, and I believe I can do more for my *compañeros* still in prison as a part of it rather than sitting here comfortably in…in the United States."

Courtney hangs up. A couple of people call to ask about the role of the church, and the hour is over.

"Good show," Mr. Gunderson says as soon as he switches off the microphones. "Good work translating, Daniel."

"Thanks."

"I hope some of the kids at your school had a chance to listen."

"I'm sure they did." I hope my physics teacher doesn't find out about my fake excuse.

"Tell your father he was excellent. I wish him good luck with whatever he does."

Papá's words race through my mind. I want to think of him as a hero and me as the son of someone who did great things. Like investigating secret prisons and bearing witness to what went on there. But there's a huge empty space in my chest when I think of all the time we missed together. Five years, three months, and sixteen days, to be exact. And when I walk out of the studio, my fists are again clenched, and my neck and shoulders ache, as I think of how he put us in danger, ordered us out of the country—and still wants to go back there.

CHAPTER SEVEN
February 26, 1986
Madison

Light floods the stage. I stand in the center, alone with my guitar. Flecks of light dance off its steel strings. I hit a power chord, then another. The audience is jumping up and down, hands waving and clapping. My heart thuds, my feet stomp to the beat, and the stage vibrates under my sneakers. My fingers race over strings alive with electric current, pressing and releasing in time to the drumbeat, the clapping of the audience. The final chord echoes; applause builds. The audience screams louder, louder.

I recognize one scream, rising above the rest.

I awaken to screaming. I throw off the covers, sit up. I shake my head, trying to clear it. The screams are dying away, but I hear my mother's voice saying, "It's all right; you're safe," over and over in Spanish and a lot of rustling in the room across the hall.

A memory flashes: *Don't get out of bed. You know what happens when you get out of bed.*

I bury my head under the covers, the way Tina must have done the night the soldiers came. A lead weight fills my stomach. I swallow the stale taste in my mouth. On one side of me are harsh, muffled cries and terrified whispers. On the other side, a tapping.

"Daniel?" The wall that separates my bedroom and Tina's is thin, and her voice is weak and scared.

"Yeah."

"What's going on?"

"I don't know."

"Can you check?"

I don't answer.

"Please."

"Okay, Tina." I fluff the covers to make it sound like I'm doing something. I hear footsteps—familiar footsteps. Not strangers, not soldiers. My door opens with a click. I jump out of bed.

It's Tina. Her face is blank in the darkness, but her voice is accusing. "I knew it. You're not doing anything."

"Okay, okay," I mumble. In my T-shirt and boxers I walk across the hall to my parents' bedroom. I tap the door with my knuckles, but no one answers. They're still talking in hushed voices in Spanish.

"Mamá? Papá?"

Tina scoots up beside me. "Are they fighting?"

"No. I don't think so."

I knock again, louder. The door opens a crack. I try to peer inside, past Mamá's face, but all I see is the dresser and part of the window. The main light is off, but a lamp glows from somewhere else in the room.

"It's all right, kids. Go back to bed," she says in English. "Your father had a nightmare." Her face is pale and her eyes huge black circles in the dim light.

"He was screaming, Mamá."

"I know. I know," she says, like she wants to get rid of us.

"Is it because he had that interview today? He was talking about his printer friend who they killed. And when he was in the hospital."

Mamá sighs. "Daniel, please take your sister and go to bed."

"Come on, Tina," I say, pushing her toward her room. She goes inside, and I shut myself in my room. Not long after, I hear Papá's unsteady shuffle in the hall and a clatter as kitchen cabinets are opened and shut. I tiptoe into the hall.

The lights are off in the rest of the apartment, except for a dim lamp in the corner of the living room. Papá sits alone at the table in the kitchen area. The tip of his cigarette burns orange in the semidarkness. In front of him is the bottle of pisco that he'd planned to serve Courtney and me in celebration, and a half-filled glass.

I retreat to my room, load a tape into my Walkman, and push the volume up. I'll go deaf at this rate, but it drowns out the screaming that echoes in my head.

* * *

The whole school seems to have found out about the interview. My band members rag on me for not arranging a gig at the radio station, and my physics teacher, who's hardly older than the kids, says she didn't know I was the son of a "freedom fighter." What that means is I get to take the makeup even though I lied about why I was out. On the other hand, I have to see the vice principal about Papá's bogus excuse note. The guy lets me off with a warning, but I know he's not going to accept anything my father writes again.

Courtney catches up to me at lunch. "Your father was awesome!"

"Thanks for broadcasting it," I mumble.

"I thought you'd be proud."

"The vice principal called me in."

"He's such an ass." Courtney pushes a few strands of hair from her face. "If we had a fascist dictatorship, he'd fit right in."

I stuff my mouth with peanut butter sandwich to avoid talking to her. I should know better by now. She's one of those girls who, if you don't say anything, just keep on talking.

"It's so amazing, how your father refused to quit, even when his friend was killed. And what he said about bearing witness in prison, how it gave him a reason to survive. I hope people paid attention."

"Yeah, but you heard him say he wants to go back."

"He's so brave." Courtney shakes her head. "But I don't know, Dan. I mean, last night I was thinking about him. Now that I've met him, I'm really worried."

"That's because you don't have enough stuff to worry about with your parents."

She stares at me. "You don't know everything about me," she says after a moment, almost whispering, so I can barely hear her.

I always thought she and her parents had the perfect relationship. And the perfect life. Maybe her mom or dad has cancer or something and she's not telling me. After all, her parents were almost forty when she was born, so they're pretty old now.

"Anyway, you know how he limps. If he went back and had to run from the police, he'd never make it." She chews a piece of celery. No wonder she's so skinny. "Did that come from the head injury he mentioned yesterday?"

I nod. "He can't use his arm or hand on that side

either."

"I was thinking," she continues, "that we could have him do something here, so he won't want to go back. He'll be safe, and you guys will be together."

"Like what?"

"Well, interviews and speaking. I'm sure my dad can arrange a few things."

So he can wake up screaming every night afterward? I don't tell her this. We all have our secrets.

"Or he can start a newspaper. You and I will translate."

"And give it out at school? Good luck."

"No, at the university. And we can send the stories to newspapers around the country. He's so incredible. They'll take them for sure."

She's practically jumping up and down in her seat. If it were anyone else, I'd say forget it. But Courtney's a great writer, and she's already convinced that Papá's story will be front-page news all over the country.

* * *

The committee that arranged Papá's interview yesterday has also arranged for him to go on a speaking tour in three weeks, once he's finished his first round of physical therapy. At dinner he tells us all the places he's going: Washington, DC, New York City, Boston, San Francisco, Seattle, and about two dozen other cities—none of which I've been to in my almost five years here except Chicago, and some I've never even heard of. I notice Tina pushing her food around her plate while staring straight at him. I realize she's mashed her pastel de choclo into a rough map of the United States and without looking down has plotted his itinerary with her fork from the Southeast to the Northeast, up and down the West Coast, and to the Midwest. Maybe it's moving across the planet at age eight, but she has this thing about geography. She won her elementary school's Geography Bee last year, which shocked everyone but to her disappointment didn't make her popular.

"I want to go," Tina mumbles in Spanish.

"Don't you have school?" Papá asks her.

"You let Daniel skip for your interview." She sticks out her lower lip.

"He had to translate."

"I can translate. I'm not a little kid."

Papá stares at the ceiling. He's mashed up the food on his plate too. "Tina, be realistic. This isn't a vacation tour or a children's adventure."

"I'll learn more than at school."

She'd learn a lot more—more than she'd ever want to know. I'm thinking of reminding her that two days ago she couldn't stand to be near Papá, and now she wants to travel around the country with him.

"The answer is no."

She turns to Mamá. "Make him take me," she says in English.

"He's right, *m'ija*. You're too young. You and your brother can help right here by studying and behaving."

Tina jumps up and throws her napkin on the table. She points at Papá and screams in English, "He won't let me do anything! Why did he come here anyway?"

I don't know if he understood her, but he leaps up and slaps her across her face. His chair falls to the floor with a clatter. He turns and limps to his room. Mamá follows him.

"Good work," I tell Tina.

She rubs the red mark on her cheek. Tears are running down her face. "Shut up, Mr. Goody-Goody. You don't even know what happened."

"Papá hit you because you were rude and made him feel like crap. All he thought about for years in prison was getting out and seeing us."

I'm making that part up. For all I know, all he thought about was bearing witness and going back to fight, which is what he said in the interview.

"No, not about that, stupid." She sniffles. "You're so busy with your girlfriend and kissing up to Papá you don't even know."

"Then tell me."

"Some eighth-grade boys tore my pictures out of my locker. Then they shoved me inside."

I clench and unclench my fists. "Why would eighth-grade boys mess with a girl in sixth grade?"

"I pulled a girl's hair because she called me a freak. One of the boys was her brother."

"You shouldn't be pulling girls' hair." And she wonders why they call her a freak.

"You never take my side. Even Papá said the boys were wrong."

I jerk up straight. "You told Papá about this?"

"He was the only one here when I got home. You were off with Courtney." She kisses the air.

"So that's why you want to go with him on his tour?"

Tina's crying for real now—loud, heaving sobs. "Do you know what it's like to walk into a class where everyone hates you?" She wipes her face with her shirtsleeve. "I'll go anywhere to get away from that."

*   *   *

Some of the members of the committee pick Papá up after dinner. They're going to plan the speaking tour. He's not back by the time I finish my homework and get to bed.

Sometime later, I awaken to doors opening, then slamming shut. And voices. My mother's and two different men's, all speaking rapidly in Spanish.

"Why'd you bring him back like that?"

"We're sorry, Vicky."

I realize they're talking about Papá and wonder what happened.

"We weren't paying attention," the other man says.

"How could you not pay attention, Pato? You were sitting right there."

"What do you want us to do with him?"

"I don't know." Mamá's voice is breaking. "Just bring him to bed."

Heavy footsteps pass by my bedroom door. I hear a moan, then syllables, badly slurred, over and over. After a few times I make out words. "I want to sleep," he's saying.

"I'll get his shoes," one of the men says. The voice sounds like it belongs to the guy nicknamed Pato. In my mind I flip through the members of the committee who've come to the apartment. Pato is familiar. His real name is Patricio, and like Mamá he's from Chile and a graduate student—though in chemistry, not sociology. If I get up and go into the hall, I can see who the other one is, but Mamá will probably tell me to keep out like she did last night. And if I stay where I am, I won't have to know for sure that my father, the freedom fighter, came home in the condition I think he came home in. I lie in bed, listening, hoping Papá will get to sleep soon and the other guys will leave.

"Help me with his sweater," Mamá says.

"I'll hold his arms."

"Stay away from his head, Gregorio," she warns.

So she knows too. I picture Gregorio. He's a grad student from Colombia, studying electrical engineering. He once talked with me about it.

"Raise his bad arm higher," Pato says.

"Vicky, do you really want him in your bed with that filthy cap on?" Gregorio speaks in a nasal whine but his *castellano* is smooth, not like the machine-gun rhythm of us *chilenos*.

Papá yells. I clap my hands over my ears and press my body against the wall, expecting to feel Tina tapping on the other side. I can't imagine her sleeping through this racket, but after what happened last night, I doubt she'll turn up in my room again. I think of the vocabulary quiz I have in the morning and pray they'll all shut up and leave me in peace. A word from the list comes to me: *Bane. Fatal injury or ruin, or the cause thereof. A deadly poison.*

Mamá tries in vain to shush Papá. Then I hear Gregorio, almost as loud as my father, as if he thinks he'll get through at maximum volume. "*Cálmate, 'mano*. We're going to take your jeans off because you really messed them up. Now try to stand."

The screams turn to groans, then a crash and a loud thud. The apartment shakes.

"Why'd you drop him, Gregorio? You could have hurt him." All the calm is gone from Mamá's voice.

"I'm sorry. I tripped on the lamp cord."

"You smashed the lamp, *huevón*," Pato says.

"It wasn't me. It was him."

"Marcelo? Chelo? *Amor*, tell me you're all right," Mamá pleads.

I hear rustling, like they're shaking him. Gregorio shouts his name.

But Pato answers, not Papá. "I think he passed out again. And his elbow's bleeding. He must have cut himself on the lightbulb."

"That's a lot of blood," Gregorio says. "He's going to wake up tomorrow and wonder what the hell happened."

"Can we help you clean up and get him into bed?" Pato asks.

"No. Just. Leave. Now," Mamá says. "And don't come back."

"Look, we're really sorry. The truth is, we tried to convince him to slow down, but he wouldn't listen to us."

"He's probably not used to—"

"Out!"

Footsteps pass my door again, and the front door clicks shut. There's silence for a moment, then water running in the bathroom. I know Mamá needs help, but I don't want to do it, and I tell myself I don't have to either. She thinks I'm asleep.

The last thing I hear before I place the headphones over my ears is my mother sobbing.

Part Three
La Gringa

Chapter Eight
February 26, 1986
Madison

Dan doesn't know everything about me.

Chapter Nine
1984-1986
Madison

The neatly printed slip of paper outside the counseling center read "Spanish Tutoring, Native Speaker. Call Dan Aguilar, 555-8425."

The name sounded promising. I needed a tutor. I had one year to make up two if I wanted to take Advanced Placement Spanish my senior year. I'd started Spanish late, but that's a story for another time.

I dialed the number. A woman with a heavy accent answered. I asked for Dan.

"*Daniel, teléfono,*" she called. That much I understood.

"Hello. This is Dan." He had a trace of an accent and a reedy voice that hadn't quite finished changing.

"Hi. I'm Courtney Larkin. I saw your sign for tutoring."

"What level Spanish?"

"Second year."

"I don't recognize your name. You must not be a sophomore."

"Are you?" I'd expected a senior, someone looking for activities to put on a college résumé or fulfill National Honor Society requirements. Not some younger kid.

"Yeah. And so are most of the Spanish Twos."

He was right about that. And they were a pretty immature bunch. Two weeks into September, and I was telling myself it'd be a miracle if I learned anything this year.

"I'm a junior. Is that a problem?" I used to care about things like this, which is why I asked.

"No. I take anyone who can pay."

"So you charge, uh, money?" I was too surprised to sound intelligent.

"Five dollars an hour."

"I didn't think they let you put up a sign in school if you charge," I said.

"They didn't say anything."

"Well, neither did you."

"Don't tell them, okay?" He sounded a little nervous. "I need to earn some cash."

"You said you're a native speaker. Where are you from?" I decided to keep him on the phone for a while, maybe all afternoon long, to listen to his hot accent.

"Chile. Do you know where that is?"

"Yes." One of those places where the government killed its own people. He was lucky to be out of there, I thought. "How long have you been here?"

"Since seventh grade. So do you want the tutoring?" I could tell he wasn't falling for my ploy to keep him talking.

"Let me think about it."

I didn't think my parents would pay when an NHS tutor would do it for free, but I wanted a native speaker. They're not easy to find in a state where the cows outnumber the people, even though Madison's a college town.

After I hung up with Dan, I went next door to the church. Dad was in his office; the door was open. Mom was in the kitchen, checking the pantry. I tried him first.

"Five dollars an hour?" he said slowly. "He's a kid, right?"

"A sophomore. But he speaks Spanish at home. I heard his mother call him."

"Did he tell you where he's from?"

"Chile."

Dad sat up straight. "Is the boy's last name Aguilar?"

"Well, yes. Do they come here?" I thought of the pantry. Dan had said he needed the cash.

Dad opened a desk drawer and took out a single sheet of paper. There was a picture of a bearded man with glasses. Below it were the words, "CHILEAN POLITICAL PRISONER."

I read, "For more than three years, Marcelo Aguilar has endured unspeakable conditions as a political prisoner in Chile."

"So his father is in *prison*?" I asked.

Dad nodded. "Some of us at the church have been writing letters to get him released."

I stared at the picture, wondering what Dan's father was like and why he'd risked being separated from his family and sent to prison. I looked up into my father's eyes, deep blue behind his glasses. His light brown hair had started to turn gray over the past few years.

Back in Michigan, they called my father Andrés. Spanish for Andrew. And my mother, Alicia. Everyone else knew them as Drew and Alice.

"Please be careful, Dad," I said. I probably shouldn't have said anything, but I didn't want to have to move again.

"It's okay, Court. We're just writing letters to his government. The family's here legally."

"So can Dan tutor me?"

"Money's a little tight. But I'll see what I can work out."

I agreed to work as a teacher's aide for free to pay for tutoring twice a week. Later Dad would hire Dan to play the guitar—Latin American folk songs—at services on Sunday mornings. I started writing letters along with Dad, Mom, and the church's Social Action Committee.

Dear General Pinochet: I am a student at West High School in Madison, Wisconsin, USA, and someday want to be a writer. I respectfully urge you to take action to free the writer and prisoner of conscience Marcelo Leonardo Aguilar Gaetani, who has been sentenced to nineteen years in prison and subjected to torture due to his nonviolent political activities…

(Dad said General Pinochet didn't care who I was and what I wanted to do with my life, that he didn't actually read any of the letters we sent to him, but I wanted him to know just in case.)

I found myself falling in love with Dan, with his accent, the sound of his voice, his music, his reddish brown hair that he wore long and promised one day he'd turn into dreadlocks, his hazel eyes that turned green in the sunlight, the way his upper lip curled like he had an overbite, even though he didn't. My old boyfriend was a senior who got into drugs and decided to go east for college anyway. He ended up taking someone else to his prom, and I spent that evening at the Jam listening to Dan's band play Bob Marley tunes.

Dan didn't talk much about his father, and I got the feeling he never really expected to see his father again. But I believed that one day my parents and I, and all the other people who wrote letters to get Marcelo Aguilar freed, would convince the dictator to let him go. More than anything else, I wanted to meet him.

He had put his life on the line so that there would be no more dictators.

And no more refugees.

CHAPTER TEN
February 27, 1986
Madison

I'm serious about the newspaper, but I know I'll have to convince Dan and his father. I mention it again to Dan the next day because I've thought of a title. *Justicia* means justice in Spanish, so we could call it *Justicia/Justice*.

"I don't think it's such a great idea," he says. I notice he's a little pale, and I wonder if he's coming down with something.

"Why not?"

"Like who's going to pay for it?" He tears his sandwich into tiny pieces and picks at the meat inside.

"I will. I earn fifteen dollars a week now that I'm teaching and not the aide. And we can start small, maybe with a leaflet front and back."

"Forget it."

"I've got it all planned out. My father's going to send some to the other Methodist churches around the country." I haven't talked to Dad about it yet, but I'm sure he'll like my idea. "We can set them out on campus and at some of the coffeehouses on State Street."

Dan sighs and stares at the ceiling. The tiles have brown spots from where the snow has melted and leaked through the roof.

"And he has a list of the other Amnesty groups that

we can send to. A lot of them wrote letters for your father, and I bet they'd be happy to hear he made it out and hasn't stopped fighting."

"No, Courtney." He's squashed some of the sandwich between his thumb and index finger. He doesn't usually play with his food.

"What's the problem?"

He glances downward. "It's Papá. It's really not a good idea that you do this."

I reach for his hand. It's warm, and his palm is sweaty. Maybe he has a fever. "Why not, Dan?"

"The other day, when he did the radio interview. He had a nightmare that night. He thought he was still in prison."

"Oh, no."

"I'm not sure it's good for him to be talking about it if that's what happens." Dan sweeps the bits of sandwich into his brown bag. "And he's supposed to be going on a speaking tour in a couple of weeks."

"Did he say where?"

Dan shakes his head.

"Or how long he'll be gone?"

"A month to six weeks."

I'd better talk to Mr. Aguilar soon if I want this newspaper to get started. But if he's going on a tour, he could report from all the places where he's speaking. That would make the newspaper even more interesting.

"Maybe the nightmare was a one-time thing. He'll be okay when he gets used to speaking," I tell Dan.

"It wasn't a one-time thing." He pitches the bag and walks out of the cafeteria.

I catch up to him in the hallway. "Your father was

probably nervous. It was his first time since he came back."

Dan simply shrugs.

"And a newspaper is different. We don't have to interview him. He can write what he wants."

"He's doing that already. Except he can only type with one hand, and it takes him forever."

"Okay. That's a start."

One of Dan's friends from the soccer team comes up to us. They slap high fives. Dan walks backward, in the direction his friend is headed, but he calls out to me, in Spanish, across a couple of people, "Fine. But I'm not going to ask him."

* * *

I cut out of school right after lunch. As a second-semester senior I can do it, though I've skipped afternoon classes only one other time since midterms. I drive straight to the graduate student apartments where Dan lives. I have to take care of this quickly, before he, his sister, or their mother gets home.

On the way, I rehearse in Spanish what I'm going to say about the newspaper. I realize I should have started talking about it that way with Dan. But he doesn't like to speak Spanish at school unless he doesn't want anyone but me to understand what he's saying. Not even the kids taking Spanish can understand us when we get going, because they don't really learn that much in class, and the Chilean *castellano* is different from what's taught in school, which is the way people speak in Spain.

A manila envelope sticks out of the half-open

mailbox for 6A, the Aguilars' ground-floor apartment. I slide it out and a couple of letters as well. The envelope is addressed to Marcelo Aguilar, with a return address from Milwaukee.

I knock on the door. No answer. Dan once told me his father has rehabilitation at the hospital every morning, but it's already one in the afternoon. I knock again. I'm turning to leave when I hear a muffled *"¿Quién es?"*

"Courtney Larkin," I call. *"La amiga de Daniel."*

"¿La gringa?"

The door opens a crack. The first thing I see is a haze of smoke. I smell it too. Dan's father is wearing a bathrobe and the same pajama pants and wool cap he wore the first time I met him. There's a lit cigarette between his lips.

Suddenly tongue-tied, I hand him the mail. He turns it right side up and frowns. He's as pale as Dan was at lunch, and he squints as if the light outside is bothering him. Inside the apartment, the curtains are closed.

"You didn't come to bring the mail," he mumbles, the cigarette still in his mouth.

"No, Señor Aguilar," I stammer. I thought speaking Spanish on the radio with all of Madison listening would get me over my nervousness, but it's much harder talking to him face-to-face, alone, with him still in pajamas and that creepy cap. "I heard your interview on the radio the day before yesterday, and I wanted to talk— "

He interrupts me. "This isn't a good time. I have a headache."

"I'm sorry. Is there another day—"

"No."

He shuts the door. I'm frozen in place, starting to realize what a truly bad idea it was to show up at his apartment unannounced, when the door opens again. Mr. Aguilar takes one step outside and flicks his cigarette. "Is this about the Spanish Club at your school?"

"No. Yes. It is, but I had another idea."

"Look, I'm not feeling well today." He sighs, leans against the door frame, and takes a long drag, which he blows toward my face. I step back, out of the way of the smoke. "Give me your telephone number, and I'll call you when I can."

I follow him inside. I've been in that apartment a hundred times, but today it feels like a stranger's place—overheated and dingy. The air is stale and sour, as though someone had a party there the night before. The manila envelope is sitting on the coffee table, and there's a pencil on the table too. I write both my home number and the number for the church, because in addition to teaching and preparing lessons in the library I'm now helping out at the pantry twice a week.

"I'll talk to my father about having you speak at the church, too," I say as I hand him the envelope.

He grimaces when he takes it. "*Sí. Sí.* I'll call you."

"Thanks. I hope you feel better soon."

"*Chao.*" He slams the door behind me.

Chapter Eleven
March 11, 1986
Madison

Five minutes after I drive away, I regret going there. I regret leaving my phone number. I imagine Mr. Aguilar telling Dan I came over while he was still in school. I know Dan said he wasn't going to talk to his father about the newspaper, but I don't think he meant for me to do it, at least not right away.

But Dan doesn't say anything. And his father never calls me.

Ten days later, Willie Mrazek, Dan's best friend and Firezone's drummer, stops me on the way to gym class third period. He's coming back from gym, and his short blond hair glistens from the shower.

"Hey, Court, did you hear?"

"Hear what?"

"Dan beat up this eighth grader who'd been bothering his sister, so they suspended him for a week."

"No way!" Heads turn in my direction. I lower my voice to just above a whisper. "How did you find out?" I hadn't seen Dan in school yet, but we usually don't get together until lunch.

"He called me last night to get his work from his teachers. He's screwed."

"I was with him yesterday. He didn't say anything about beating up a kid."

"He walked to the middle school to pick Tina up. I guess earlier this boy ripped up her notebook and wrote something on it. Dan completely bugged out. When Tina pointed the kid out to him across the street, he dashed through four lanes of traffic and went whaling on him." Willie punches the air with both fists.

"Dan told you this?"

"Yeah. He's scared shitless. The kid's family called the cops, and they want to press charges."

"They arrested him?"

"They brought him to the middle school office, and the cops met him and his mother there."

"The police didn't go to his apartment?" I can't imagine what Dan's father would do if police showed up at their place. For all I know, his father doesn't yet have his papers to be in the country. Thoughts of what happened to Dad rise up in me. I push them away.

"No."

"You sure?"

"Yeah." Willie scratches himself behind the ear, like someone would do to a dog.

"You don't think they'll go there?"

"Why?"

"I just want to know." I lift my bag to my shoulder. "Why didn't he call me?"

Willie shrugs. "Because you'd overreact, maybe?"

I don't like getting dissed by junior boys, especially mediocre drummers and keg stand champions, so I show Willie my back and leave for gym.

I skip out after lunch, this time with Dan's books and assignments for the week, which, according to the teachers, Willie hasn't even started collecting. At least

Dan has one conscientious friend.

He answers right away when I knock on his door. His hair is a mess, and there's a purple mark on his cheek where the kid must have landed a punch.

He takes the books. He's still standing in the doorway, even though it's below freezing outside. "So you heard."

"Willie told me." I can't keep the hurt out of my voice. "Why didn't you call me last night?"

Dan stares at his unlaced sneakers. His entire face starts to match the mark. I begin to feel sorry for him, and when I feel sorry for Dan, all I want to do is hug him until he feels better. This time, though, he has an armful of books, so I slip around him, embrace him from behind, and bury my face in his hair.

"Okay," he murmurs. He puts his free arm around my shoulders and leads me inside.

We sit next to each other on the sofa, and I take his hand. "Tell me what happened," I say.

He goes through the story, not much different from the way Willie told it, but he doesn't say anything about the police. I ask him about that part, and he shushes me.

"If they come here, Papá's going to go apeshit. Thank God he's leaving tomorrow," Dan whispers in English.

"Is your father here?"

"In his room. Packing for that speaking trip."

"Does he know what happened yesterday?"

Dan nods.

"So did they, like, ground you forever?"

Dan points to the mark on his cheek.

"Way to show that violence never solves anything," I mumble.

I realize it was Mr. Aguilar, because Dan's mother has

never hit him in the year and a half that I've known Dan. She's grounded him a couple of times, once when his grades slipped, and once when he came home from a party drunk after curfew. Mr. Aguilar's good arm must be pretty strong, because close-up the bruise is dark and bears the imprint of a pair of knuckles. I trace Dan's cheekbone around the ugly mark, which is mushy and swollen beneath my fingers.

How could Mr. Aguilar have done that? I thought he opposed violence.

"I saw the soldiers beat Papá up. When they came to arrest him." Dan blinks and wipes his face with his shirtsleeve. When he touches the sore spot, he winces.

"So you think that's why he hit you? Because they beat him?"

"I don't know. He has plenty of reason to be mad at me." Dan pauses. "And it doesn't take much. He whacked Tina a couple of times just for mouthing off."

"That must have been scary."

"Yeah, I don't remember him being like that before."

He pulls his feet up onto the sofa, wraps his arms around his legs, and rocks back and forth. I rub his back.

A while later, he begins talking again. "Those boys have been bothering Tina all year, and she kept calling me a coward for not doing anything. I only wanted to talk to the kid, but when I saw he wrote 'crazy spic' on her notebook, I guess I snapped." He sweeps the hair from his face.

"Eso no es coraje."

We both look up. Mr. Aguilar stands over us, reeking of cigarette smoke. I wonder how much English he understands. Dan said his father refused to take classes.

Dan switches to Spanish. "I know. I said I'm sorry."

Mr. Aguilar nods at me. "I don't want your gringa thinking you're some hero for beating up a kid three years younger and half your size."

"He wasn't half my size. He was at least as tall as me," Dan whispers in English.

The word "gringa" grates on my ears. I want to make Mr. Aguilar understand that even if our government brought Pinochet to power and still supports him, we don't all agree with our government. But I'm more concerned right now that he hit Dan. I rehearse the words in my head before opening my mouth. "I told him violence doesn't solve anything, Señor Aguilar."

I expect Mr. Aguilar to see my point and tell Dan to listen, too. Instead, he dismisses me with a grunt.

Inside his clawed left hand is an empty aspirin bottle. He asks Dan, "Does your gringa have a car?"

I feel fingernails on my eardrums again. I jump in before Dan can answer. "Yes. Would you like me to get you more aspirin?"

"Please."

"Then would you please stop calling me 'gringa'?" I take the bottle and hold it in front of his face. "I don't support what our government is doing any more than you do."

"Daniel, you have a feisty one." He waves his finger. "Watch out for her."

Mr. Aguilar shuffles off. He's still wearing the pajama pants and robe, and the creepy wool cap is starting to unravel in the back. Something glistens on his left ankle, and I make out a brace that goes into his fuzzy suede slipper.

I grab Dan's arm. "You want to come to the drugstore with me?"

"I can't. I'm stuck here until the end of my suspension. Anyway, if the cops come back, I have to keep them out of the house."

"How will you do that?"

"Just go with them quietly." He shakes his head. "They can try me as an adult, you know. I'm seventeen."

"Wow. They wouldn't do that, would they?"

Dan shrugs. "They might if the boy's family presses charges."

"Do you want me to talk to my dad?"

"I doubt they're members of the church."

I make Dan give me the kid's name. While I'm out getting the aspirin, I stop by the church and check the membership directory in the library. Dan was right; they aren't members. The librarian and a couple of pantry volunteers want to talk. One of the volunteers has a daughter in my Sunday school class, and she's telling me how much the girl likes the class. I listen to her for a while, not only to be polite but also because it's really cool to hear that I'm doing a good job. By the time I leave, it's almost four.

On the way to Dan's apartment I get caught behind the school bus. It stops at the far edge of the parking lot, and a dozen kids get off. One of them is Tina. The others walk in clumps of two, three, and four, but Tina is alone. I park and run to catch up with her.

"Hi, Tina," I say.

"Hey." She holds her hand out for me to slap it. She's a small, slender girl with olive skin and thick, straight, dark brown hair.

"How was school?"

"Sucked, as usual." I imagine her in black, pierced and tattooed, in a year.

"Did those boys bother you again?"

Tina turns to me. There's a wide grin on her face. "No. Nobody came near me."

I guess violence does solve problems sometimes. But it probably won't be worth it, especially if Dan is charged with battery. There'll be court costs and probation, at least, and since he's an adult, he'll have the conviction on his record for the rest of his life. Sooner or later, the boys will figure out that he can't beat them up again unless he wants to be expelled from school and go to prison, so they'll pick on Tina even more.

"We have to find another way to deal with this," I tell Tina.

"Why?"

"You're not making any friends this way."

"It doesn't matter. Papá says we're all going back this summer."

"To Chile? No way."

She nods. "And when we get there, I'm going to help Papá with his newspaper. I'm going to answer the telephone and run the office and help deliver the paper when it's printed."

"Tina, your father didn't have an office. Or a telephone. He published his paper in a secret place, and it was dangerous." I don't know why I'm telling her this, because she's just a sixth grader. But I don't want Dan to have to go back, and I want Mr. Aguilar to start a newspaper here so I can translate it and send it all over the country.

Tina sticks out her lower lip and stalks off ahead of me. I don't try to catch up with her this time but let her think about what I just said. She gets to the apartment and throws the door open. "I'm home," she yells out.

"¡Cállate!"

I hear Dan next. "Shh, Tina. Papá has a headache."

"Again?"

Dan shepherds Tina to the back of the apartment. Mr. Aguilar sits at the kitchen table, his good arm propping up his head, his bad arm outstretched and inert on the table. The sleeve of his bathrobe is pushed up a little, and his wrist looks like bone covered with a layer of shriveled, translucent skin. A cigarette burns in the ashtray in front of him, and there's an open manila envelope like the one I brought in to him a couple of weeks ago.

"I have the aspirin for you," I say in Spanish.

"Thanks. Get me a glass of water, please."

I fill a glass from the sink and set it on the table. He doesn't move. I slide into one of the metal chairs, open the bottle, and set two tablets next to the water glass.

He raises one eyebrow, glances at me, mumbles, "Spanish Club. Maybe when I get back in April."

"I have another idea too," I begin. "It's a kind of newspaper that we can start here. You can write about the situation when you left Chile and about the trip you're going on now." I fish for more words in Spanish, but they all seem to have flown out of my head.

"And where do you plan to get the money for this newspaper?"

"I've saved my teaching salary. I already have thirty-five dollars." I'd have ten more, but I couldn't pass up the new Sting album.

"And how will you get people to read it?"

"I'll translate it into English. We can make it bilingual."

"Where will you find these people to read it?"

He doesn't look at me while he grills me. His head is still resting on the palm of his raised arm, and I notice he hasn't shaved in a couple of days. The little bits of hair on his chin are mostly gray. Dan says he'll turn thirty-eight later this month, and I'm amazed someone not even forty looks like this.

"We can send it to the people who wrote letters for you. My father can mail a bunch to other churches." I still haven't talked to Dad, though. I'm waiting to see if it ever happens.

Mr. Aguilar reaches for the manila envelope. "It's being done already. People from the committee have been translating some articles I've written. I've sent them out. Nobody wants them."

He holds up the ripped-open envelope. His eyes catch mine. They're the same shade of hazel as Dan's, but red-rimmed and drained of light. His left eyelid droops, nearly closing that eye. His expression—bitter and sad, as if the weight of the world has crushed his face—freezes me, speechless.

When he opens his mouth again, his voice is almost inaudible. "You think you can do a better job?" He slides the envelope in my direction. Inside is a bunch of typed, dog-eared pages. "Take them."

Chapter Twelve
March 13-14, 1986
Madison

I don't know who translated Mr. Aguilar's articles, but no newspaper will print ones that have so many mistakes in English, like misspelled words and nouns and verbs that don't agree.

But I don't really understand Spanish that well. And there's a lot of history and information about political parties and leaders and words like *hegemonía* that I don't understand either. I end up going back and forth between my Spanish-English dictionary and another big dictionary that keeps falling off my undersized desk, and I still can't make sense of most of it. Mr. Aguilar's gone, Dan's suspended, and his mother has grounded him entirely, so I'm not even allowed to ask him questions over the phone.

I write on the top of one of the translated pages: *1. Who are the members of the "committee"? 2. Where else did they send these articles?*

I still have the leaflet my father gave me more than a year ago, and it has a phone number. Not Dan's, fortunately. I call it.

A woman answers, "Ballard residence." She has a Southern accent.

"Is this Mrs. Ballard?"

"Yes. May I ask who's calling?"

"My name is Kara Slater." Kara Slater is the name of my best friend back in Michigan. Like me, she's eighteen years old. I glance at the return address from the manila envelope. "I'm an editor at the *Milwaukee Free Press*. I have an article from Marcelo Aguilar that was translated into English and this phone number."

As I'm talking, I'm thinking, *How does a preacher's kid get to be such a smooth liar?*

I finish by asking, "Are you by chance the person who did the translation?"

"I know Marcelo Aguilar, but I haven't translated his articles." She sounds suspicious.

"I'm sorry to bother you." I make my voice as sweet as possible. "But if you could help me, I'd really appreciate it. Mr. Aguilar submitted the translation for publication along with the original, but the English version isn't very clear and we don't read Spanish. We'd like to contact the person who worked on it to see if he or she can do it over."

"Might you want to publish the article?" Now she sounds less distrustful. More hopeful.

"Yes. If we can get a good translation."

Before I hang up, she gives me the name and phone number of Gregorio García, who she says is a member of the Latin America Solidarity Committee at the University of Wisconsin in Madison. Right around the corner from me, but Mrs. Ballard doesn't know that. She thinks I'm calling long-distance from Milwaukee. The thought makes me smile. No, more than that. It makes me want to jump up, dance around the room, and sing "We Will Rock You" as loud as I can.

Afterward, I call Gregorio. After several no answers

and a busy signal, a man picks up. "*Eló.*"

I decide to go with English. It's easier to spin lie after lie in your native language. "May I speak with Gregorio García?"

"I'm Gregorio."

I give him my real name and explain, "Marcelo Aguilar asked me to look over the translations because I've had some things published."

"Did he give you my number?"

Gregorio's guarded tone makes me hesitate. And he speaks English with even less of an accent than Dan does. He could easily check my story with either Mrs. Ballard or Mr. Aguilar. I glance down at the *Gregorio Garcia, 555-4946* on the back of the translated version's final page. "Someone wrote your name and number on the article," I say. *Yeah. Me.*

"I translated most of the articles, and Patricio Wheelock did the rest," Gregorio replies.

"Could I meet with you two to talk about them?"

"Sure. Did any of them get accepted?"

"Not...yet." Thinking of the quality, I grimace. I'll have to keep a straighter face when I meet these guys in person.

I arrange to have lunch with Gregorio on campus the next day. Another skip-out. I love senioritis.

At the Memorial Union, he sees me first. Natural blondes are hard to miss. The other guy, Patricio, is with him. Gregorio is tall and skinny, with short, dark brown hair and a light brown complexion. He'd be attractive if he had more muscles and a deeper voice. Patricio is a bit lighter in skin tone, overweight, with long, stringy brown hair that looks like it hasn't been washed all winter. He's disgusting by anyone's standards.

Over cheeseburgers and fries, I hand them the envelope with the article and the form-letter rejection.

Patricio glares at me. "How did you get this?"

"Mr., uh, Marcelo gave it to me a couple of days ago. I'm a friend of the family. I've been published in newspapers and magazines and have some connections, so I said I'd help."

Gregorio looks at the article. "Yeah, I did this one."

Then Patricio asks, "How well do you know Nino?"

"Nino?"

"*Nombre de guerra.*" Patricio explains, "That's the name he used when he was working underground. So no one would know who he really was or go after his family."

"I guess it didn't make much difference. They took him in front of them."

"You're a smart girl, whoever you are," says Patricio. "The *milicos* usually figure these things out. But the great *guerrilleros*, their names are of legend. *Como el Che.*"

"Guevara," Gregorio adds.

Like I don't know that. I lift my lip to bare my teeth on one side. Having grown up with two much older brothers, I know when I'm being patronized and how to fight back.

"And…Nino?"

When Gregorio speaks again, there's a hard edge to his voice. "Whatever he did to them, they really fucked him up for it."

"He had that newspaper."

His mouth full, Patricio says, "Yeah, that took *cojones.*"

"Balls," I add before one of them does it again.

"So are you a writer for one of the campus papers?"

Gregorio asks.

"I've done some work for them. Human rights issues with a local angle." In fact, it was a short story about Mayan refugees from Guatemala that won a contest and was published in a campus literary magazine last fall, but these two don't need to know. "I offered to help with the articles' translation," I say, avoiding Gregorio's face, "because they weren't getting taken."

Gregorio taps the envelope on the table. "You have to understand. We didn't have a whole lot to work with."

"Oh?" I twirl a fry in my ketchup.

"When he arrived, he asked the committee for volunteers to translate the articles he was writing, and we said we'd do it," Gregorio continues. "Once we saw them, we didn't want to put a lot of time into them."

I remember the second question I'd scribbled on the page. "Where else did you send them?"

"I don't know. He was mailing them out himself, from a list a professor on the committee gave him. Mostly alternative magazines, but also some local newspapers that might print them—if they were really, really good. Which they aren't."

"As you *norteamericanos* might say, he's lost his edge." Patricio scoops up the last of his fries and dumps the salt from the bottom of the carton onto them and his fingers, too. "Back when I was in high school in Chile, I read *Justicia* whenever I could get my hands on it." He shakes his head. "He was a great writer then." Patricio shoves the salty fries into his mouth, licks his fingers, and stares covetously at my half-finished carton.

I push it toward him. "Do you have a copy now?"

"You'd get into a lot of trouble for having it in your

possession. I think I even ate one to avoid getting caught." He picks up a long fry. "Maybe it was being in the middle of it that made his writing so exciting, but these new articles are unreadable. They're just cold facts and theories. There's no feeling."

"I think it's because of what they did to him." Gregorio taps his head.

"Nino has some problems." Patricio looks at me as if he's unsure of how much he wants to tell me.

Gregorio has no such inhibitions, though. He tips his head back and pretends to hold a bottle to his lips.

"He drinks?" It would explain his headaches and his disheveled appearance. But Dan has said nothing about his father coming home drunk.

Patricio glares at his friend.

It doesn't stop Gregorio. "Sorry, kid," he says. "We're as upset about it as you are. I hate seeing a good man end up like this."

Patricio leans back in his seat and locks his hands behind his head. His belly strains the buttons of his checked flannel shirt. "So are you going to take over the translating from us? We'd really like that."

"You can come to our committee meetings too," Gregorio adds. "Second and fourth Mondays of every month. We used to meet at the Aguilars' apartment, but Victoria kicked us out. We're looking for a place."

For a moment I consider volunteering the church, but something stops me. A feeling of dread, of fear for my parents. These guys don't know me, but I don't know them and what they're up to either.

They called him Andrés. And her, Alicia.

"How about the Memorial Union?"

Gregorio drums his fingers on the table. "This week *compañero* Nino got us kicked out of here, too. For bringing a bottle of tequila to the meeting, drinking about half of it himself, and trying to pass the rest of it around before he passed out. I don't know how he got it by her."

"*Flaco*, if he got the names of torturers out of prison, he could hide a bottle of Cuervo from his wife."

"Anyway, she was distracted. Her kid had just got into a fight."

"O-kay," I say, trying not to wince. I need to exit before my boyfriend becomes the next subject of Gregorio's gossip mill. Quickly, I write my phone number on a napkin and hand it to Patricio. "Call me before the next meeting and let me know where it is."

Patricio folds the napkin and slips it into his back pocket. Gregorio picks up the manila envelope. "Are you going to take care of this, or do I have to give him the bad news?"

"I'll do it." I reach for the envelope. "By the way, do either of you know his tour schedule?"

"That's my department." Patricio lifts a filthy backpack to the table and pulls out a binder. He opens it to a page with a plastic cover over it. "He left on the twelfth. Today's the fourteenth. Washington, DC."

"May I see that?"

Patricio flips the binder around. I scan the list of dates and places. Good Friday is March 28, and that's when spring vacation begins. Mr. Aguilar has three speaking dates in Boston: April first through third.

It's time to pay my brother Matt a visit.

CHAPTER THIRTEEN
April 1-2, 1986
Boston

"Mom, Dad, I'd like to visit Matt in Boston for spring vacation."

My mother's face breaks into a smile. "I think that's a lovely idea. You two should spend time together."

I hardly see my brothers. Tim is twenty-six and lives in Michigan. He was already out of college when we had to move. Matt's six years older than I am and was a junior at the University of Michigan then. Now he's a graduate student in architecture at MIT.

My parents thought they were done having kids with Tim and Matt. I was a surprise.

When we call him, Matt's excited. But it's his last semester, and he's busy with his master's thesis project. "She'll have to go around a lot on her own," he says.

That's my plan.

With his father away, life returns to normal at Dan's place. Or almost to normal. Dan gets charged with misdemeanor battery for bloodying the boy's nose and leaving him with a split lip that needed five stitches. He has a court date in May to make his plea. He's got a job after school, weekends, and through spring vacation bagging groceries at the supermarket to pay the attorney's fees. Even so, he tells me he likes it without his father around. "It's the way it always was. Mamá, Tina, and me."

I don't say I met with the guys from the committee, but the day he returns to school I tell him I'm going to Boston to visit my brother.

"That's cool. I'm kind of tied up for break anyway." He crumples his brown paper bag with all our lunch trash. "I think Papá's supposed to be there around then."

"If he is, I'll get Matt to hear him with me."

"Papá would like that. He says the audiences have been pretty small."

"Bummer."

"Yeah, like at one place three people showed up."

I twist my finger around my braid in front. "I can't believe it, Dan. How can people not care?"

Dan shrugs. "I guess they have other stuff to do."

"Like what? Watch TV?"

* * *

I fly to Boston the Monday after Easter. It's my first time on an airplane by myself. Matt picks me up at the airport and drives me to his place near Central Square in Cambridge. He shares a three-story wooden row house with two other guys in his program. He has the attic bedroom and has left a sleeping bag for me in the alcove under a dormer window.

Mr. Aguilar's speaking at MIT on Tuesday, at the Harvard Medical School on Wednesday, and at Boston College on Thursday. I convince Matt to come with me for the first one.

When Mr. Aguilar enters the room, accompanied by a translator, it occurs to me that this is the first time I've seen him wear something other than a T-shirt, a bathrobe, and pajama pants. He has on jeans, a wool sweater over a button-down shirt, and hiking boots that cover his leg brace. His hair, without the cap, is mostly gray with streaks of red and brown. It falls nearly to his shoulders, about the same length as Dan's but not as thick. The harsh light reflects from his glasses. I sit toward the back behind a tall guy, because I don't know if Dan told his father I'd be there and I don't want to surprise him before his speech. I count twenty-three people in a room that holds about sixty. Better than three but not great. Maybe some will show up later.

"Which one is your boyfriend's father?" Matt whispers.

"The one with the gray hair."

"He's almost as gray as Dad. How old is he?"

Our dad is fifty-six. He has gray hair for a reason. "Thirty-eight."

"Sheesh." Matt shakes his head.

Mr. Aguilar scans the room. He nods in my direction, then limps toward where Matt and I are sitting.

"Daniel said you might come."

Matt looks confused. He doesn't know Spanish. Like me, he took French back in Michigan because we lived so close to the Canadian border.

I introduce them, which is kind of tricky when neither one speaks the other's language. Then the translator comes up and tells him they're going to start. Mr. Aguilar has a tough time negotiating the few steps down and almost trips, but he waves away the translator's offer of help.

As the organizer introduces Mr. Aguilar, I see Matt's

expression turn to awe. "Not bad, little sister," he says over the applause when Dan's father steps up to the podium. I grin, as much because I've impressed my older brother as out of excitement at hearing Mr. Aguilar speak in person for the first time.

He speaks clearly despite his injury, mainly because he doesn't talk as fast as I've heard him at home. I can understand almost every word, and I translate silently along with the serious-looking young man standing beside him.

A lot of what he says I remember from his radio interview in February. He talks about his printer friend who died while being tortured and describes in more detail now the terrible conditions in prison. He shows people his withered wrist and hand. I take notes but think I should have brought a tape recorder. No problem. I brought fifty dollars in spending money and can go shopping for one before his talk tomorrow night.

It's time for questions. My hand shoots up, and Mr. Aguilar calls on me first. "How did people get copies of *Justicia*?" I imagine Patricio picking one up on campus like I'd pick up our local free paper, *Isthmus*.

"We'd drop them near schools and in certain neighborhoods when no one was looking. Because of the curfew, we couldn't do it late at night, so we waited until the weather was bad. Winter was easier because it got dark early." He stops and waits for the translator, then adds, "We put them in places where the wind would scatter them."

Other people ask questions, and soon the presentation ends. I want to talk with Mr. Aguilar, but Matt has to return to the studio.

"Are you free to see him with me tomorrow?" I ask my brother.

"No, but I'll show you how to get there."

* * *

The talk at Harvard Med starts at five in the afternoon, and when I get to the room at the hospital, there are a lot of people. And food. South American food, like the empanadas Dan's mother makes, along with salad and a beef stew. They're not as good as hers, but the tape recorder cost more than I'd thought, so I'm happy to have the free meal. I get in line behind doctors dressed in their hospital scrubs and med students in jeans and sweatshirts, but I don't see Mr. Aguilar. Finally he comes in with a young woman who wears a long peasant skirt and blouse. I glance down at my peasant skirt and blouse and my face reddens. Fortunately, hers is mainly green and mine is mainly purple, because I didn't come here to find a fashion twin.

I head over to them, tape recorder in hand. "*Buenas tardes, Señor Aguilar.*"

"You're back." He gives me a lopsided smile. "Where's your brother?"

"He had class. But he asked me to tape your talk because he liked the one last night so much. Is that all right?" My father once told me I should get permission from a person before I taped them.

"That's fine." Mr. Aguilar introduces me to Sarah Grossman, the medical student who's organized this presentation and will be translating.

I look down at my plate of food. "Would you like me

to get you anything?"

Sarah asks for cookies and a diet pop. Mr. Aguilar shakes his head. "I can't eat before these things."

This talk turns out not to be what I thought but a panel discussion on treating people who've been tortured. There are two doctors who speak along with Mr. Aguilar, and none of them gets very much time. Especially Mr. Aguilar, because his part has to be translated into English. Because it didn't occur to me to ask the two doctors for permission, I turn off the tape recorder and take notes instead. I don't understand the medical terms but try to follow what they're saying. I'm thinking about what Gregorio and Patricio told me, and I wonder if anything these doctors say can make Mr. Aguilar better.

At the end, Sarah comes up to me. "Were you able to understand it?"

"Sort of."

"Marcelo said you're a high school senior, a friend of his son. I think it's really cool that you're here."

"Thanks."

"The talk tomorrow night will be more for you. You can look at BC while you're there."

I suppose that's an indirect version of the "Where did you apply?" that every senior gets asked a thousand times. "I'm going to Wisconsin."

"Are you thinking about premed?"

I shake my head. I was doing well in AP Bio until I started cutting class. "Something with writing. Maybe journalism."

She glances over to Mr. Aguilar, who's talking to a guy with blue scrubs from the audience. "Well, there's your man."

One of the other panelists whispers something to Sarah and points to his watch.

"Okay," she whispers back, and then turns to me. "Marcelo's meeting with one of the doctors tonight, but there's a party after his talk tomorrow. Would you like to come?"

My eyes go wide. "You bet!"

She writes out the address and directions, and I'm on my way.

Chapter Fourteen
April 3-4, 1986
Boston

Boston College is at the end of the Green Line. Matt says it takes a long time to get there, and I'll have to leave the party before twelve thirty because the transit system shuts down at one. He gives me a key since he's pulling an all-nighter at the studio, and he warns me to be careful.

About twenty people show up for the talk, but Sarah, who invited me to the party, isn't there. I wore jeans and a UW T-shirt so we wouldn't end up dressing alike again, but I should have chosen the skirt. Now I feel like a total slob, and I worry that I'll have no one to talk to at the party, either.

The translator from the MIT talk is there again tonight, for a talk that's almost identical. I notice that Mr. Aguilar has a black nylon splint on his left wrist.

I raise my hand to ask another question.

Mr. Aguilar points to me and says, "She's a friend of my son's from Wisconsin. She's been following me all over the country."

A few people in the audience laugh. When the translator finishes, even more do. One man calls out, "Your son sent her to make sure you behave."

Everyone laughs, including Mr. Aguilar. I ask, "Did you have any way of knowing how many people were reading *Justicia*?"

Mr. Aguilar turns to the translator. "She's obsessed with that newspaper." The translator doesn't repeat the comment in English. Mr. Aguilar faces the audience. "The military read it. And they knew a lot of other people were reading it too. Otherwise, they wouldn't have been so afraid of us. We measured our audience by the amount of repression against us."

An older woman raises her hand. "Why do you think they were so afraid of your newspaper?"

"We told the truth not only about the conditions in the poor neighborhoods and in the prisons, but also about who was responsible for them. Most of our readers knew the former, but they didn't have the information to hold the responsible parties accountable. And not just the dictator and his top officials, but the people who ran the prisons, and the spies in the neighborhoods."

While the translator finishes, Mr. Aguilar walks away from the lectern toward the audience. He paces in front of the first row of seats and speaks without the microphone.

"When I uncovered information, I gave it to the investigators with the Catholic Church, the *Vicaría de la Solidaridad*."

I see heads nod in approval. BC is a Catholic university.

"I also published the names so people could protect themselves. If your neighbor was a spy, you needed to avoid talking about certain things with him. Even the weather could be dangerous, because when we said a storm was coming, that meant a raid was coming."

A man in the back raises his hand and stands when

he is called on. He has short hair and glasses with thick black rims. He wears a black jacket.

"Some of those people you named were assassinated. In your newspaper, did you advocate or promote the use of violence against those whose identities you revealed?" The man speaks in English, but with a heavy Spanish accent.

Everyone turns toward the questioner. Several people gasp. Mr. Aguilar stops pacing. He appears calm, in control. "Our readers made their own decisions. We did not tell them what to do with the names." He steps toward the lectern, detaches the microphone from its stand. "In the United States, you may not have the most perfect democracy, but you have a judicial system that is fair, that protects you, that keeps those in power from taking your freedom and even your life, which they can do simply because they have power and you don't." He stops. The translator catches up.

"In Chile, we don't have that. There is no system of justice. There is no justice." He repeats the words, *no hay justicia*, and his emotion echoes inside me. "People do what is necessary to protect themselves. I would like to see the murderers and torturers, the spies and collaborators, brought before a court of law and punished, but until that happens, it is regrettable but understandable that people deprived of justice will take the law into their own hands."

I twist around to see the man's reaction. A lot of other people are watching him too. Slowly, he sits down.

Mr. Aguilar returns to the lectern. "In answer to your question, I did not personally use or advocate violence." Most of the people in the audience applaud.

When the lecture ends, I see Sarah, who must have slipped in late. Today's peasant skirt is blue. She offers me a ride to the party, which is in Newton, nowhere near the T line. She promises that someone will drop me off at a station on the way home.

The party is at a typical suburban house. Just like at our parties, most of the people hang out in the rec room, but they don't make nearly as much of a mess. There's no spilled beer or pop, for instance. At home, I usually hang out in a corner with one or two of my girlfriends and laugh at the boys doing keg stands, who then stagger around the room making no sense and end up outside, puking in the bushes. Of course, if it's Dan or one of my friends' boyfriends who decides to do a keg stand or play beer pong, this instantly stops being funny.

Here I don't know anyone, and they're all years older. At first I'm afraid I'll be standing around by myself or clinging to Sarah, but I'm wrong. Being a high school student all the way from Wisconsin has made me an attraction. People stop to ask me how I like Boston and how I know Mr. Aguilar and where I'm going to college. They listen to what I say, too, though I'm a little bummed when a couple of them tell me I should have applied to an Ivy League university (which my parents couldn't afford) rather than going to UW. Still, I'm glad to be around people who think it's cool to be smart, and it's fun being the center of attention for once rather than sitting around watching stuff happen. Besides, the empanadas are awesome.

New people come in soaking wet or carrying umbrellas. I've finished dinner and am trying to decide between the flan and the chocolate-chocolate-chip cookies when the man with the thick glasses steps into the kitchen. He isn't wet, and he comes in alone.

In the next moment, he's alongside me. "Are you the high school student?"

I count him as about the twentieth person to ask me, but the first with a Spanish accent. "Yes?" I answer. I haven't forgotten the man's earlier attitude toward Mr. Aguilar and his newspaper.

"You asked a good question."

Aha, a suck-up. He looks the part too. Besides the glasses and short hair, he wears a long-sleeved white shirt, black pants, and a loosened tie. The black jacket he had on earlier is gone. Seeing his smooth face close up, I estimate midtwenties but trying his best to appear forty.

"Thanks," I say, still wary.

"You can't accept everything you hear at face value. What we do has consequences, whether or not we intend them. And that goes for the newspaper."

I'm about to ask him how he got into the party, but he holds out his hand.

"I'm Samuel. What is your name?"

I don't like the way he's eyeing me now. He's leering at me, almost as if he owns me. He steps toward me, into my personal space. My skin crawls; I slide backward into the dessert table and feel my left hand land in the icing of one of the cakes. I give Samuel a fake-sweet smile, but with the tooth-baring lip lift, and hold up my hand, which is now smudged with chocolate. *See what you made me do*, I want to scream at him. Instead I say, "I'm sorry. I have to go wash up."

I walk away, licking the heel of my hand.

Sarah stands next to the fireplace. "Having a good

time?" she asks when she sees me.

"Yeah, except for that weird guy." I point to Samuel, standing by the food table. "Who is he?"

"A graduate student. He knows the professor whose house this is," one of the other women with Sarah says. "He comes to a lot of these talks and likes to argue with the speaker."

"Devil's advocate?" Sarah asks.

"I'm not so sure," the woman replies.

"He was in my face. I backed into the table to avoid him and stuck my hand in the icing." I show them my gooey hand.

The woman wags her finger at me. "You'd better watch out."

On my way to the bathroom, I check out the living room, where the hard-core drinkers are hanging out. Mr. Aguilar is seated in a corner, in a cloud of smoke with four or five other guys. All night long, they've been doing tequila shots with beer chasers. The tequila bottle sits next to Mr. Aguilar's feet. The other men are eating, but when I ask Mr. Aguilar if he wants any food, he says, "I can't eat after these things." I notice the new black wool cap covering his head. It matches his sweater.

Now I see Samuel in the room, on the other side of a set of French doors. He's standing with an older man and munching an empanada. Samuel says a few words, which I can't make out, and the man writes something on a folded piece of paper.

I feel a hand on my shoulder.

"*Permiso.*"

I realize I'm blocking the door and step aside. Mr. Aguilar stumbles past me and into the door frame with a dull thud. He reaches out with his good hand to steady himself.

I glance in the opposite direction. Samuel and the other man are watching the spectacle. "Pathetic," the other one says.

"Don't kid yourself. He isn't harmless," Samuel remarks.

"I didn't say he was," the other man replies. The two turn away and keep eating.

When I come out of the bathroom, Mr. Aguilar is waiting, leaning against the wall by the door. He grabs my arm.

"I have to get out of here," he says, breathing hard. I have a tough time understanding him, between the noise of the party and his slurred speech.

"Is everything all right?"

"I'll tell you later."

He teeters a few steps in front of me, then his bad leg buckles, and he falls to the ground. I go to help him, but he waves me off. He gropes for a doorknob and pulls himself to his feet.

"Do you have a jacket?" I ask him.

He describes Dan's denim jacket. I dig it out from under the pile, along with my poncho and shoulder bag. The tape recorder and cassettes rattle inside my bag. I hold Dan's jacket while Mr. Aguilar struggles into it, and, with him hanging on to me, we slip out the back door.

It's a light rain, but hard enough for me to see the drops hit the driveway, which glistens in the floodlights. We stand in front of the garage under the eaves, and I wonder what to do next. We're miles from the nearest T stop. It's raining. Neither of us knows our way around, and he's so drunk he can barely stay upright. I want to ask Mr. Aguilar if he has any ideas on how to get out of here. I can't think of the words in Spanish, so I just stare at him, my mouth open.

"*Puta silla*," he mumbles.

I wonder what any of this has to do with a chair, since *silla* means "chair" in Spanish. "Did it break?" I ask.

"Say. Ee. Ah. *La C-I-A*." He bares his jagged front teeth; one of the upper ones on the left side is completely missing.

"CIA? Like spies?" I ask in English. He nods. "*¿Quién?*"

"The *huevón* with the glasses. And the one next to him." Mr. Aguilar spits a few more expletives. I suck in my breath. I should have guessed. The guy asked a hostile question. He was trying to start up a conversation with me. He and the other guy were watching Mr. Aguilar in the living room.

"Have you seen them before?"

"The younger one, maybe. The other night."

He takes out his cigarettes, puts one in his mouth, but doesn't light it. After a while he shoves it back in his jacket pocket.

A couple of people leave the house. One is the woman I talked with earlier, the one who told me about Samuel. I run up to them. "Can we get a ride to the T?" I ask.

"Sure," she answers, pointing to her car.

I grab Mr. Aguilar, and we stumble to the car, him leaning on me. "Thanks," I say breathlessly when we get in. He sinks down in his seat and says nothing.

They drop us at the Boston College stop. We wait under the shelter for the streetcar. Mr. Aguilar wedges himself into a corner and again sticks the cigarette into his mouth. He tries to light it but misses the tip several times. His glasses are streaked with rainwater. "Will you light it for me?" he slurs.

While he smokes, I step outside into the rain and scan the area for the two men, in case somehow they have figured that we've gone and where and are coming after us. I see no one. Before Mr. Aguilar finishes his cigarette, the streetcar arrives. I help him up the steps and into a seat.

My eyes struggle to adjust to the bright light. Mr. Aguilar rests his arms on the back of the next seat and drops his head into his hands. His eyes are closed. His breath—actually, his whole body—reeks of alcohol.

"I've got to stop drinking like this. It's not safe," he murmurs.

"No kidding," I whisper in English. I glance around. There's one other passenger in the car, an older black woman.

"So where do we go?" he asks me.

"Where are you staying?"

"I have no idea," he says.

"Do you have a phone number or address?"

"Yes. But the people are still at the party."

"We can ride around for a while. The T doesn't shut down until one," I tell him.

The streetcar jerks to another stop. Mr. Aguilar grimaces. "I'm going to be sick before then."

"We can get off. You might feel better if you eat something."

He pushes himself against the window. "I want to get to a safe place. Not in public."

"I'll take you to my brother's house. He's not there."

We switch trains and walk the few blocks through steady rain to Matt's place. Helping Mr. Aguilar up and down all the stairs along the way is surprisingly easy because he's so thin. Even with the heavy wool sweater, Dan's jacket is loose on him. I can understand him being underweight coming out of prison, but he's been back almost two months. I don't think he's eating at all.

The house is dark and still. I guide Mr. Aguilar through the tiny living room into the kitchen to a small table pushed up against the wall under the stairs. There are three chairs. He drops into the corner one.

I hang my damp poncho on the hook by the back door and set my bag on the table. Mr. Aguilar asks me to light another cigarette for him. There's no ashtray because neither Matt nor his roommates smoke, so I hand him a saucer.

I open the door to the small pantry. "Would you like me to make you some soup, Señor Aguilar?"

"Marcelo. Call me Marcelo." I read out the choices. He picks minestrone. "Something to drink, too."

I fill a glass with water.

"No. *Un trago*."

I pretend not to understand him while I wash a pot from the dirty dishes left in the sink and heat the soup. Even though Matt and his roommates have most of a case of beer in the fridge, Mr. Aguilar doesn't need any more alcohol in him. I glance in his direction. He's pushed his chair into the corner. His arms are folded on the table with his head resting on top of them. The cigarette is burning out on the saucer, next to his glasses. He trembles.

I step toward him. "Would you like some hot tea?"

He shakes his head without raising it. I don't hear his teeth chattering, which they would be if he were cold, but his clothes are damp. "I need to be numb."

I stir the soup, wondering what he means. Then I hear a loud scream. Mr. Aguilar is sitting upright, his back arched. His eyes are wide open and in them is an expression of complete terror. At first I think he's having a seizure, but he doesn't fall to the floor, and he's still screaming, one eardrum-piercing shriek after another.

I drop the spoon into the pot. Each scream cuts through my chest. I can't breathe. My heart thuds.

Jesus, help me. Please help me.

I scoot my chair beside Mr. Aguilar and put my hand on his back. In the next instant, I pull it away. Whenever Dan's upset, I rub his back, and it calms him down. But this isn't Dan—it's his father. He's still shaking and shouting words that I can't make out, the same sounds over and over.

Please, God, let me help this man.

I don't think Mr. Aguilar sees me. He's someplace else, far away and terrible. My mind flashes to the talk last night, one of the doctors saying something about the healing power of touch, but the notes I took are two flights upstairs. I slide my trembling hand between Mr. Aguilar's sweater and shirt and rub his back in wide circles. In his rigid muscles, I feel the power of whatever it is inside him. "It's all right. You're safe," I repeat in Spanish. All the words are coming to me in Spanish. I pull myself closer so my body is against his, keeping him warm. Keeping him safe. "It's just me here. Nobody is going to hurt you."

It seems like forever before he calms down. He gulps air. "Sorry," he gasps. "I get these flashbacks."

"Is there anything I can do?"

Mr. Aguilar sags against the wall. "I'll take the soup and tea."

I start to worry about doing something that might make him panic. "What causes your flashbacks?"

"A lot of things," he mumbles.

"Do you want to talk about it?"

He shivers a little. "I should. The doctor said it would help me."

I slide his glasses out of the way and set the soup bowl and a mug of apple spice tea on the table. "I'm here to listen. I won't leave you."

"Thanks, but aren't you a little young?"

"I was eighteen in January."

"*Bueno.*" He sips the tea and takes a deep breath.

In the moments before he begins to talk, I slip my hand inside my bag, slide a fresh cassette into my tape recorder, and push the buttons: record and play.

Chapter Fifteen
April 4, 1986
Boston

Mr. Aguilar slurs so badly I understand less than half of what he says, but even that leaves me wondering why he's sitting here in front of me and not insane or dead. I fill an entire sixty-minute cassette and part of another. He's so far into what happened that he doesn't notice when I reach into my bag to flip the tape. Or when Matt's roommates come home together.

I shush the roommates and promise to explain tomorrow. They go upstairs.

Just after two in the morning, Mr. Aguilar quits talking in midsentence and slumps onto the table, almost crushing his glasses. My bag with the tape recorder is under his face. When I slide the bag out to stop the cassette, he jerks upright. His breath is sour and his face gray in the weak light from the back porch. A glistening stream of saliva runs from the side of his mouth down his chin.

"You should go to bed," I say. He doesn't respond. I pull off Dan's jacket, put Mr. Aguilar's arm around my shoulders, and help him to his feet. He shudders. I hear a rumble deep within him.

He grabs the edge of the sink and pitches forward, sick, into the dirty pots and dishes. I lift him up and hold his forehead. He mumbles an apology.

"It's okay. Get the poison out," I whisper in English, as I would to a classmate on his hands and knees in somebody's backyard.

He groans. "I want to die."

He tears at his insides even after there's nothing left but air, still repeating those awful words, *quiero morir*. I tell him to relax, that he'll feel better in the morning.

"Don't...talk." His body stiffens. "Just...don't...talk." I try to reconcile my image of him speaking in front of all those people with the sick, scared man in my arms, but the only words running through my head are, *I can't tell Dan this happened.* After Mr. Aguilar passes out, doubled over, I drag him to the sofa and lay him on his side—the recovery position, they called it in the first aid class I took to get out of gym last year. His breathing, at first shallow, becomes regular and deep.

I turn the faucet on high until the sink is clean and open the back door to let in fresh air. I sit on the porch steps, wrapped in my poncho, until my neck starts to hurt. I consider listening to the tapes, but I don't want to be reminded yet of what Mr. Aguilar went through and how he ended up tonight. It makes me too sad. I go upstairs to bed.

The next thing I hear is my brother's voice. "Court, what the hell is going on?"

"Nothing, why?" I roll onto my back. The sun feels warm across my face.

"There's a stinking drunk passed out on our sofa downstairs." Matt stands in the doorway to his bedroom. His eyes are bloodshot from his night in the studio, and there are dark circles underneath.

"What time is it?" I ask.

"Seven thirty." Matt glances into the hall. "Who is he?"

I hesitate, wondering how much to tell Matt. Three nights ago he was in awe of Dan's father, and I don't want him disillusioned now. I crawl out of my sleeping bag, push past my brother, and race downstairs, where Dan's jacket is draped over a kitchen chair and Mr. Aguilar's glasses and my bag with the tape recorder are on the table. I pick up my bag and throw the strap over my shoulder.

Matt points into the living room, but I make no move to look. "Did one of my housemates do this?" he asks.

I shake my head.

"Did you have a party?"

I shake my head again.

"Did you pull a Dad and pick up a homeless person?"

I shake my head a third time.

"I don't have the patience for Twenty Questions, little sister."

"It's Dan's father, Matt," I whisper.

"And how did he come to...that?"

I shush my brother so he doesn't wake Mr. Aguilar.

"Don't worry. He's dead to the world," Matt replies.

I step out on the back porch, and Matt follows. The sun has climbed above the rooftops of the triple-deckers behind his house. A woman hangs laundry on a clothesline across the low, weed-covered fence that separates the yards. The sky is deep blue, but the day hasn't warmed up yet. I pull my poncho around my shoulders.

I keep my eyes on the woman across the yard, avoiding my brother's face. "After the talk, I went to this party in Newton where Mr. Aguilar and a couple of other guys were doing shots. Then some CIA guy showed up, and he panicked. He asked me to get him out of there, so I brought him here."

"Why did he think the guy was CIA?" I expect Matt to say Mr. Aguilar was hallucinating, but he doesn't.

"He asked a hostile question at the talk."

"What kind of question?"

"If Mr. Aguilar ordered assassinations of government officials."

"So he accused the newspaper of being a hit list?"

I nod.

Matt runs his fingers through his uncombed hair. "Do you remember what the guy looked like?"

"Short, dark hair, glasses with black frames. He was wearing a black jacket and a tie."

"Yeah, I think I saw him at the MIT talk."

Relieved that my brother doesn't think I'm crazy, I continue, "And at the party, he came up to me and tried to start a conversation. Saying stuff about the newspaper and trying to get my name."

I sit on the top step. Matt sits next to me and puts his arm around my shoulders. "I shouldn't have let you go out there alone," he says.

"I can take care of myself."

"And your boyfriend's father, apparently."

"I think I did okay." I twist my finger around a strand of hair. I didn't braid it for the party because I wanted to look older.

"Court, that is not cool." Matt clears his throat. "Just like Dad, you find random, desperate people and bring them to houses that aren't yours."

I can't believe Matt's dragging that into the morning

sunlight. I scoot away from him, out of his grasp. "Dad did the right thing. The refugees would have been killed if he hadn't helped them." Picking at a loose thread on my poncho, I add, "His only mistake was getting caught."

"There were other places they could have stayed. He didn't have to bring undocumented immigrants to the church when the members didn't even know. Or to the house with you there." Matt sighs. "I knew the FBI was watching us, and I told Dad I'd drive the refugees to Canada, where they'd be safe and so would we."

Matt once told me about two teenage brothers from El Salvador he'd smuggled across the border, even though the kids knew no English and Matt, no Spanish. In all, he said, he made four runs and delivered eight refugees to Canada while at Michigan—not your usual college extracurricular activity.

Matt stands and stretches. "I better go check on your pickup again. You should never have left him alone." I follow my brother inside. He kneels and lays his hand on Mr. Aguilar's back, timing his breaths. He was right about the stinking drunk part: a strong odor of tequila mixed with vomit and urine rises from the sofa. I can't think of anybody, at any party—Willie included—who's ever gotten this wrecked.

Matt gives Mr. Aguilar a gentle shake. "Hey, buddy, are you okay?" he asks.

I scoot closer to Dan's father and call his name. Getting no response either, I squeeze his shoulder.

He opens one eye, coughs, and licks his lips, which are covered in a white crust. "Jaime, *otra ve' me sacaron la cresta*. Let me sleep," he croaks.

"What's he saying?" my brother mouths to me.

I didn't understand Mr. Aguilar's first sentence, except for the name of his friend from prison. Another flashback, I guess. I step away and join Matt in the kitchen, where he's rinsing the coffeepot.

"You're lucky nothing irreversible happened to either of you," he says, a hard edge to his voice. "I suppose you have no idea how much he drank."

"No. And not all of it stayed in him."

"Which probably saved his life. Do you plan to tell your boyfriend?"

"No way."

"You have to say something. If not to Dan, to his mother." He spoons coffee into the filter. "The man needs some serious psychological help."

He needs to get his articles published so he doesn't have to do these tours. I pat my shoulder bag and hear the rattle of the cassettes. "I've got it under control."

"This isn't a high school kid acting silly." Matt returns the green coffee can to the shelf above the sink. "It wouldn't surprise me if he intended to harm himself."

He said he wanted to die, though I can't believe he meant it after surviving all that he survived in prison. "Okay, I'll talk to Dan's mother." I think of how Mr. Aguilar smuggled the bottle of tequila into the committee meeting. "But I'm sure she knows already."

"Doesn't matter, Court. You've gotten yourself into something that's a lot bigger than you are."

"Like the refugees," I say.

Matt nods. "And you're going to have to see it through."

CHAPTER SIXTEEN
1982-1983
Bloomfield Hills, Michigan

They called my father Andrés. And my mother, Alicia. Everyone else knew them as Drew and Alice.

I remember hushed voices. And words in a language I didn't understand.

One day at the beginning of ninth grade, my parents came up to my room. They came together, which meant it was really important. A knot like a cry rose to my throat. The last time they visited me like this was when Gram died.

"We need you to do something for us," Dad said.

That's how it began. With a very big favor.

"Your father and I are helping some people who will be killed if they stay in their country. They may have to live at our house for a while."

"Do you need my room?" I couldn't see why. Mom and Dad had just finished our basement.

"No. You keep your room," Dad said. "But we can't let anyone know about these people."

"Are they in danger here?"

Dad nodded. "What that means is, when our guests are here, you cannot invite anyone over. No one."

"Not even Kara," Mom added.

"And you can't tell anyone that people are staying with us." Dad put his hand on my shoulder. "This is very serious. Do you understand?"

"I understand," I said.

* * *

It was after that when I started hearing the voices. They were men, women, children, and babies too young to speak. Their words and cries came up from the basement, carried through the heating ducts. I couldn't tell what they were saying, but I could tell they were afraid. It wasn't only the tone of their voices. Sometimes I could even smell the fear, and I knew this was a secret I had to keep.

We were a group of four—my best friend, Kara, and Heather and Jen. We were planning a sleepover for my fifteenth birthday. Three days before, a family from Guatemala—father, mother, two little girls, and a baby boy—showed up.

"You'll have to cancel," Mom said.

"Can't they go somewhere else for one night? Like the church?"

"Not with the homeless shelter there."

Why couldn't my birthday have been in July instead of January?

Why did there have to be homeless people?

And refugees from places most of my classmates couldn't find on a map?

* * *

I blinked back tears when I told my friends my birthday party would have to be canceled.

"My mother has to go for surgery," I said.

"Omigod, what's wrong?" Kara gasped.

I thought of Gram and felt warm tears on my cheeks. The sobs rose from my throat. "Biopsy. They think she might have cancer. They're taking her in day after tomorrow."

* * *

"My mother's fine. The tests were all negative," I told my friends the following Monday.

But I'd had no birthday party. And the Guatemalans were still there.

"I have an idea. We can have the party this weekend," Kara said.

"My mom's kind of worn out. From all the stress, you know. Maybe we can do it out somewhere."

We ended up going to a movie and sharing a giant sundae at Friendly's afterward. I promised my friends we'd have a big party for my Sweet Sixteen the following year. That's what I'd make Mom and Dad do for me for wrecking my birthday.

But the following year never came.

No, it came.

In a way that I could never have imagined.

* * *

Right before final exams freshman year, it happened.

The phone rang nonstop that afternoon when I got home from school. My mother yelled at me through her bedroom door not to pick it up. I saw the door to the basement wide open, with huge muddy footprints on the new carpet and everything down there gone. Carried off.

Unable to concentrate on studying, I buried myself in the Stephen King novel I'd checked out from the school library and forgotten to return. *Firestarter*.

After the phone finally stopped ringing, my mother came into my room alone. She said my father had an emergency meeting at the church, but she had to talk to me.

"Your father and the López family were arrested this morning."

The López family—two parents, two little kids from El Salvador. López wasn't their real last name. They'd arrived at the house two days ago, in the middle of the night. The kids wore no shoes and had cuts and blisters on their feet. Dad was planning to take Mr. López to the mall to buy the kids new shoes.

"Is Dad in jail?" I asked. She'd said he had a meeting at the church, but now I didn't believe her.

"I bailed him out this afternoon."

"What about the family?"

"The police won't release them." She inched closer to me. "They'll probably be deported."

"Can't the people in the church help them? They must know someone."

My mother sighed. "We didn't tell anyone, except for a few people we trusted. Most of them wouldn't support what we're doing."

"But the refugees are going to die if we don't help them. Can't Dad tell them that?" My face grew hot. Dad should have tried to convince them. Or he should have tried harder.

"This congregation is very conservative," Mom answered. "Your father knew that, but his conscience wouldn't let him stand aside. That's why we agreed to keep it a secret."

The next day, when the story appeared in the newspapers, I stayed home. I didn't know what to tell my friends. I faked sick for the rest of the week too, missing exam reviews. By the time exams started, everyone had forgotten. I just had to hope colleges didn't pay much attention to freshman grades.

In the following weeks, new words rose from the heating ducts. Words like "pastor-parish relations committee" and "formal complaint" and "district superintendent." And other words like "felony transport," "illegal aliens," and "adjournment on contemplation of dismissal."

My mind raced. Would Dad go to jail? Could the church fire him? If so, where would we go? What about school? What would I say to my friends?

As the days grew longer, I would stare out the window, watching the sun go down. I figured I wouldn't have much more time to look through this window, to inhabit my room, with its light rose walls and lace curtains.

In the middle of June, Mom and Dad told me he had been appointed to another church—in Madison, Wisconsin, hundreds of miles away. The government dropped the charges against him but sent the López family back to El Salvador, even the little kids. We would never hear from them again.

My mother told me to start packing. We had only two

weeks before the move. "Sort through your things—things you need and things you can live without," she said.

"You can throw all my stuff out. I want to stay here with my friends."

"Courtney, this is no time to act childish."

I glared at Mom as if I could reduce her to a pile of ashes with my eyes. Like the girl in *Firestarter* did. And after I finished with her, I'd go to the cops who arrested Dad. And the people in the church who didn't want to save the refugees.

Look at me. Sizzle. Ssssss.

When I told Kara about moving to Madison, she and I hugged and burst into tears. "You have to come over the night before you leave," she said.

Mom had warned me to say good-bye quickly; it would make leaving easier. "Okay, but I might have to sneak out." No problem—I had done it before.

When I got to her house, it wasn't just Kara and me but about twenty of our friends from school. The kids I'd known since kindergarten. And Mom was right about quick and painless good-byes. When I saw my friends all together, I couldn't stop crying until Ronnie O'Shea said, "Oh, quit blubbering," and poured Jack Daniels into my Coke.

Kara gave him the finger, which made me laugh for about a minute, and then she and I started sobbing together. We ended up passing around plastic cups with spiked Coke until everybody was tipsy and giggling, and half of the addresses they gave me so I could write to them were unreadable.

* * *

"Mom, Dad, I want to switch to Spanish," I told them in August, as we were filling out the forms to register me for high school in Madison. Our new parsonage had creaky floors, noisy plumbing, no dishwasher or air conditioning, and a leaky roof. My bedroom walls were painted pea green and had water stains.

"But you've put so many years into French," my mother said. "It's a shame to start over."

"I can't really do anything with French. We're not near Canada anymore." I was staring at the wall, wondering how soon my parents would get the roof fixed so I could repaint the room.

Blue. It would be blue this time. Like a cloudless sky.

"You won't be fluent in either language if you switch now," Mom said.

"If I study enough, I will."

"Why Spanish?" Dad asked.

"Because of you guys."

He smiled. "I think we've gotten you into enough trouble because of our Spanish."

"We've promised not to shelter any more refugees who don't have legal status," Mom said. "It was a condition for dismissing the charges against your father."

"Don't worry. I'm not sneaking any refugees into my room." I added, "Not in this dump," in case they thought I was happy about the whole thing.

* * *

Someone from the church came to fix the roof, and I

did repaint my room blue. I found some fishnet curtains and decorated my wall with Frida Kahlo posters—a self-portrait with a pyramid, skulls, and broken machines, a bright picture of a Mexican village, a portrait of two Fridas with their hearts visible. I discovered her when I started Spanish and loved the way she turned her suffering into art. That was how the textbook described it, making it sound simple and magical—like Rumpelstiltskin turning straw into gold.

That's when I began to write. I won my first prize that year, with a story about ghost children from a made-up land based on El Salvador.

But it wasn't enough.

I wanted to do something.

Bigger and better than what my parents had done.

And I wasn't planning to get caught.

Part Four
Nino, Resurrected

Chapter Seventeen
April 15, 1986
Madison

Since she's come back from Boston, Courtney's been acting really weird. I see her staring into space with a dreamy expression. She's beautiful that way, soft and glowing, her mouth slightly open to show her smooth lips and perfect teeth. I want to kiss her for a long time, long enough for her to carry me away to wherever she is. I want her to take me away from my upcoming court case and the drumbeat at the back of my head: *You are a criminal*.

Sometimes we kiss, but it's never long enough. Other times, I reach for her and she stays frozen in place. "What's going on, Courtney?" I ask.

She snaps to attention and says, "Sorry," or "Nothing," and then our lips lock. But it doesn't feel the same.

The week she returns, she arranges an independent study that excuses her from AP English and AP Spanish. If she gets out of gym, she won't have to show up for school until sixth period, but she says she'll come for lunch fifth period to keep me company.

"Or at least to keep you away from bad influences," she says, even though Willie and my other bandmates have either fourth- or sixth-period lunch.

At lunch the next Tuesday I notice she has the beginning of a shiner around her left eye. It's bright red, going to purple, and swollen. It's not pretty, so I focus on the rest of her.

"How did you get that?" I ask her.

"Gym class. We were playing volleyball, and I guess I zoned out." Her voice sounds weak and far away. "A ball hit me in the face."

"Ouch." I bring her some ice from the cafeteria kitchen, wrapped in a dishtowel, to replace the melted icepack I now see behind her shoulder bag.

She holds the towel to her face. "Thanks. But I'm getting out of gym for the rest of the year. The teacher told me to bring in a doctor's note."

I'm surprised the teacher didn't accuse her of being on drugs and send her to the vice principal, because she's doing a very good imitation.

"So what's your plan?" I can't help the envy that creeps into my voice. "Sleep late? Watch *Jeopardy!* reruns?"

"Write some more stories. Try to get them published."

"I hope you have more luck than Papá's had."

She lowers the ice pack. "What happened?"

"He sent out some articles before he left on tour. They got rejected." I gaze down at the table. There are initials carved in it: J. S. + C. N. Whoever J. S. and C. N. are, they'll probably get more attention than Papá. "When he calls from the road, he asks about his articles, and Mamá and I don't know what to tell him."

"Don't tell him anything. It'll break his heart."

"That's what we figured." I remember listening to him on Mamá's electric typewriter before he left, as he typed with his one good hand. Tap, hummm, tap, hummm, tap. And he wouldn't let either of us help him. He said we all had our jobs, and this was his.

Courtney gives me a ride home after school and comes

inside with me. I'm no longer grounded as of yesterday, but I've had to keep working at the supermarket because the lawyer costs a fortune. The ride has just given me the only half hour of free time I have all day.

I make Courtney a new ice pack. Mamá arrives about ten minutes after we do, and she brings the mail with her. She's asked me not to pick it up because she doesn't want me to see the rejections, but she tells me about them anyway, which doesn't make a whole lot of sense.

There's another manila envelope in the pile that she dumps on the kitchen table. The return address reads, *"Los Angeles Worker."*

Mamá notices the ice pack right away. While I'm explaining the volleyball incident, Courtney pulls the envelope toward her and examines it with her uncovered eye.

Mamá sighs. "Yes, another one turned him down."

Courtney leans back in her chair so that the pack sits on her face without her having to hold it. "You don't really know until you open it, Señora Fuentes," she says in English, but addressing Mamá the way we do in Chile, by her father's rather than her husband's surname. "Sometimes they ask for revisions."

"We've only had form letters," Mamá says.

"Where are the others?" Courtney asks.

"In our bedroom. I'll get them."

Mamá goes into the bedroom and comes out with a stack of torn-open envelopes. I wonder why she lets Courtney see them and not me. My question is soon answered.

"I heard from some people on the committee that you've volunteered to translate," Mamá says.

Courtney nods. She's removed the pack now, and the side of her face is red and damp. "Señor Aguilar gave me one before he left, and I noticed mistakes. That's why I offered to help."

Mamá tenses. "What kind of mistakes?"

"Spelling. Grammar. Things that would get the articles rejected without an editor reading beyond the first page."

My mother relaxes. "So you think these weren't even read?"

"Probably not."

"Maybe you can fix the spelling and grammar and he can send them out again." Mamá sets the pile on the table in front of Courtney, who lays the most recent one on top and slides them all into her bag.

"I just arranged an independent study for the rest of the year to give me time to work on them." Courtney sets her bag on the floor.

So that was her plan all along. Why didn't she tell me?

Mamá goes over to the stove and fills the teapot with water. She turns on the flame and sits with us at the table.

"He's taken those rejections hard," she says after a while.

"I do too, Señora Fuentes. If you don't care about getting rejected, it means you haven't been putting your heart into your writing."

My mouth falls open in awe of her. Courtney can come out with the most amazing things sometimes, like she understands totally what we're going through.

Mamá stares at Courtney, apparently as stunned as I am. The teapot whistles. She asks us what kind of tea we'd like and fixes three mugs of mint, sharing one bag among us. Courtney gets the first turn; Mamá's cup goes last.

Mamá takes her seat again and sighs wearily. "These articles are the only things he has here. He says if he can get them published and people read them, they'll pressure Pinochet to free the other prisoners. But each time an article is rejected, he sees it as another day his *compañeros* rot in jail."

Courtney nods and sips her tea. Mine's too hot, so I blow on it. I'm pretty loud, and Mamá flashes me a disapproving glare.

She continues. "If he can't get them published, I'm afraid he's going to try to go back. He thinks that'll be the only way left to him to do something for the others." She shakes her head. "I don't want him in that…place. If the soldiers don't kill him, the death squads will."

"Don't worry," Courtney says. "I have some ideas for the articles."

Mamá smiles. "Good. So many more people read those newspapers. And the speaking takes a lot out of him."

I think of the nasty cold Papá caught somewhere in California. He's now in the Pacific Northwest, and the last couple of times I talked with him over the phone he was coughing so badly I could barely understand him. But at least he's there and not here, threatening to take us all back every time a manila envelope shows up in the mail and drinking himself into a stupor afterward.

I glance at my watch. I'm going to be late for work. The only way I'll make it to the supermarket on time is if Courtney drives fast. I tap her arm and whisper to her, "I have to go." She wants to keep talking with Mamá, so I raise my arm with the watch right in front of her face. That gets her attention.

Courtney and I run to her car. She screeches out of the

130

lot.

"How's this for fast?"

I'm struggling with my seat belt while she jerks the car onto University Avenue. Maybe it wasn't such a good idea to ride with someone as spacey as she's been these days. "It's okay if I'm a little late—as long as I get there alive."

"Sorry, Dan. Your mom wanted to talk. She's really worried, you know. So am I."

"Yeah, if Papá keeps getting rejected, he'll do something crazy."

"Why do you say things like that?"

She pulls up to the front of the supermarket, where six hours of bagging and carrying groceries to cars stares me in the face. "I don't know." I take a deep breath and mutter, "I've got problems too, and it's like nobody gives a crap."

Chapter Eighteen
April 24-26, 1986
Madison

Courtney says nothing about my outburst—not then and not in the days that follow. But by the end of the week, she begs out of lunch. "I need to work on the articles," she tells me. "I want at least one acceptance before your father gets home."

Those stupid articles again. "Not much chance of that," I grumble. "You have, like, a week."

"And I've got great stuff. They can't turn it down." I wish I could love her confidence as much as I used to.

Courtney smiles at me. Her eye is really scary looking—purple and black swirled together. If I were in her place, I'd wear sunglasses. She leans over to kiss me, and I shut my eyes, trying to imagine myself far away from here.

"I hope you don't mind," she says when our lips part. "You have no idea how important this is."

I start hanging out with Willie more because he doesn't talk about Papá's articles all the time, and he makes me laugh. But he doesn't have the same lunch period that I do. I use the time to finish my homework, since I'm working thirty hours a week on top of going to school, playing guitar at Sunday morning services, and rehearsing with the band.

Mamá and I meet with the lawyer. He says he's talked

to the district attorney, and they're willing to plead my charge to disorderly conduct instead of battery. It's the lowest misdemeanor instead of the highest. I'll pay a five-hundred-dollar fine and get six months' probation. If I keep away from trouble until I'm twenty-one, my record will be expunged, and I can apply for my citizenship then. As much as I want to become a U.S. citizen when I turn eighteen this November, I don't have much choice. I take the plea.

Willie gives me a ride home from rehearsal that night, and I tell him. He slaps me on the back. "Congratulations, Aggie-boy. You stayed out of jail."

"I won't even have to do community service."

"Yeah, it would be the pits to have to work at the church pantry alongside you-know-who." He pops a stick of gum in his mouth. "So will you cut her loose?"

"Where did you get that idea?"

"She abandoned you to eating alone."

"I'm not Tina. I *do* have other friends." I think of Tina, who now respects me. The mean kids haven't bothered her since, so maybe beating up that little jerk was worth it after all.

"I don't know how you can go out with someone who sincerely believes she's better than everybody else." He spins around a corner on two wheels. I grab the dashboard. "I mean, she's hot-looking, but she must be awfully good in bed for you to stick around as long as you have."

"You hate her that much?"

"I told you last year when you first started going with her. She's not right for you. If you think she has an attitude now, wait till next fall. I'd be amazed if she didn't dump you for a college guy by the end of freshman orientation."

I'm about to tell Willie that I believe Courtney when she says she chose UW so we can stay together. But then I think, *She's kind of dumped me already for Papá—or at least for his cause.*

Willie honks at a car that's slow moving on the green light. "Okay, I get it. You're enjoying the sex while you can. It's not like she's good for anything else."

I take a deep breath. "She helped get Papá out of prison."

"Her letters made the difference?" Willie lets go of the steering wheel in the middle of University Avenue. "She's one person, Aggie. One person. Miss Jesus Freak may have convinced you otherwise, but she isn't that important. She could disappear tomorrow, and everyone would simply feel better about themselves."

I think about Papá's radio interview, about the people in our country who opposed the government and disappeared without a trace. "Willie, that's not funny."

"Sorry, man." He takes control of the van just in time to avoid the median.

Papá returns the next evening. Our band has a gig at the Jam, so I miss him coming in. When I get home from the after-party at one in the morning, I hear him coughing from the bedroom. Mamá's at the kitchen table, grading papers. She usually waits up for me. Anyway, I don't know how she can sleep with all that noise.

"How was the concert?" Her voice sounds far away.

I brush my sweat-salty hair from my forehead. "Awesome. The Jam was packed."

She shushes me. I realize my hearing is still dulled from the gig and the crowded party. I leave my electric guitar in a corner of my room and come back for a glass of juice.

"Papá doesn't sound so good."

"He has walking pneumonia. When they dropped him off, I took him straight to the doctor. He should have cut his tour short and not let it get to this."

I remember what Willie said about Courtney yesterday, that one person wasn't so important. Obviously Papá disagreed, or he wouldn't have put himself through the full speaking tour in the hope that it might get someone else out of prison. "Is he going to be okay?"

"They gave him a lot of medicine and told him to rest for a while."

I spot a flattened pack of cigarettes on the coffee table and pick it up. "He can start by getting rid of these things."

Mamá takes the cigarettes from my hand. "With his nerves, don't count on it."

I lower my voice to a whisper. "Did he ask about the articles when he got in?"

She nods. "I said we hadn't heard back. It's a good thing Courtney took them."

Except now she's ditched me for the articles, I mutter on my way to bed.

I get up at eight the next morning so I can catch the bus to the supermarket. Tina lies sprawled on the living room sofa watching cartoons. Mamá and Papá are still asleep. I grab a granola bar and muss my sister's hair as I pass her.

Something hard whacks me on the elbow. I look back at Tina, who waves a library book and smiles at me. I realize she'd only had the TV on for background noise. The book is thick, much thicker than I'd expect for a sixth-grade assignment. I squint to read the title: *A Tree Grows in Brooklyn.*

I grin at her. "Are they making you read that for English?"

"No. I wanted to. Courtney said it was good."

So she's brainwashed my sister, too. Before Courtney started coming over, Tina was like me: she wouldn't read a book unless she absolutely had to for school. "What's it about?"

"A girl whose family comes to New York from Ireland. She's poor and her father's a drunk." Tina blinks rapidly. "But at least he loves her and she has a nice brother."

"Are you saying I'm not nice?" After almost wrecking my future on account of her social problems, I'm hurt.

She sets the book facedown on the coffee table. It's open to a page about two-thirds of the way through. "No, you're okay." She lowers her voice to a whisper. "It's Papá."

I lay my hand on the top of her head. Her hair is silky and warm. "Tina, it has nothing to do with you. He's so beat up I don't think he can love anyone right now."

She looks down. "Yeah, that's what Mamá says too."

At Kohl's, it's a typical workday. Bag groceries. Deliver bags to cars. Push empty shopping carts back into the store. At least it's not raining. Near the end of my shift, I almost drive a train of carts into a familiar gray Toyota that makes an illegal turn into an exit lane.

"Jeez, Courtney, watch where you're going!" I shout.

She can't hear me. Her windows are closed. She whips into the closest space and steps out of the car.

"Dan!" She jumps up and down. In her hand is a piece of paper. "Look! They accepted it!"

"What?"

"*Milwaukee Free Press*. They took one of the articles!"

I snatch the letter from her. My eyes zero in on the words, "We are pleased to inform you that we would like to publish your story, 'The Hole.'"

"Did you tell Papá yet?"

"That's where I'm going. Do you want a ride?"

I talk my boss into letting me punch out early. Courtney and I run to her car like we used to. Her shiner is now just light brown and yellow patches on her pale skin.

When we get to the apartment, she lets me enter first to avoid startling Papá. He's propped up on the sofa, wrapped in a blanket. His eyes are closed, and his glasses are on the table. Mamá's cutting vegetables. I don't see Tina, but she's probably in her room.

"Good news, Mamá," I whisper. Courtney shows my mother the letter.

Mamá gives her a hug. "*Gracias. Gracias.*"

"They're going to pay, too," Courtney says in Spanish.

"That's wonderful. How much?"

"Fifty dollars. It's not a lot, but if we make some big papers..."

"*Oye*, Courtney..."

Papá's eyes flicker open. Whatever he was planning to say next is lost in a fit of coughing. He's sunk down into the sofa and is having trouble catching his breath. Mamá goes to him, but he waves her off and struggles upright on his own. He reaches for the box of tissues on the coffee table.

"That's a bad cold he caught on tour," Courtney says to me.

Mamá joins us in the kitchen. "Viral pneumonia."

Papá wraps his good arm around his chest. "I got sore ribs I can't blame on Pinochet." His effort at humor ends in another coughing fit.

"There's this Chinese stuff you should try, Señora Fuentes. You rub it on his back. It'll take some of the soreness away, help him to relax and breathe more easily." She tosses back her little braid. "I had pneumonia my first winter in Madison, and it worked for me."

"You can also find a *botánica* and buy herbs and statues of saints," Papá says.

"*Amor*, don't be sarcastic. She's only trying to help." Mamá points to the letter that Courtney's still holding. "Anyway, she has wonderful news. *Milwaukee Free Press* took one of your articles."

Courtney brings the letter to Papá. I follow. Papá puts on his glasses and takes the paper from her. "I thought they rejected it."

"I retranslated it. Those guys didn't do a very good job."

"'Tay ... O-le.' What does this title mean?"

"*El hueco*."

"I thought it had another title."

"Well ... I ... kind of shortened it. You need something to get people's attention and make them want to read more."

"So when are they going to publish it?"

"Two weeks."

"Very good." Papá hands the letter back to Courtney, and when she takes it, he grabs her wrist. He gazes at her with his one good eye and says, "It seems our luck has started to change."

CHAPTER NINETEEN
May 10, 1986
Starlight Motel

When she drives me home from work two weeks later, Courtney has half a dozen copies of the *Milwaukee Free Press* that just arrived in the mail. She also shows me a letter of acceptance that came yesterday from a magazine in Chicago. She says it's the only other letter of acceptance she's gotten since taking over the translations, but she hasn't heard from most of them yet.

We all sit at the kitchen table except for Tina, who remains standing, ready for a quick escape. Papá's taken to calling her La Coneja, the Rabbit. Courtney hands Papá fifty dollars in cash.

He stares at the bills—two twenties and a ten—before dropping them on account of a coughing fit.

"What's this?" he manages to choke out.

"They paid for the article," Courtney answers. "They made the check out to me, so I cashed it."

"We should all celebrate," Mamá says. She picks up one of the papers from the pile and starts to read the article. "This is very well written, *amor*. I don't know why you won't let me read what you write."

"Because you're not objective. You always thought everything I wrote was brilliant." He opens the next paper to the page where Courtney points.

Tina and I reach for a paper at the same time. Papá

slaps his hand over the pile. "You're too young, Tina."

Tina's lip turns out in a pout. Unable to get a paper either, I look at Courtney with a pleading expression. After all, she's a grand total of ten months older than I am, and she got to translate the article. She rolls her eyes in the direction of the parking lot, as if to say, *Outside, in the car.*

Mamá shakes her head as her finger moves down the column. Suddenly she quits reading and leaves the kitchen. I hear the bathroom door shut and the fan click on. Tina slips off to her room.

I follow my sister and knock softly on her half-open door. I've been meaning to spend more time with her, to give her advice on how to act around other kids, so she doesn't get picked on. But my work schedule has made it almost impossible. And what she really needs right now is advice on how to act around Papá, or at least how to avoid him without being showy about it, so she doesn't piss him off all the time.

"Hey." I step inside her room.

"This sucks. I can't do anything because I'm too young." For the last three words, she imitates Papá's Spanish, but with a whiny, sarcastic edge that's all her own.

"I'll make sure you get to read the article," I say.

"Thanks a bunch." She doesn't sound excited, but I'm glad she doesn't doubt me or call me a wimp like she used to. "I'm tired of being treated like some stupid person who doesn't know anything." She stops talking, and I use the time to read the titles of the paperbacks on her desk. *The Catcher in the Rye. The Outsiders.* A volume of Pablo Neruda's poetry in Spanish that Papá brought from Chile. "I'm not stupid, okay!" Tina's shout makes me jump.

"I didn't say you were."

"You weren't even paying attention. Like everyone else around here."

I look at my sister, flopped on her stomach on her unmade bed. "I was checking out your books. And no, you're not stupid. I'm sorry."

Tina smiles at me.

"So how was that other book you were reading? The one with the tree?"

"*A Tree Grows in Brooklyn*. Awesome!" Tina's expression turns serious. "What do you think Papá's article says?"

"I don't know."

"He's even weirder since his trip." She stares at her bitten-off fingernails. "I can't believe he's really my *papá*."

"I wish he was different too. We all do. Even him." With a shudder, I recall the night he arrived at the airport and I first saw what they did to him in Chile.

"Is he always going to be like this?" Her voice breaks. I realize I'd never thought about how all this has affected her—and she had enough problems before Papá showed up.

"He should be happier now that his articles are getting published. That's what he wanted to do when he got here." I see Tina's face soften as I speak. I'm on a roll. "Now they're paying him. Maybe soon he'll start English classes and learn enough to get a job writing for a paper."

"You think so?"

"You should offer to speak English with him. You know, to help him." I pat her shoulder. "You're home a lot more than I am."

"Yeah." Tina grins. I'm starting to believe my own fantasies—even though Papá still refuses to sign up for any language classes. I bet he can't even read the article in the *Milwaukee Free Press* that Courtney translated. And as far as his ever being normal, two days ago Tina told me she heard him screaming in his room after a coughing fit, something about a submarine. When I asked Mamá, she said Papá probably had a flashback about being dropped into a vat of sewer water to force him to confess—that's what *el submarino* is. Mamá made me promise not to tell Tina.

I return to the kitchen, to Papá and Courtney. Papá's on the phone to one of the people from the committee. After hanging up, he hands me a newspaper and fills a drinking glass with red wine from a jug under the sink.

"I didn't want your sister reading it, though I don't really remember what I wrote." He coughs, clears his throat, takes a drink. "This doesn't look like what I remember."

Courtney jumps in. "They edited it. Shortened the paragraphs and put some of your comments in quotes." There's a catch in her voice that I don't understand. Maybe she's shocked at the amount of wine he poured and how he's drinking it like water. And I can tell from his breath that this wasn't his first glass today.

Papá continues. "*¿Cachai?* I want her to be able to go back to her country one day. To think of it as a place of great beauty—of sun and sea and mountains—and not of violence and death." He looks at me with a mournful expression. "I'm sorry, Daniel. You've already seen too much."

As I'm unfolding the paper, Mamá comes back. Her eyes are red and puffy, and her face is damp. I push the article aside. I'm eager to read it, but also scared because

Papá didn't want Tina to see it and it upset Mamá like that.

Papá dangles the ten-dollar bill in front of Courtney. "Here's your share for translating. You two go out and have a good time."

"I thought we were going to celebrate together," Mamá says.

"Pato's picking me up. I want to show the article to the boys. Let them see what a real translator can do." He stuffs the two twenties in his pocket. "Maybe they can learn a thing or two from La Gringa."

"You're in no condition to go out. Especially with Pato." Mamá's voice is low, hard.

He ignores her. "And since Daniel has to be at church early in the morning and I don't want to disturb him coming in, I might stay over."

"We have plans tomorrow," Mamá says.

I lean over the table and whisper to him, "It's Mother's Day, remember?"

He slaps his hand on the table. "*Chuta*, that's right. I'll have Pato bring me home in the morning."

"When you'll be good for nothing. Absolutely nothing," Mamá says. "I'd think, after all these years, you might want to spend some time with your family."

"There'll be other times." Papá glances at Courtney. "Didn't she say another newspaper took my article?"

"I don't care," Mamá says. "You need to be here. Start being a father to your kids—now."

Papá glares up at her. "This is my article, my job. You don't tell me what to do, woman," he growls.

Mamá touches my shoulder. "Daniel, take your friend and go."

Papá gestures the same with his head—it's the only

143

thing they can agree on. I slip my trembling hand inside Courtney's and we go out the door, leaving the angry voices behind. As soon as the door closes, I realize I've forgotten the newspaper.

"I have another one in my car," Courtney says when I tell her. After a moment, she asks, "Do you think they'll be okay?"

"I've never seen him hit her, if that's what you're asking." My mind flashes to poor Tina, who has gotten whacked. And to the time he hit me. "Maybe I ought to go back and make sure."

But as I'm on my way back, Papá steps outside and slams the door behind him. There's a cigarette in his mouth. His eyes lock on mine. "¡*Vete!*" he shouts.

I scram like he tells me to and catch up to Courtney. "It's okay. He's chilling," I pant.

"That's good. I was worried."

"Typical Latin male? Drunk, beats his wife?" I don't know why I said that, but now that I have, I can't take it back.

Courtney stammers, "I didn't mean it that way. Believe me, Dan." She puts her arm around my waist and squeezes. "And I'm sorry about the last few weeks. I got caught up in those articles and totally forgot about you."

I twist my head toward her, and she kisses me, pressing her lips hard against mine as if she's not just saying words; she really wants to put aside everything that's gone on between us for the past month. I run my tongue along her perfectly straight teeth. My stomach swirls, and my jeans suddenly feel too tight. I wonder if our problems are finished like neatly solved math questions, because my body is celebrating.

Our mouths separate. We're about an hour from sundown, and it's still warm enough that we don't need jackets. "Let's reopen the Starlight Motel tonight," I say.

"Good idea." Courtney kisses me again.

There are three big lakes in the city of Madison. At various places on their shores, the city's trucked in sand to make a sort of beach. They're not like the beaches in Chile, which has nearly four thousand miles of coastline and volcanic lakes too, but they're nice, especially when the sun's setting over the lakes' still waters. Most of the beaches are in parks that don't open until Memorial Day, but we have our methods for getting in. Courtney found out about the Starlight Motel from her ex-boyfriend, who left for college last fall, and we checked in several times in September and October before it got too cold for anything that required the removal of clothing.

We make a couple of stops on the way: Courtney's house, where we pick up a blanket and pop and flashlights; and the deli, where we spend her translation fee on sandwiches and cookies. We leave her car about a quarter mile away from a park on Lake Wingra, cut through woods, and slip through the gap between the gate and the fence. I have Courtney's copy of the *Milwaukee Free Press* to read while we're there.

In the fading light I read. The article starts when Papá awakens in the hospital, not knowing where he is or what happened to him on the day they crippled him. My hands are shaking. My chest is tight; I can hardly breathe. I can see why he wouldn't want Tina to read his article. I don't care what I promised her; I'm not letting her read it either. If this is what Courtney translated, it's no wonder she was standing around, practically catatonic, while volleyballs smacked her in the face.

She comes up behind me and wraps her arms around my shoulders and chest. I want her to hold me like that forever, as if she could protect me from all the cruelty in the world.

"It's pretty rough," she whispers.

"Yeah. He wrote that?"

"*Más o menos.*"

I don't know what she means when she says more or less. The sun has almost finished setting over the lake. A breeze from the south blows little ripples that flash red and purple, the color of Courtney's shiner at its worst, or the old cigarette burns on Papá's neck, back, and shoulders. Mamá and I saw them when I helped her rub the medicine on his back so he could breathe more easily. She was so upset she could only bring herself to put the medicine on once. I didn't put it on again either. He said it made no difference and was a waste of money. Mamá told me afterward there wasn't a part of his body they didn't violate.

Courtney lets me go. I reach for her arms. My throat is clogged, and I can barely swallow. "Stay with me like this, okay?" I whisper.

"Sure." She smoothes her skirt and again kneels behind me. Her head is on my shoulder, and I smell a hint of lemon in her hair. In my mind, we're in the midst of a war and we're lovers who've sneaked away from the battlefield for the night.

"I can't believe he survived this," I say when I'm finished reading. I knew Papá had done great things back in Chile, with his investigations and the newspaper, but I had no idea what it felt like for him to go through what they did to him. Even when I saw the soldiers beat him up, it wasn't me they were beating up. I didn't feel the pain then, or during the days afterward when his bones were still broken and his muscles torn. "How did he do it?"

"He's the one you should ask. Not me."

"He doesn't want to talk about it." Instead he drinks. He smokes too much. And he yells at us all the time. It makes sense, though. I tell myself I'm never going to complain about the way he treats us again.

Courtney crawls around to face me. She crosses her legs under her long skirt and pushes her hair back. Her eyes, dark blue in the twilight, hold mine. "Dan, I really care about your father. He's the most courageous person I know, and believe me, I know a lot of courageous people."

She takes both my hands in hers. For a moment she closes her eyes, and then she moves her lips like she's praying.

"All the hurt that he describes in that article—and it wasn't just his body, Dan; you see how they messed with his mind, too."

I think about the guard who had the bet on him dying first.

"Everything they did to him in that prison…" She lets go of my hands and touches her chest, just above her heart. "It's all in here now. And he's barely hanging on."

"How do you know that?"

"You can see it if you really pay attention. Like the way he abuses his body. Or how he snaps at you guys to make you hurt like he's been hurt, or to make sure you don't get too close to him."

She's a hundred percent right, and I don't know what the hell I'm supposed to do. I don't want to lose Papá after all he's been through, but I see him slipping away from us.

"Don't let him push you away," she says finally. I take her hand. God, I love her. "Just stay with him, okay? Whatever he does."

It's pitch-black by the time we finish our sandwiches. Blown in from the breeze, little waves lap at the shore. I imagine that I'm nine years old, back in Chile, and we're camping out beside one of the lakes near Chillán. In the darkness, you can't see that the trees are different, or if there are mountains behind you or flat land as far as you can see. There's just the new moon, thousands of stars, and black water.

Courtney runs her fingers through my hair. I play with her skinny braids. She has three of them today. We kiss. We hug. As much as people can hurt other people, we want to be kind to each other tonight. So we crawl between the blankets in a place we call the Starlight Motel.

CHAPTER TWENTY
May 12-13, 1986
Madison

Something happened at the committee meeting tonight. At ten thirty, about a half hour after I finish putting Tina to bed, Mamá rushes through the door. Papá lurches after her, yelling about someone named Lucho and calling her a whore.

All along, I've promised myself to stay out of whatever's going on between them. After reading his article, I've also promised to cut him slack for his drinking and the way he treats us.

But this is crazy.

I step between them, with no idea what to say to them besides to shut up or they'll wake Tina.

Papá tries to push past me and trips. I catch him, hold him in a bear hug, and whisper for him to calm down. A sharp odor—hard liquor, and lots of it—rolls over me. He's too weak and uncoordinated to get away. I feel his ribs underneath the gray UW sweatshirt he borrowed from me. He still wears a wool cap even though it's now spring, almost summer. Mine fell apart. Someone must have given him this one on his speaking tour, because he doesn't know enough English to go to a store and buy one himself.

He coughs and gasps. I worry that I'm squeezing him too hard or that he's going to be sick.

He grabs my T-shirt with his good hand. His breathing

slows down, though the muscles of his shoulders and back are still hard.

"I'm fine. Let me go," he says.

I don't. I'm afraid he'll go into the bedroom and hurt Mamá. Suddenly I feel my shirt yanked and a shove into my side that sends me into the living room chair.

I steady myself against the chair and dash after Papá. He stumbles past the bedroom into the bathroom. I hear the fan and the water running. Harsh, choking noises rise above them, and I can't tell whether Papá's sick or crying or both.

I knock on the bedroom door and call out softly, "Mamá? It's Daniel."

She comes to the door. Her hair is messed up and her makeup streaked. "I have to get out of here for a while. Come with me."

I'm in pajama pants. I change into jeans, dirty from six hours at the supermarket, and follow her out.

We sit in her car. She taps a cigarette from a pack in her purse. Now she's smoking too.

Before I can ask her about the meeting, she begins in English, "I wouldn't drag you into this, except that some of it concerns your friend."

"Courtney?"

The glowing tip of the cigarette moves up and down. She takes it from her mouth, holds it between her fingers. "Two of the committee members who first worked on the articles with your father read that one she translated."

"Yeah, it was pretty upsetting."

"They said Marcelo didn't write it."

My heart drops to somewhere around my stomach. "What?"

"They don't know where Courtney got it."

My mouth is dry, almost too dry to speak. "So they're saying she made the whole thing up?"

Mamá nods.

"Well, screw them. Courtney doesn't make stuff up." Well, actually she does, it occurs to me. Until this, the only things she's had published are short stories—which are all made up. Maybe these guys are right.

But maybe the guys are wrong. Two nights ago, Courtney sounded so convincing about Papá and what he went through. And he has the scars and the battered head to show for it.

"Maybe Papá gave her some new articles that nobody knows about."

"It's possible. The committee called a special meeting tomorrow night, and they want her to be there. I doubt they're going to let her continue translating."

That would crush Courtney, who has dedicated most of the semester to this project, with at least one more article waiting to be published. "It's not their decision. They're Papá's articles. What does he think?"

Mamá takes a long drag and blows a stream of smoke toward the windshield. I roll my window open. "What if they're not his articles?" she asks.

"Are they or aren't they?"

"That's the problem. He thinks they're his, but he doesn't remember writing them." Another drag. Another stream of smoke. My eyes sting. "Because of his injury, he has problems with his memory. The drinking doesn't help."

I shrug. "I guess Courtney will have to clear it up, then."

I recall Papá questioning her, twice. Could she have made the whole thing up? Could she have read a book or newspaper article and combined it with that radio interview or one of his lectures in Boston?

Mamá stubs out the cigarette. "I hope to God they're his."

"Yeah, she'd be in deep trouble if they weren't."

"I don't care about Courtney." Mamá's voice hardens. "Your father is on the edge of...I don't know what. He's scared that because of his injury, he can't write anymore. And if he can't write, he says he's worthless."

That's nothing new. I've heard it from her—and him, along with his threats. "So if he can't do anything here, he'll drag us back to Chile."

Mamá shakes her head. "He says the people on the committee humiliated him by even suggesting the articles aren't his. He got hysterical and yelled at them, saying they all knew he'd lost his ability to write and were just playing with him."

"That's hard-core," I say.

"And he accused me of sleeping with one of the guys while he was in prison. Luis, from Argentina. Lucho and I are friends. He's gay, for God's sake."

Papá sure managed to make an ass of himself, I think. But then I hear Mamá crying.

"After the meeting...on the way home...he said he wanted to kill himself."

I throw the car door open. "Then what are we doing sitting here?" I shout at my mother. "We left him in the apartment—alone!"

Mamá grabs my arm. "Daniel, he was angry. Anyway, nothing's going to happen with Tina there."

"Like Tina's going to stop him? She'll hand him the freaking razor blade." My face is hot. My legs twitch. I slam the door and run back to the apartment.

The moment I step inside, I feel like a fool. Papá's crashed on the sofa. No pools of blood next to his wrist. No empty pill bottles. I turn off the lights and crawl under my bedcovers so Mamá will think I'm asleep when she comes in.

I wait about an hour and slip out of my room. The door to my parents' bedroom is shut. There's no light coming from underneath, so I assume Mamá's sleeping.

I tiptoe into the living room. Papá lies curled up on his side. I kneel next to him, listen to him snore, sniff his rotten breath—the smell of a liver decomposing, I imagine. Once in the middle of a nasty hangover, he said he expected to live no more than five years, and I guess the cause will be liver failure unless he makes good on his threat. Killing himself one way or another, and I wonder if there's anything we can do to stop him.

I sit in the chair for a while. Papá has horrible nightmares that leave him moaning and thrashing. I don't want to touch him, because I can't tell if he's awake or still asleep and how he'll react. Around four in the morning, he calms down. I decide that he'll be safe on his own and return to my bed.

* * *

I'm dead tired at school. Courtney has started showing up for lunch again to keep me company. I'm slow to react when she sits across from me, which gives her an opening to start the conversation and then chatter on and on.

"I'm working on my summer plans," she says. "I want to study advanced Spanish for three weeks—total immersion, no English. I mentioned this program in Estelí, Nicaragua, but my parents aren't too thrilled about me studying Spanish in a war zone. They said Mexico, Argentina, or Spain."

"Forget Argentina. You'll end up with some mishmash of Spanish and Italian."

"Yeah, I'm thinking Mexico. You know how much I love Frida Kahlo."

Her whole room's covered with Frida Kahlo posters. It's practically an obsession with her. But Courtney's summer can wait.

"Listen, we need to talk," I say.

"What is it?"

"The article that came out last week. The guys on the committee said Papá didn't write it, that you made it up."

Courtney was holding a sandwich, but her arms drop to the table. "I figured this would happen," she says. She stuffs her sandwich into her brown bag, along with the can of pop she hasn't opened yet. "Let's go, Dan."

I follow her out of the cafeteria and to her locker. She flips the combination. Inside, her woven shoulder bag hangs from the hook. She grabs the bag and leads me into the language lab.

She dumps the bag's contents onto a table. Three cassette tapes fall out along with her other stuff. "I brought these to school because the equipment's better. Some of it's hard to hear."

I pick up a tape. She's written on it, *Marcelo Aguilar, April 3-4, 1986. Boston.*

"I recorded him. One tape has his talk at Boston

College. I was planning to make him a copy here."

"And the other two?"

"That night I took him to my brother's place after a party. Some CIA guy had been, like, stalking him."

"You sure he wasn't being paranoid?"

Courtney shakes her head. "I saw the guy. And so did Matt." She slips the tape inside one of the school's machines. "When we got back to Matt's, your father had a flashback. I suggested he talk about it, and while he was talking, I recorded him. That's what I used for the articles. They're all his words." She hands me the headphones. "So he didn't actually write them, but I didn't make them up, either."

"Does he know you taped him?"

Again, Courtney shakes her head.

I put on the headphones and press the play button. I hear my father's voice, muffled because she probably had to hide the tape recorder. The words all run together. I lift off one earpiece. "He's drunk."

"A little."

"Yeah, right. You secretly recorded him when he was wasted. I'm sure he doesn't remember that he even talked to you."

"I'm sorry. He wanted to get those articles published, and what he'd written wasn't very good. I was planning to use his lecture, but—"

"But what?" This was a worse situation than I'd ever imagined.

"He was in such bad shape I thought getting him to talk about it would do him some good."

My face burns. "Did you get that idea from a daytime TV show?"

"No. From couple of doctors at Harvard Medical School. Your father was part of a panel on treating torture victims."

I stop the tape and yank off the headphones. "So you taped without permission, translated articles that didn't exist, and practiced psychology without a license after thinking one panel made you the expert. How could you do this to Papá?" My voice cracks. The language lab aide glares at us.

Courtney glares right back at him. When she speaks again, it's in Spanish and almost a whisper. "Listen, Dan. The most important thing is for him to get his message out. That's what he'd tell you. I know it."

"You know nothing about my father, so stop acting like you do."

"I read his articles, the ones he wrote. They never would've gotten published." She locks her eyes on mine. "Did you read them?"

"No. He never showed them to me. Or to Mamá." I can't hide the resentment in my voice. Why did he keep his articles from us—his own family? Because he thought I was too young? Or that Mamá would lie to him?

It occurs to me that either of us could have read the articles when they came back rejected during his tour, and we didn't. As if we didn't want to know the truth of what happened to him.

I fight the sinking feeling in my chest. My teeth are clenched. I snap back, "But you know what, Courtney? You're screwed, because the committee has called a special meeting to ask you about your fake translation. Tonight. Seven thirty. I'll give you the address. You're going to have to figure out what to tell them."

"I have to talk to your father first."

I stare at the rug. "If you thought he was in bad shape then, you should see him now—after those guys on the committee told him the articles weren't what he wrote."

"What did he do?"

I whisper, "He threatened suicide."

I expect her to look shocked, but she only nods. "Did you hear him?"

"No. Mamá did." I stop, take a deep breath before I reveal what else he accused her of and how I had to keep him from hurting her. "You knew this would happen."

"Uh-huh." Courtney stands and collects her stuff.

"How?"

"He said it himself. On one of the tapes. The guards didn't only tell him he threw himself down the stairs; they kept baiting him. They said he'd go insane from the torture, so even if he got out alive, he'd end up killing himself."

I clench and unclench my fists. It feels like a hundred degrees in the language lab. I want to kill the guards who treated Papá like that. I want to rip their tongues out and kick them down a long flight of stairs into the center of hell. But here I am, fifty-five hundred miles away, with physics, PE, and U.S. history in the way of my doing anything.

"All right. I'll call work and cancel. We'll talk to him together."

Chapter Twenty-one
May 13, 1986
Madison

Obviously Mamá's not too worried about Papá's suicide threat, because she's left him home alone again. He's napping in their bedroom when we come in. The curtains are drawn throughout the apartment. "Papá, Courtney's here. She needs to talk with you."

He stands, grimaces, and rubs his neck with his good hand. His bad hand feels the nightstand for his glasses, which he manages to get to his face. He's in pajamas. His leg brace lies on the floor next to the wall, and he makes no move to put it on. He limps into the hallway, where Courtney meets him. I'm shocked to see the two of them hug, especially after what must have happened at the committee meeting.

We sit at the kitchen table. Courtney shows him the tapes. "Remember that night in Boston, when you slept over at my brother's place?"

"*Sí, sí*." He nods like it's all coming back to him.

"When you told me what it was like for you in prison, I taped it without your permission. That's what I used for the two articles that were accepted, and all the others I sent out. I'm sorry."

Papá picks up a cassette, flips it back and forth. For a while he says nothing. Then he asks, "Can you make me a copy?" His voice is calm. The word "detached" sticks in my mind. "Make several. This is evidence against the bastards."

My mouth falls open. Even Courtney looks surprised.

"If they're ever put on trial for crimes against humanity, we would submit these to prove what they did." He sets the tape down. The boulder sitting on my chest all afternoon finally rolls off. If he's talking about submitting tapes for a trial that's probably going to be a long time off, he's not planning to kill himself. "Do you have something to play it on?"

Courtney pulls out her small recorder, loads the cassette, and presses the button. On the cheap machine, he sounds even less coherent.

Papá shakes his head slowly. "I must have been *medio cocido* that night." He shrugs. "I guess we all have things we're less than proud of."

"Aren't you even mad at her?" I'm still confused. If someone had taped me without telling me, especially if I was as trashed as Papá, I wouldn't have let them off so easily.

"Danielito." He reaches across the table and squeezes my shoulder. "One of these days, I might have to forgive a lot of what was done to me, and secretly taping my *testimonio* is probably the least of it." He falls silent and listens for a while, his head resting in the palm of his good hand. "Anyway, this tape is very powerful. It's raw. People pay more attention to that than something that sounds rehearsed."

He hands the three cassettes back to a smiling Courtney.

"Where did a nice gringa like you learn to be such a good journalist?"

"You inspired me."

"Which has now come back to haunt me." Papá leans back in his chair and groans. "When there's democracy and I get my newspaper back, I'm going to hire you. That is, if the television channel doesn't get you first."

It's time to end this lovefest, especially since there's no way Courtney's ever going to live in Chile. "Mamá says Courtney has to be at the emergency meeting tonight. What should we do about this?"

"I'll explain everything. You two don't even have to come."

"I should go, Señor Aguilar," Courtney says.

I reach for her hand. "And me too, since I heard the tapes," I say.

* * *

It seems like everyone has shown up for the emergency meeting at the Ballards' house. Besides Professor and Mrs. Ballard, there are the two guys who first translated Papá's articles, Pato and Gregorio. I glare at Gregorio, because he was the idiot who dropped Papá onto the floor a couple of months ago. Gregorio doesn't even know why I'm angry at him. In a bizarre way, it's a good feeling. If Willie's right, Courtney goes around feeling that way all the time.

I also see Luis, who was so kind to Mamá when Papá was gone. He gazes at her from across the room with soft, pitying eyes, and I wonder if anything really did go on between them. Mamá didn't have much of a life all those years on account of taking care of us, and I can't say she has much of one now that Papá's back. If anything, it's worse with him here.

They've set out a chair at one end of the living room for Courtney, like they're going to grill her. That pisses me off. Papá must feel the same way I do, because he rearranges the side chairs so that they're all part of a long oval, and he sits in one of the chairs next to hers. I stay across the room with Mamá so she's not alone.

When everyone sits, Professor Ballard clears his throat. He glances at Courtney, then at the rest of the dozen or so people there, and says in English, "We've called this meeting to clear up a misunderstanding and come to an agreement on where to go—"

"Bob, that's enough," Papá interrupts in Spanish while rising to his feet. "Courtney's a friend of my family. To me, she's like a daughter, so I'm not going to sit here and let you people put her on trial. The translations came from a series of *testimonios* that she taped when I spoke in Boston."

Pato raises his hand and shouts out at the same time, "So why didn't you tell us this yesterday?"

"Because I didn't know she'd recorded them, and after a five-week speaking tour, I didn't remember what I'd said."

The gringo sitting next to me whispers to his friend, "He wouldn't remember what he'd said the next morning." They giggle like little girls.

Rage burns in my chest. "That's my father you're talking about," I snap at them.

"*¡Cállate!*" Mamá slaps my arm.

"Courtney, show them the tapes."

Courtney takes the three cassettes from her bag and holds them up for all to see.

"Can we hear them?" Pato asks.

"After she makes copies, I'll give one to the professor. These should be put into an archive as evidence, along with any others Courtney and I might record, any interviews I do, lectures." He jabs a cigarette into the corner of his mouth, picks up the half-full jug of wine from which the Ballards had served the committee members, and signals for Mamá and me to stand. "That's it. We're leaving. Carry on."

Papá, Courtney, and I go out into the warm evening. Papá raises the jug in triumph.

"Where's your mother?" he asks.

"I think she's still there. Shall I get her?" I reply. I thought she'd join us. She drove Papá and me to the meeting, and she's our ride home.

"No. Leave her." Papá waves his hand. I glance at Courtney, my face going from sticky to hot in a split second. She gives me a pitying look, not much different from the one Luis gave my mother. Papá continues, "Maybe they'll do something useful, like plan a fundraising concert, instead of drowning themselves in gossip." He hands me the jug and lights the cigarette. A coughing fit accompanies his first puff. "Did you bring a car, Courtney?"

"Yes. Would you two like a ride home?"

Papá checks his watch. "Let's get something to eat. Tina's fine alone for about an hour."

It's the first time I've seen him show any serious interest in food. Usually Mamá has to force him to the table, and after about four bites, he's done. Having pneumonia for weeks didn't help his appetite.

We end up at the Middle Eastern restaurant near

campus where Courtney has landed a summer job, which means the dinner's on her. By the time we're done, it's almost dark. Papá calls home from a pay phone.

"Good news," he tells us. "I talked to Tina. Your mother's back, so we're free for the night. Homework all done, *m'ijo*?"

"Yes." Committee meetings tend to run late, so I made sure I finished this afternoon.

"So where do we go for a good time around here?"

"Depends on what you want to do, Señor Aguilar," Courtney says. "Do you want to hear some music, or see a movie?"

"No."

I wish I could suggest something. I have no idea what my own father likes to do in his free time, what makes him happy. Before he went to prison, he played soccer and basketball and liked to dance the *cueca* and carried Tina and me around on his back or shoulders, but these things are impossible now.

After a while he says, "Maybe we can sit and talk. Someplace where no one else is around."

There's one place, though if we take Papá there, I know we won't be able to use it as the Starlight Motel again. Courtney drives to where the trail begins. We get out. Papá cradles the jug he swiped from the Ballards. "You'll have to leave it," Courtney says. "They don't let you bring alcohol into city parks."

We follow the trail, each carrying a flashlight. We walk slowly so Papá can keep up with us. I carry the blankets from Courtney's trunk over my shoulder like a bandolier. Tonight, we're guerrillas slipping through the woods in search of a safe encampment.

We come out at the beach, stars and the half moon shining on the glassy lake. Courtney and I spread out a blanket. Papá lowers himself to the ground, trying to make his bad leg, along with the brace, go where he wants it. We sit on either side of him. He shudders.

"I don't like people surrounding me." I hear the tension rising in his voice. "One of you needs to move."

Courtney stands. As she passes behind me, she takes my right hand and sets it on Papá's back. His breathing is rapid and shallow, his muscles tight. I think I can feel his pounding heart through ribs, skin, and layers of clothing. "Papá, it's okay," I say.

He sucks in a deep breath, holds it, then lets it out with a loud sigh, followed by a cough. I rub the space between his shoulder blades. "Is that better?" I ask.

"I...think." He reaches inside his jean jacket. It's really my jacket. He's borrowed it permanently. He spins the top off a pint whiskey bottle with his thumb and takes a swig. After another gulp, he wipes his mouth on his sleeve and passes the bottle to me. I take a sip and hand it to Courtney. She sets it in the sand out of Papá's reach. Good move. I don't want to have to carry him back to the car when he's too drunk to walk.

Courtney pulls me closer. I feel the warmth of her body, sniff her fruity perfume mingled with the aroma of pine needles and fallen leaves. It's a narrow beach, and we're not far from deep woods. I listen to the crickets chirping and the rhythmic brush of my hand as I rub Papá's back through the jacket.

"Doesn't this remind you of the place where we camped near Chillán?" I ask him.

He nods. I can tell he doesn't want to talk anymore. He's in another place now. As Courtney would say, it's a good place, and I know because I'm there too.

CHAPTER TWENTY-TWO
May 28, 1986
Madison

Papá asks Courtney and me to take him to the lake the next night, and for every other night that it's not raining or cold.

"As soon as our country's free," he says, "I'm going south and camping by Lago Llanquihue, and I'm not coming back for weeks." Llanquihue is the second largest lake in Chile and amazingly beautiful. At least that's what I've heard. I've never been there.

"And then I'm going to find a deserted beach, build a fire, and all night long listen to the waves come in."

He's smoking and drinking less, and eating more. He reads the books he brought and a lot of the time seems calm, as if he's meditating. Instead of yelling at us, he mainly ignores us when we're home.

Tina doesn't understand the changes. She tries to get his attention, saying she promised she'd teach him English.

Mamá steers her away. "Leave him alone. He's healing. It's hard work."

I sense the irritation in Mamá's voice. I want to tell Tina not to be such a pest, but my sister isn't the problem. More than once I've heard Mamá mutter to herself about when Papá's going to act like a father to his kids instead of like some strange person who happened to move in with us. Since the incident with the committee, he's started sleeping on the living room sofa. At separate times I ask him and Mamá why. They give me the same answer: "It's the only way both of us can get a good night's sleep."

He really meant it when he told the people on the committee that Courtney was like another daughter to him. She's begun calling him Papá, too. They recorded another tape, talking about how he survived prison. This time, she asked his permission.

They used the recording to write another article, which the *Milwaukee Free Press* accepted. A couple of other places took some articles too—none of the big newspapers and magazines, but alternative ones with an interest in politics. Papá says Courtney's teaching him to write again, that he's had to learn it all over the same way he had to relearn how to walk and talk.

School ends right before Memorial Day, and Courtney graduates the Wednesday after the holiday. My whole family attends the graduation and the party the Larkins give at the parsonage. We get home around sundown, and as we're coming through the door, the phone rings.

Mamá rushes to get it. "Marcelo, it's for you."

Papá takes the receiver from her. He's standing, but as he listens, his face drains of color, and he drops to the sofa. "The sons of whores," he mumbles over and over. Several times he asks the person on the other line how it happened, and then he hangs up.

His entire body is shaking. Mamá goes to sit next to him. He's staring into space, his eyes as glassy as the still lake.

"Jaime Lozano. *Compañero* Jaime, he's dead. They killed him in prison."

CHAPTER TWENTY-THREE
June 16, 1986
Madison

After his friend's death, I expect Papá to slip back into his depression. Instead he arranges to return to his therapy sessions at the hospital and asks me to install a pulley over the bedroom door so he can work out at home. Mamá gets a summer job teaching Spanish at the university, so Courtney drives Papá in the mornings, and I come along too. Even when he's hung over, pale and barely able to hold his eyes open, he goes. Courtney and I hang out at a nearby coffee shop, and when he's done, she drops us off on her way to work.

One morning we get back to the apartment to find Pato Wheelock waiting for us outside.

"Where the hell were you, Nino?" he asks in Spanish, using Papá's *nombre de guerra*.

"Therapy," Papá fires back. He wiggles his fingers in front of Pato's eyes and growls. Pato laughs and jerks backward, pretending to be attacked by Papá's clumsy arm. The two hug—my scrawny Papá and big, greasy-haired Pato.

Papá unlocks the door. I follow the two of them inside.

"*¿Está aquí La Bruja?*" I assume it's my mother Pato's calling a witch. I give him a dirty look before Papá answers.

"*No. Tiene clases.*"

"Good."

Papá takes three glasses from the cabinet and a pitcher of orange juice from the refrigerator. While he pours juice into the glasses and sets them on the table, Pato lifts a bottle of tequila from his backpack. He unscrews the top.

Papá holds his hand over the top of his glass. "I'm cutting back. I have to get healthy." Then he glances at the glass and takes his hand away. "*Bueno. Un poquito.*"

Pato pours some tequila into Papá's glass and then into his own. "And the boy?"

I pick up my glass and drink from it. "I'm good," I say in English, then switch to Spanish. "I have to go to work in an hour."

Papá takes a pack of cigarettes from the pocket of his work shirt and hands it to Pato. Pato taps out two cigarettes and lights one of them for Papá.

"So what brings you here, man? We're supposed to meet tonight," Papá says.

"An emergency. Something's come up." Pato looks at me. "Do we want the boy here?"

Papá shrugs. "He's going to find out eventually anyway."

Find out what? My mouth is dry. I drink, but all of a sudden the juice tastes sour.

"Can we trust him?"

Papá turns to me and smiles his lopsided smile, cigarette dangling from the dead corner of his mouth. "Can we trust you, *m'ijo*?"

I nod. *I'm not getting out of bed, or telling anyone anything.*

"The plan is off," says Pato. "I'm flying to Santiago tomorrow. My mother's having surgery."

"*Mierda. ¿Qué pasó?*" Papá's face crumples.

"Diabetes, man. They have to amputate her leg." Pato pours another shot into his glass. "That won't give you enough time."

"Give her my best wishes, okay?" Papá claps Pato on the shoulder. He inhales and blows smoke across the table. "Is there another plan?"

"They're leaving it to you how you're going to get in. They say you're a smart boy; you'll figure something out. But I have the money." Pato digs into his backpack and comes up with a wad of bills. He counts them out, hundreds and fifties and twenties, on the table. "Eight hundred from the committee. That's for your plane ticket." He counts more bills. "Three hundred for documents and incidentals."

"Not from the committee."

"Exactly." Pato chugs the rest of his juice. I know not to ask where that money came from.

Papá stands and puts the eleven hundred dollars inside a coffee can he takes from a cabinet above the sink. He pushes the can to the back and replaces the drinking glasses and mugs in front of it. It's a load of money for a trip they were going to make together. I think of possibilities for what it could be, possibilities besides what I'm afraid it is.

Maybe it's only a conference. Papá's giving a lecture somewhere in Latin America or Europe. He needs a ticket and a visa. Pato was going to help him get around, and now he'll have to go alone.

After Pato leaves, Papá and I sit at the table. We finish our juice, spiked and unspiked, without speaking. I can tell he's disappointed. More than disappointed. Crushed.

First his friend dying. Now this, whatever it is.

"I have to catch the bus to work," I say. "You going to be okay here?"

He runs his lower lip under his jagged teeth. His eyes are shiny.

"You can trust me, Papá. I can help, if you give me a chance."

He rises from his chair, gripping the edge of the table for balance. "I'll walk you to the bus stop."

Outside, he rests his hand on my shoulder. "After Jaime died," he says, "I realized there's no way I can stay here. I'm not getting anyone out of prison. But since they've banned me from my country, Pato was going to help me sneak in."

My chest tightens. What I'd feared since the day he arrived has come true. But it'll be him going back, not the whole family. It's as if he cannot exist in the world we—Mamá and Tina and me—have made for ourselves, so he's ditching us, too. And right when I'm starting to get close to him, like a real father and son.

This sucks, I mutter under my breath.

Then I think of the money. Pato said the money for the plane ticket came from the committee.

"Does Mamá know about this?" I ask him.

He presses his lips together and nods.

"It's okay with her you're going back?"

"This reunion wasn't quite what she expected. I've changed. She's changed." He squeezes my shoulder. "It's a complicated situation, Daniel, and it's probably for the best that we're not going to be living together." He takes a deep breath. "That is, if this thing works out."

"What does that mean? Are you guys getting a

divorce?" I blurt out.

"No, I'm leaving. We'll deal with that later." Papá sighs. "If we have to."

The tightness turns to a slow burn. I know how hard it's been for Mamá since he got back, but I never thought she'd want to get rid of him. Or if she isn't actually throwing him out, because he wants to go back on account of his friend, she's making it easier for him to leave by getting him the money. And now that he can't go because of Pato's mother, how else might Mamá make it easier for him to check out, besides leaving him home alone with liquor, painkillers, razor blades, and who knows what else?

I step in front of Papá and grab both his shoulders. He shudders.

"Papá, how was Pato going to get you into Chile?"

"We were going to fly into Argentina and cross over the mountains. As if we were there to go skiing."

"No one's going to believe you can ski."

"I was working on it."

My mind flashes to the pulley I installed, to the bands he uses to strengthen his arm, to the ball he squeezes all day long. His long walks. The floor exercises, with his feet pressed against the wall. Stuff that we do without thinking he practices day after day, covered in sweat, his face twisted in effort and pain.

"Would you let me bring you back?" I pause. "Nino?"

For a few moments, he hesitates. Then he pulls me to him and holds me tight, in the middle of a soccer field on the way to the bus stop. "Welcome to the struggle, *m'ijo*," he whispers.

CHAPTER TWENTY-FOUR
June 16-17, 1986
Madison

I slide into the first empty seat on the bus. After it pulls away, leaving my father leaning against the shelter, I begin to realize the craziness of what I've promised to do. He may have cash for the plane ticket, but I don't. After my fine and the lawyer's fee, I have next to nothing in my savings account and one year before I have to pay for college. I have no experience smuggling people or anything else into a brutal dictatorship and a police record for losing my cool. And I have no idea what Papá wants to do when he gets back to Chile. For all I know, he intends to blow up the prison or gun down whoever he thinks was responsible for Jaime Lozano's death.

Then, there's my mother and whatever role she has in this. I guess you can fall out of love—it almost happened with Courtney and me a few months ago. But after waiting for him all these years—if in fact she did wait for him as opposed to sneaking off with that Lucho guy—and after all they've been through, you'd think she wouldn't actively encourage him to do something crazy.

Freshman year, the guidance counselors organized a workshop for all the students to teach us to deal with problems without drugs or alcohol. Ours asked us what we do when we're upset or angry. Some kids went out running. Willie said he smashed things in his house. I practice my guitar, and if I can't, I try to do something useful and completely unrelated, the best that I can do it—which is why, unlike Courtney who got kicked out of gym and almost failed biology, I made the high honor roll for the first time ever. And now I'm a candidate for Kohl's Bagger of the Year.

Usually Courtney picks me up after work, but today my mother meets me inside. She's doing her shopping, so I bag our own groceries and walk out with her. We have less than usual—Tina's off at Girl Scout camp and away from all this mess.

"What happened to Courtney?" I ask in English as I unload the bags into the trunk.

"I called her and said I'd pick you up tonight."

I push our cart, and another three I pick up along the way, back into the store and trot to the car. The moment I shut the door, Mamá starts, "Whatever Marcelo says, you are not going to Chile with him."

Bagging's done. My anger boils over. "What do you care? You want to throw him out."

"I'm not going to lose another family member to this insanity."

My apron's still on. I yank it off to toss it into the backseat, but my plastic name tag—DAN A.—is pinned to my T-shirt underneath. I hear ripping. "Shit!" I yell.

She slaps my arm. "Don't talk to me like that."

"It's not you. My shirt tore." I examine the hole in the red UW shirt that Courtney gave me when she got her acceptance letter. "Anyway, you can't stop me."

"I'm still your mother."

"He's still my father. Is he home?" I realize the person I really need to talk to is Willie. He's the expert on parents' failed marriages—and he got to live with his father.

"El Jardin. They're saying good-bye to Pato. I left them to pick you up."

"I want to go there. Now." I'm guessing I haven't much time before Papá drinks himself incoherent and can't take my side.

"No. I don't need you creating another disturbance." She turns onto University Avenue. "We'll discuss this tomorrow. But I've locked away your passport, so you can forget about Chile."

She drops me off. She's going back to Pato's farewell party. I think about calling Willie, but except for telling him we're Splitsville here, I have nothing to say to him. There's so much I have to keep secret.

Stuck inside without a car, I crank up Springsteen and play along on my electric guitar. Soon enough, the people upstairs come banging on the door, yelling at me to turn it down. I pace the apartment for a while. It's too late to call Courtney, even if I could think of something to say to her.

The telephone rings. The digital clock next to it reads 10:42. Willie should know better than to call at this hour, even if he just found out about a keg in the woods.

"Dan. It's Matt, Courtney's brother. I'm glad I got you. Is Courtney there?"

"No."

"She didn't pick you up from work?"

"No. My mother called her and told her not to come."

"Great," Matt mutters. "I need the car, and she took it."

Matt's been home for a week now, waiting for a job to start in Chicago. He doesn't have a car yet, so they're four people with only two cars. And one's a brand-new minivan that Mrs. Larkin won't let anyone else drive until it gets a scratch or two.

"Have you called her other friends?"

"I thought I'd try you first. I called earlier, but you didn't answer. I figured you two were out together."

"I must have missed the call. Guitar practice."

"Do you have her friends' numbers?"

I give him two possibilities. Courtney doesn't have a ton of close friends. It's what happens when you spend all your time studying, at church, or with a boyfriend.

Ten minutes later, Matt calls back. "Nobody knows where she is."

Now I'm worried. "I don't have a car either," I tell him. "Maybe you can use the minivan."

"Dad took it. He's at a funeral up in Eau Claire."

"That's a long way."

"Sister of one of the board members. Mom's gone too, so my ass is in a sling if anything happens to Court."

"Our car's on State Street with my mother. Let me run up there." It's a little less than three miles from the apartments, if I cut through the woods next to the lake and through campus. I estimate it'll take me half an hour.

"Thanks. Will you pick me up when you get it?"

"Sure."

I take off sprinting, slow to a jog through the woods to avoid outrunning my flashlight, and don't stop until I'm in front of El Jardin. I could use a drink of whatever they'll serve me. The committee people are sitting at a large, loud table in the back.

"*¡Danielito! Ven aquí.*" Professor Ballard still hasn't lost his Anglo accent.

I squeeze past a half-dozen tables. Despite the air

conditioning, my face feels like it's going to explode. I can't find either one of my parents.

"Where are my mother and father?"

Several people shake their heads, one of them Lucho. Professor Ballard answers, "I thought your mother was with you. She said she had to pick you up from work."

"That was more than two hours ago." I know I should have been more polite, but my parents and my girlfriend are missing, and I'm desperate.

Gregorio speaks up next. "And your father went to the bathroom a while ago, and we haven't seen him since."

Of course, nobody went to check on him. I ask a waiter for directions and barge into the men's room.

"Papá!" I scan the damp floor, push open the stalls. Nothing. I'm swearing, over and over, under my breath.

There's an emergency exit into the back alley. I call Papá and run up and down the alley, looking behind garbage cans and Dumpsters.

I run the possibilities through my head. Mamá and Papá aren't together. At least she's not with Lucho. She could be with one of her friends, plotting strategies to make sure I go nowhere this summer.

On the other hand, Courtney missing and Papá missing probably have something to do with each other. I get an idea.

I run back into the restaurant, to the committee's table, and squeeze into a seat. "If any of you need to get home, I'm a sober driver," I announce.

Various people look at one another. Gregorio stands, belches. "I've had enough," he says.

"You old enough to have your license, kid?" a woman asks. She winks and gives me a full-lipped smile. Her *tetas* jiggle under her see-through peach T-shirt. She's at least twice my age, so it's pretty disgusting.

Pato lifts his head from the table. A pile of shot glasses surrounds him. "I told you the boy looks just like Nino," he slurs.

Outside, Gregorio hands me his keys. He's leaning on a woman with dyed red hair. Or she's leaning on him. "Remember where your car is, Goyo?" she asks in Spanish-accented English.

"Over there." He points to a black Jeep Renegade parked in front of a pharmacy. Yes—my dream car.

I wait until they stumble inside and ask them where they're going, hoping it's one place instead of two. The woman gives me an address on the East Side.

"So who's the kid?" she asks.

"Vicky and Nino's."

She switches to Spanish, forgetting in her wasted state that I'm as fluent as any of them. "God help him, with that marriage made in hell."

"They got along fine before his arrest," I tell them. *Or did they?*

* * *

I used to think of their voices as a duet. A duet that seemed to harmonize if I didn't listen to the words. Papá's voice was low, tight, harsh. Mamá's was high, insistent, pleading.

Sometimes shots would ring out, blocks away. Papá would grab his denim jacket and the keys to the taxi. Mamá would clutch his arm. "It's after curfew."

"Curfews are for cowards."

She would struggle to hold back her tears after he left, even though she told me it was probably just a street fight and someone needed a ride to the hospital. That was what the newspapers always said too. By the time I learned the truth, Papá's voice had vanished.

* * *

The woman apologizes, and she and Gregorio shut up for the rest of the trip. I promise to return the Jeep the next day and check the gas tank.

First I have to pick up Matt at the parsonage. He's waiting for me. It's now almost midnight.

"Cool Jeep," he says, climbing in.

"You wouldn't believe what I had to do to get it."

He slams the door. "Do you have any idea where she might be?"

"You bet."

Now that it's summer, the park is open until midnight, and the Starlight Motel is no longer ours. But it's still worth a try. I screech into the parking lot next to Courtney's Toyota. The beach is deserted, but behind a shelter, there are barbecue pits and picnic tables. Courtney and Papá are sitting across from each other at one of the tables. In front of them is the tape recorder.

"What the...?" Matt says.

I hold my arm out so Matt doesn't startle them. "It's okay. They're making tapes, that's all." But I'm still jealous he's talking to her and not me. And neither of them told me this is where they'd be.

"I don't have all night. I was supposed to be somewhere an hour ago." He sticks his fingers in his mouth and whistles loud enough to be heard on the other side of the lake.

Both of them look up. Courtney drops the recorder in her bag.

"It's closing time, little sister."

Courtney snatches the bag and runs toward us, tripping on the uneven ground in her sandals and long skirt.

"I'm sorry, Matt. I lost track of the time."

Matt grabs her skinny wrist. "You didn't even bring a watch." He snaps the fingers of his other hand. "Give me the keys."

Courtney pulls a key ring from her bag and hands it to Matt, who's gone in an instant. His tires spin on the gravel at the edge of the road.

I slip my hand inside Courtney's. Papá catches up to us in the parking lot.

"How did you get Gregorio García's Jeep?" he asks.

"It's a long story, and I'm thinking of not returning it."

Courtney jumps up and down. "Let's drive it to the Twin Cities."

Papá looks at me, expecting, I imagine, an explanation. "Minneapolis-St. Paul," I say. "Only five hours away."

"I can make it in four." Courtney says. "Except that there won't be anything open when we get there." She twirls a braid around her finger. "We can ride around for a while and talk."

"Thanks. Drop me off at home," Papá says.

I wonder if Mamá's home and if she's worried about Papá, and where the hell she went when she said she was going back to El Jardín. Her car's in the parking lot, so I leave Papá to deal with their imploding marriage. It would take a trip all the way to Minnesota to tell Courtney everything that's happened today. The Jeep only has enough gas to go a couple hundred miles. I get on I-90 West.

But before I can speak, Courtney says, "Papá told me you're going with him to Chile. I've decided I'm coming with you."

"You?" Shocked, I drive onto the shoulder. Rough pavement jolts me to attention.

"Yes, me."

"You've never been there. Where are you going to get the money? And if your parents won't let you study Spanish in Nicaragua because there's a war—"

"Number one, it doesn't matter. Number two, graduation gifts. Number three, they can't stop me."

Yeah right, they can't. I still have to figure out a way to get my passport back, unless Pato gave Papá enough money to buy me a fake one too. "How are you going to tell them?"

"I'll fill out an application for a nature tour in Argentina. Nature tour—no phones."

Clever. My mind races to find other ways to talk her out of it. It's my last chance to spend time with my father for a while—maybe forever—and she's managed to stick herself in the middle.

"Look, Courtney. It's going to be hard enough to sneak Papá in without you attracting attention. I mean, you're a…" The word "gringa" sticks in my head. I can't think of another word that won't piss her off.

"Gringa," she says. "That's the whole point."

"What?"

"You two need me. I'm a gringa, and I make stuff up. How I've caused you guys the most trouble will get you into Chile, nice and safe."

"And how's that?"

She tosses her braids back. "I'll give you an example. You have a passport problem."

Good job, Papá. Tell my life story to my girlfriend.

Courtney continues. "Did you really think you were going to cross into Chile as Daniel Gerardo Aguilar Fuentes, *hijo del subversivo Nino?*"

"Yeah, yeah. Phony documents. So where do you come in?"

"I'm paying for yours and mine." She rubs her thumb and index finger together. "From what I made on the articles. And Papá thought we should pretend to be a gringo family, so I offered to make up names and do the talking at the airport."

"So it's *his* idea you come along?" My first thought is, *What the hell is going on between them?* My second is, *Someone with serious brain damage devised this scheme, and our lives depend on it working.* Or maybe Courtney's lying, and she's got Papá and me twisted around her finger like her little blond braids.

"I wanted to come, and he had a role for me. But I promise I'll stay out of your way. This is your time with him." Courtney slips a tape inside Gregorio's in-dash cassette player and pushes the rewind button. "You've got to hear this. It's the tape we made tonight."

"I can't. I need to keep my mind on the road." It's bad enough that she's messing up my plans to travel to my homeland with Papá. The last thing I want to do is think about the horrors of his time in prison there while riding the interstate in my favorite kind of car. One with fuzzy dice, rosary beads, and a Colombian flag hanging from the rearview mirror. I want to crank up some tunes, sing "Sherry Darling" or "Born to Run," and forget about my life.

"He's talking about what he wants to do when he gets to Chile."

"I hope it doesn't involve weapons or explosives," I say. "I'm not a terrorist."

"Neither is he. He wants to find out the truth about his friend and document it." She hesitates for a moment, then adds, "We've got to go through with this."

"Okay, play the tape."

She presses the button and turns up the volume. Papá's voice fills the Jeep. It's a bit slurred, not nearly as bad as on the first tape I heard.

"In a way, it was Daniel they were looking for."

He's talking about me. When I got out of bed.

"It's why soldiers break down the doors at midnight and arrest people in front of their families. They knew where we printed, and they could have picked me up there. They didn't for a reason."

There's silence on the tape. In the background, I hear leaves rustling. Courtney hits the stop button. "Do you understand what he's saying, Dan?"

"That it wasn't my fault he got arrested?"

"Why would it be *your* fault?"

She sounds surprised, and I realize I never told her everything that went on that night. "When the soldiers came, I got up, and one of them found me. They held a gun to my head and made Mamá tell them where Papá had run." I switch to Spanish. "They should have taken me instead. I was stupid and a coward."

"It wasn't your decision. Your mother did the right

thing to protect you," Courtney says in English. "Anyway, it was all part of their plan. Do you want me to play what he said again?"

"No."

Courtney presses fast-forward, and a few seconds later Papá's voice returns. "Torture isn't directed only against the prisoner, but against the community as well. The regime's goal is to make an example of the prisoner, to scare others."

I pause the tape, letting Papá's words and hers sink in. *I had nothing to do with what happened to him. He wants me to know that.* But what they did worked. Even in Wisconsin, I've avoided getting involved in anything political, and I don't know what will happen when I go back and it's in my face.

Courtney hits the fast-forward once more. The cassette spins for about thirty seconds. Then I hear her voice, sped up like one of the Chipmunks.

"This is it, Dan," she says.

Her voice slows to normal on the tape. "So where do you fit in?"

"Me." Papá's laugh is sharp, bitter. "I'm what Pinochet fears most. I got involved because I couldn't *not* do it. I was raised with this sense of justice, of right and wrong. It's in my blood. And right now, I'm so thoroughly and permanently fucked-up that I'm no longer afraid to die."

CHAPTER TWENTY-FIVE
June 25, 1986
Chicago

The thing about smuggling yourself into a military dictatorship with a fiction writer is that she's got the entire process scripted. Courtney's done a full character study for each of us, complete with our phony names, ages, and what she calls backstory, which is how we got to where we are today.

On the way to Chicago to get our fake passports and other papers, she reads aloud in Spanish what she's come up with for each of us.

"Dan, your name is Brian Shepherd. You're nineteen years old."

"Can you make me twenty-one?"

"Drinking age is eighteen in Chile," Papá says.

"This isn't a one-time thing. I'm planning to use it as my fake ID when I get back."

I hear a pen scratching in the backseat of Willie's van. "No. We can't risk it." Courtney flips a page in her notebook. "My name is Alexandra Shepherd, but everyone calls me Ali."

"How'd you come up with Ali?" I ask. I'm guessing the Shepherd part has to do with her leading Papá and me around like we're a pair of sheep.

"Are you planning to be a pain for the entire trip?" Courtney asks, then adds, "I've always liked the name, but it's too close to my mother's name."

"So?" Papá cuts in. "I wanted to name this one Marcos. My best friend beat me to it. Two days."

"Did I know them?" I ask, not remembering any kids named Marcos whose parents were friends with mine. It's a cool name, though.

"No. The whole family went into exile after the coup."

Courtney slaps her pen against the notebook. "Anyway, you'll call me Ali. I'm twenty-two years old. We're United States citizens, from Bloomfield Hills, Michigan. It's where I grew up, so if anyone asks me about a place there, I can answer them."

"I just thought of something," I say. I'm sick of Courtney deciding everything, and anyway, this is something I've wanted her to do for me for a while.

"What is it?"

"I want dreads."

Courtney groans. "What does that have to do with anything?"

"*Chilenos* don't have dreadlocks." I hold out a tuft of my hair, now three to four inches long. "White boy with dreads—a gringo for sure."

"He's right," Papá mumbles. He's leaning out the open window, gulping air, his chin on his folded arms. He told us his head injury makes him prone to motion sickness, which is why he's glad we're flying directly into Santiago rather than taking a car over the mountains like he and Pato planned to do.

"Fine. Brian Shepherd is a white Rastafarian."

"And you're going to spend a few hours tomorrow giving me a backcomb and rubber-banding my locks," I tell her in English.

"I'm looking forward to it." I detect the sarcasm in her voice and hope she doesn't screw up my hair.

She turns a page and talks to herself as she writes. I treat her to an a cappella rendition of "Ride Natty Ride."

Another page flips. "Papá…Papá."

Courtney taps Papá on the shoulder with her pen to get his attention. He jumps, almost hitting his wool-capped head on the top of the door frame. "Damn, I have a long way to go," he says. One of his goals before we leave is to desensitize himself to being touched. He says if the immigration police put their hands on him and he cringes, they'll know for sure he's one of their torture victims and not a tourist.

Courtney slides up in her seat so she's almost between us. She holds her hand to the back of Papá's neck. "Papá," she says, "since you can't speak English, we're going to have you not speak at all."

"What's my name?"

"You're our father, so we'll call you Dad. Not Papá. *Dad*. You're fifty-five years old. Your first name's Thomas."

"Tomás," he repeats.

"Thomas Shepherd. And I'm sorry I have to do this, but I'm killing you off. You have a brain tumor, and your dying wish is to travel to the Lake District and Patagonia. We're your kids, and we're taking you there."

Papá stares at his hands. "That'll work."

Courtney scoots closer, close enough that her shoulders are touching mine. She's making it hard for me to focus on the road. "But remember, you can't speak. Period. Except when we know we're alone."

"Or in a safe place," Papá adds.

"And you can barely see."

"Take away my glasses and I can barely see."

"You'll have a cane."

"For walking, or one of those blind canes?"

"Strong enough to walk with."

"Are you done?" Papá presses his fingers to his forehead. "I feel a headache coming on." He leans against the open window. Courtney returns to her notebook.

Even when he's not hung over, Papá gets wicked headaches. We didn't realize it until he cut back on drinking. They're mostly on the right side, and when he gets them, he sticks his finger in his ear and then in front of his face to examine it, as if expecting to see blood on his finger. As if somewhere deep in his damaged brain, he registers every detail of the beating that changed his life.

When I follow the directions Papá gives me, I imagine a run-down neighborhood full of potholed streets, weed-choked lots, and drug dens. I think I'm lost when I see a typical middle-class suburb with split-level houses of almost identical design and well-kept sidewalks and lawns. I pull up to an orange-brick house with a toddler swing hanging from a tree in the front yard.

We get out of the van.

"Are you sure this is it?" I ask Papá.

He reads the paper with the address, matches it with the number on the mailbox. Some kids are playing street hockey at the end of the block.

Papá rings the doorbell. A short, skinny man with black hair and a thick mustache greets him like they're old friends.

"Nino! *¿Cómo estai?*"

"Could be better, Raulito." Papá squeezes his eyes

shut. I can tell his head really hurts him now. "Nice house."

"We moved at the end of April. That your son?"

"And his girlfriend. We adopted her—or rather, she adopted us."

He introduces us to Raúl but doesn't tell us the man's last name. We follow them inside. Even without the telltale Chilean greeting, *Cómo estai*, and the accent, I know Raúl is *chileno*. There are posters of Allende and Che and of concerts by popular musicians. A charango—a small ten-string guitar made from an armadillo shell—hangs by a peg on the living room wall. In the kitchen is a "Free Chile" rally poster with a guitar, a rose, and a rifle.

"So, Nino, you're going back. What doesn't kill you makes you stronger."

"You could say that. Anyway, there's no life for me here."

"Pato told me about you and Victoria. I'm sorry." Raúl opens kitchen cabinets, takes out cheese, crackers, glasses, and a bottle of red wine. "A drink before we start?"

"You got some aspirin?"

"I got stronger stuff than that. Look."

Raúl rummages through a closet next to the kitchen. He drags a case of wine out onto the tiled floor. Behind it is another box. He opens the flap to reveal pill bottles, morphine patches, vials of who-knows-what, sandwich bags of marijuana, and postage-stamp-size bags with white powder that could be smack or coke.

My heart pounds. I glance over to Courtney, who's gone sheet-white.

"Put it away, Raulito," Papá says, his voice dropping an octave. "You're scaring the kids."

Raúl picks out an orange bottle and hands it to Papá.

"Vicodin. That's what I gave you last time."

"And it wrecked my stomach. The gringos I stayed with that night had to lift my head out of the toilet to take a piss." Papá hands the pills back.

"Very funny," Raúl says, but no one's laughing. "It's because you washed them down with a bottle of wine and whatever else you poured into you."

"Cough syrup. I turned out to have pneumonia."

"You're supposed to take Vicodin with water." Raúl fills a glass from the faucet and sets it down hard on the counter. "Plain water."

"I'll stick with the aspirin."

Raúl shoves the box back into the closet and replaces the wine in front of it. "Let me know if you change your mind. The pharmacy's always open." He slides the aspirin bottle to Papá, who flips the cap off with his teeth.

"How old's the baby now?" Papá asks after swallowing two tablets with water.

"Carlos turned two last month. I'd bring him out, but he's taking his afternoon nap." Papá and Raúl move to the kitchen table and start on the wine. Papá lights a cigarette.

While the two of them talk, I drift to the downstairs den with Courtney. The guy has some amazing computer equipment—a tower CPU, two monitors, a laser printer. It must have cost him a fortune. There's a laminating machine, an embossing machine, and a lot of file boxes like the one where Mamá stores her recipes. Next to one are half a dozen green cards—permits for an immigrant to be here legally—except the cards are really blue. I figure they were green at one time, and that's how they got the name. Courtney just stands around, speechless.

"The drugs?" I whisper in English.

She nods. She looks like she's about to cry. I squeeze her shoulders. Then I brush aside her hair and kiss her neck.

When we first started going out, she told me her ex-boyfriend used drugs and got really nasty when he was high—a major reason she broke up with him. I said I didn't use. At first she didn't believe me—she thought all musicians were druggies. I told her it was a stupid stereotype, like the one that says all Hispanics have brown skin and eyes and black hair.

She holds me tight. "It's like I'm in *Scarface*," she moans into my chest.

I feed her lines from the movie to make her laugh. I have the perfect accent, and I know she loves it. Clowning around helps me to relax too. When she lets go of me, I show her all the computer equipment and what it can do.

Papá and Raúl join us. Raúl now has a cigarette. He's talking about his headaches, how he has to take more and more pills to get rid of them. "And they didn't even smash my head in," he says. He picks up a camera and points to Papá's cap. "You'll have to take that off."

Papá reaches up and yanks off the black wool cap. Underneath, his hair is stringy and greasy. With his pale face and pinched expression, he looks wretched, the way I imagine a fifty-five-year-old guy dying of a brain tumor would look.

Raúl comes closer and reaches out his hand. "Don't touch it," Papá says, holding his palm up. I notice he's shaking.

Raúl steps back. "The sons of whores," he mutters.

Papá grimaces. "I know I'm no movie star. Take the picture and get it over with."

Raúl photographs all of us, Courtney writes out the information, and Papá gives him instructions on what we need— U.S. passports, Michigan driver's licenses, labels for half a dozen pill bottles in the name of Thomas Shepherd, an international driving permit for Alexandra Marie Shepherd in case we rent a car, and credit cards. "They won't work for buying anything," Raúl explains, "but you can use them for identification."

"That's fine. We weren't planning on shopping." Papá hands over two hundred dollars from the cash that Pato gave him.

"I'm sorry to charge you, but we all have to eat," Raúl says. "I'll give the kids a discount, though. A hundred fifty apiece."

Courtney takes an envelope from her bag and counts out the money she and Papá made from the articles.

Raúl rolls up the bills and sticks them in the back pocket of his jeans. "Come back in two weeks, and I'll have the documents for you."

The last thing I want to do is come back to this guy's place. In fact, I want to run out immediately in case the narcs already have the house under surveillance. But then Raúl brings the baby out. Little Carlos is a chubby, olive-skinned boy with huge, sparkling brown eyes. Courtney seems to have forgotten where we are and is cooing over the kid. Papá slides to the living room floor and lets Carlos tug at the Velcro strap of his wrist splint.

Raúl signals me toward the kitchen. I edge over to him, wondering if he's read my mind about the dreads and plans to offer me some weed.

I'm ready with a polite *no, gracias* when he glances toward the living room and whispers in heavily accented

English. "You two need to watch out for Nino."

"Why?" I let my arms drop to my sides. My fingers are numb.

"I did papers for seven other *compañeros* who've gone back in the last three years. We lost almost all of them." Raúl ticks them off on his fingers. "One shot. Two suicides. One fled to Europe. We don't know where the hell another one is. And your father's the worst case I've seen."

"Because he's crippled?"

Raúl leans over the kitchen counter. He's not even looking at me. "Because they destroyed him. The way he is now, there's nothing he can do for the struggle." Raúl stands up straight, at least a head shorter than me. "I told him he should get help here first. Try to pull himself together. Things are about to explode over there."

"What did he say?" My throat hurts, and my voice trembles.

"He said going back will either cure him or kill him, and he doesn't care which."

"I'm not going to talk him out of it, if that's what you're thinking." I shove my hands into the pockets of my loose cutoff jeans. The tape Courtney played for me that night in the Jeep echoes in my mind.

"I know," Raúl replies.

I walk a few steps from Raúl, stand in the archway from the kitchen into the living room, and gaze at Papá while he plays with the little boy. They're building a tower with unpainted wooden blocks, a crooked, crazy structure that has no hope of standing but keeps getting taller anyway. Each time a new piece goes on, the two of them laugh. Courtney urges them on.

I remember when I was a kid with wooden blocks.

Since age three I've wanted to be an engineer. I liked to build neat structures with the heaviest, most solid blocks on the bottom. But Papá would bring in scrap wood, twigs, and a lot of other trash, and we'd have fun figuring out how to raise a tower with things that didn't have flat sides and square edges.

Lo que no mata, engorda—that's the way Raúl described Papá. *What doesn't kill him makes him stronger.* But I want him to care about surviving, to make the choice.

It's four o'clock when we get out of there. If we hit no traffic, we'll be in Madison by dinnertime.

"July ninth we pick all this up," Papá says in the van, on the way to the interstate. He sounds tired. The aspirin didn't appear to do a whole lot for him either.

"Can't he mail it?" I ask.

Papá stares at me like I've got the sense of the two-year-old he was playing with.

"Sorry. I'd kind of like to avoid..."

"The drugs?" Papá finishes.

I nod. I don't want to say it in case Raúl was a good friend of Papá's back in Chile.

"Don't worry. I only need you to drive. You can drop me off and wait somewhere else."

"But...but he's a dealer," Courtney sputters.

"*M'ija*, people do what they have to do to survive." Papá's voice is strong and steady. "I'm not going to sit here and judge Raúl. He has a family to support and a lot of anger because of what happened to him."

"Was he tortured too?" I ask.

"Yes." Papá takes off his glasses and rubs his eyes and forehead. "After what they did to him, it's a victory he was able to father that little boy."

* * *

Raúl was right when he said things were about to explode in Chile. A week after our trip to Chicago, we hear on the news that soldiers set two teenagers on fire at a demonstration in Santiago. One of them is Rodrigo Rojas Denegri, who was born in Chile but came to the United States after the coup. At the age of nineteen, he'd gone back to take photos and learn about his country. Day after day, I follow the story. By the time Papá and I return to Chicago for our false papers, Rodrigo's dead. And the more I think about it, the more I realize that kid could have been me.

CHAPTER TWENTY-SIX
August 1, 1986
Madison

Mamá and I have always been close—I guess it comes with me being *el hombre de la casa* for so many years—but after the death of Rodrigo Rojas, she starts acting really cold to me. She hardly talks to me when I get home from work, and she spends her free time taking Tina places or reading with her. In a way, she has the right idea because Tina needs more attention, and she doesn't have friends, music, and sports like I do to keep her busy. Maybe if Tina had gotten more attention in the first place, she wouldn't have turned out so weird, and I wouldn't have ruined my chances for citizenship in November on account of trying to stick up for her.

Still, it's hard not to feel a little jealous or to wonder if Mamá's avoiding me because she thinks she's already lost me. If I could have been Rodrigo, she must be putting herself in the place of his mother. I read an interview with the mother in the newspaper, where she talked about sitting at her son's bedside at the hospital and having to change his diapers like when he was a baby because he'd been burned over eighty percent of his body.

We have to take the bus to O'Hare Airport because Courtney's parents still don't know about her plan. I have no idea what story she has in mind for when one of them sees Papá and me at the bus stop, but I expect it to be creative. She's managed to convince her parents she's going to a nature program in Argentina and even squeezed a couple of pairs of khaki pants, two plaid shirts, a pair of new hiking boots, and a colorful assortment of bandanas out of them. But when she shows up for dinner at our apartment the night before we leave, her cheeks are pink and her eyelids puffy.

I ask her what happened.

"Can we get out of here?" she says.

We go to a picnic table next to the apartment complex's soccer field.

"Mom and Dad found out. I left my ticket on my desk like an idiot, and they saw it," she says.

I suck in my breath. We really need her fictional skills to get past immigration. "Are you grounded?"

"Mom wanted to. But Dad took my side and helped me convince her."

My sigh of relief can probably be heard all the way to Santiago. "What did you say?"

"Number one, I'm eighteen already, so they can't stop me. Number two," she counts on her fingers, "I'm paying for it with my own money. Number three, we're going to be careful. And number four, who are they to tell me what to do? Back in Michigan, they were smuggling Central American refugees out of Mexico, across the United States, and into Canada."

"What?"

"That's why I came here in the middle of high school and was so far behind in Spanish. Why I needed you to tutor me. Dad got arrested and the bishop sent him to another church."

"So your parents were smuggling refugees out of their

country, and you're smuggling refugees back into their country?"

She smiles. Her cheeks have gone from blotchy to radiant. "Exactly."

I stand to leave, but she grabs my arm. A worried expression crosses her face.

"Do you think we're doing the right thing, Dan?"

I sit next to her again, put my arm around her shoulders, and slide the hair from her face. I want to kiss her all night long, and that's just the beginning. I make a mental note to pack condoms. We have a hotel room all to ourselves for most of the trip.

"Of course we are," I say. I have no idea which she's most upset about—deceiving her parents and getting caught, sneaking into a country with a fake passport, or eleven days by ourselves that are going to make the Starlight Motel seem like a quickie in a pup tent.

"No, I mean it." She clutches my arm so hard it hurts. "Remember Raúl?"

"You're worried because of *him*?" I'm astounded that it's eaten at her this long. I put him out of my mind five seconds after Papá and I picked up our documents.

"What kind of people are we bringing Papá to?"

"They're risking their lives to free their country. They're not drug lords." I stand and pull her to her feet. We've got a lot of packing, and a lot of rehearsing, left to do.

* * *

I'm still in bed when Mamá knocks on my door the next morning. I'd awakened earlier, but I'm thinking I can lie here all day, that having to take a bus three hours, fly twelve, and enter a police state illegally using forged documents is just some crazy dream. Like a story Courtney would make up. But then I think of the mountains that I could always see from wherever I was standing, the stars in the southern constellations, the lakes, and the endless beaches, and my heart races with the thought of the place that I once called home.

I smell eggs frying and coffee brewing. I hear Papá singing a folk song and the television in the living room. Tina must be awake too. I'm the straggler. It's the committee's custom to celebrate someone's departure by drinking the person senseless, but last night, Courtney, Papá, and I slipped out after two rounds and let Matt drive us to the park for our final rehearsal. Papá said we shouldn't start a difficult journey feeling like crap, which gives me hope for him.

"Time to get up, *m'ijo*. I have to leave," Mamá says.

She has an appointment with Professor Ballard this morning to discuss the courses she's teaching in the fall. I wonder if she could have made more effort to reschedule it. After all, I'm leaving for two weeks, and Papá probably forever.

I drag myself out of bed into the kitchen and pour a cup of coffee. My dreads have developed nicely. I don't even need rubber bands for them to stay in place. Maybe I'll keep them for the start of school, to go along with all the stories I'll be able to tell.

Mamá pulls me away from the table and hugs me like she's never going to see me again. When she releases me, she turns to Papá, her eyes narrowed.

"Marcelo, you're a lost cause. But you better make

sure nothing happens to my boy."

Papá raises an eyebrow and returns to nibbling on toast he dips in jam.

If I come home safely, is there any way they'll get back together? I dismiss the thought. It's almost as hopeless as asking God to take back a day.

After Mamá leaves and I clean up from breakfast, I get the Kohl's bag from my room. Courtney brought it over the night before; inside is an electric razor, surgical tape, cotton pads, a roll of gauze. To make Papá look like a guy dying of a brain tumor, we're supposed to shave off his hair, stuff the dented spot with a pad, and wrap his head. But because of her fight with her parents yesterday, Courtney hasn't finished packing. Now I'm going to have to handle this operation by myself, or with Tina.

Tina hasn't moved from the armchair since breakfast. She uses the chair now that Papá's sleeping on the sofa, where his pillow and a threadbare blanket lie. She's reading a thick hardcover, and when I get close enough, I see it's a textbook with the title, *Our Physical World*. On the armrest is a spiral notebook, open near the beginning, with a pencil on it.

I lower the top of the book. Tina frowns at me. "What's that?" I know it's not her usual reading material.

"Oh, I guess no one told you." She pauses. "Mamá met with my counselor and the principal. I'm supposed to learn the first four chapters of this book, and if I pass a test, I'm going into the honors track *and* skipping seventh grade."

"You're skipping a grade?" In a way it would make sense. Both of us got held back when we moved here, but since my birthday was just before the cutoff anyway, it didn't make as much difference. Still, I always thought you had to be a genius to skip, and I wonder if Tina is one of those weird geniuses who doesn't fit in at school like Edison or Einstein and we didn't realize it until now.

"Yeah. I'm going to take two sciences instead of a language. They gave me credit for knowing Spanish already." She closes the textbook and sets it on the floor. "Maybe school will be less boring now."

"And you'll be in class with different kids."

"Yeah. Eighth graders."

It's a good plan, though I can't believe Mamá has never said a word about it to me. In the time she's been spending with Tina, she's made this deal happen. I'm proud of her, and I'm proud of my sister, who I guess isn't such a loser after all.

"That's super," I say. "And I promise when I get back, I'll help you with those chapters so you can pass the test."

Tina grins. "Thanks, Daniel."

"But I need you to help me now."

She folds her arms across her chest. "What?"

I explain how Courtney and I have planned to sneak him in, then tell her, "We have to shave and bandage Papá's head for the trip."

"But he's so scary."

I shush her even though he's packing in Mamá's bedroom and can't hear her.

"Does he know you're skipping a grade?" I whisper.

Tina shakes her head. "What does it matter? He's leaving anyway."

"That's not nice," I tell her.

"So what? He's totally useless."

I know Tina's repeating what Mamá has said, but I

201

can't let it go. There's way too much hostility around here. "He's still your father, Tina. You should talk to him."

It's probably too late for a reconciliation between Tina and Papá, but I need her to talk to him for another reason—to distract him so I can shave his head. Courtney told me that one of the things prolonged torture does is remove a person's body from his own control. It's as if his body has been reprogrammed to do what his torturers want—cringe or vomit at another person's touch, suffer horrible flashbacks caused by ordinary things like getting wet or coughing, feel jolts of pain like electric shocks upon lying down.

I wish Courtney were here. For some reason, he always feels safe with her. And I wonder what's going to happen once she and I drop him off, because where he's going is not safe.

I knock softly on the bedroom door to avoid startling him. "Are you ready, Papá?"

He nods and stubs out his cigarette. He's already pale, and we haven't even started. "Let's do it," he says.

He sits in one of the kitchen chairs, away from the table. I take his glasses and drape the blanket from the sofa over his clothes.

"Come on, Tina," I say, motioning her over.

She shuts off the TV and walks the eleven steps from the living room into the kitchen so slowly I count them. Papá starts to tremble. This isn't the way I want my sister to act. I root through the cabinet below the sink and hand Tina a plastic bucket.

"Hold this in front of him. He'll need it," I tell her in English.

"Oh, no," she mumbles. She looks like she's going to

cry.

Papá turns to her. "Listen, *m'ija*, I'm sorry you have to see me like this." His voice fades out. He swallows hard.

I crouch in front of him and touch his shoulder. I describe what I'm going to do and tell him to let me know if I should stop at any time. Then I add, "Tina has something to say."

He puts his good arm around her back and draws her to him, tight. "What is it?"

"I'm going to skip a grade." She repeats what she told me, all in perfect Spanish.

"I always knew my girl was smart." I can't imagine how—she'd just turned seven when they arrested him.

"Now I only have five years of school instead of six."

"What about university?" Papá asks.

"Like where Mamá is? That's different," says Tina, grinning.

While they talk, I lift off Papá's wool cap and flip the razor's switch.

The vibration makes me think of my guitar, as I plug it in before I hit the first chord. I'm singing a song in my head, Springsteen's "Adam Raised a Cain." My lips move. I shave off handfuls of gray hair streaked with brown and red.

I've been so busy worrying about how Papá would react to having his head shaved that I'm not prepared for my own reaction. I have to go over the uneven right side carefully to avoid nicking him. When I see the indentation and the jagged purple scars that cross it like a tic-tac-toe board drawn by a madman, my hand jerks away. The razor vibrates against my fingers. Papá and Tina haven't yet noticed. I say to myself, *I can do this*. I force my arm steady and finish shaving.

Papá's telling Tina about his university days in Chile, when he and the other students worked to elect the country's first socialist president. And she's listening. *Good*, I think. *That's the last thing she'll remember about him.*

His ears are huge next to his misshapen skull. I squeeze an almond-scented cream on my hands and rub it into his scalp. He shudders at first, then goes still. I hold the pad to the right side of his skull and start wrapping, making a good, tight wrap neatly finished off with the surgical tape. "How does it feel, Papá?" I ask.

"Good." He tosses the empty bucket into the sink and runs his hand over the bandage at the back of his head. "This should hold for a while."

He stands and hugs the two of us at once.

Like Raúl fathering a child, this is a victory.

Chapter Twenty-seven
August 2, 1986
Santiago

It was summer when we left Madison, but when we land in Santiago, it's the middle of winter. Snow covers the mountains almost to the city's eastern edge, the sky is a dull gray, and even inside the airport it's cold.

Papá hasn't spoken since we stepped up to the check-in at O'Hare Airport. It's too dangerous; anyone on the flight could be a spy. At the gate, before we boarded, we held each other's hands and Courtney led us in prayer. I could tell Papá wasn't into it, but he couldn't argue.

In the airport in Santiago, just as we're about to go through immigration, she takes our hands again. I clasp her right hand. Around her thin wrist, she wears a single black rope band with a gold heart charm. On my other side, Papá's hand is limp and clammy. Without the wrist splint, he has little control over his fingers.

"Dear God. Please protect us and lead us along the path of righteousness. Watch over"—She hesitates, glances at Papá—"our father and make him strong as he struggles against the forces of darkness and death. Amen."

I carry our two suitcases to the immigration booth and place them on the counter for inspection. Two men with machine guns approach us. My guts squeeze tight. The soldiers are carrying real guns, the kind that can kill. The kind they carried the night they took Papá away.

"*Pasaportes.*" The first soldier is tall and muscular. He glares at me with dark brown eyes.

I glance at Courtney, pretending not to understand. She's doing all the talking. She's perfectly fluent but has a definite accent.

"Hand him the passports, Brian," she whispers in English. She has her arm around Papá's waist. He holds her forearm like he's blind and she's leading him. A cane hangs from his arm. I wonder if his guts are cramping as bad as mine.

I hand the soldier the three U.S. passports. He flips through each of them. I pray silently that Raúl did them all correctly.

"*¿De donde son ustedes?*"

"Bloomfield Hills, Michigan," Courtney answers.

He asks us what we're doing in Chile.

"We're on vacation. My father, my brother, and me."

The other soldier eyes Papá. The one asking the questions turns to me. "What is the purpose of your trip?"

Courtney cuts in. "They don't speak Spanish. And my father can't talk at all. He has cancer of the brain and doesn't have long to live. He wants to visit Patagonia before he dies."

"*Ay.*" The soldier asking the questions nods. "It's very beautiful."

The other soldier circles Papá. His machine gun swings from a shoulder strap, and its barrel taps Papá's stomach. Papá stands motionless. His eyes are closed.

"How did he find out about our country?" the first soldier asks.

"When he was in the hospital. He wanted to see places he'd never been, so we brought him travel books."

"I'm sorry he's coming in winter. Unless you ski, January and February are the best months."

Courtney steps toward the soldier, whispers, "The doctors say he doesn't have that long."

"I'm very sorry."

The second soldier places his hands on the two suitcases. He's a head shorter than I am, and his face is pockmarked. "Open them, please," he says.

Courtney turns to me and says in English, "Open them, Brian."

I unsnap Papá's suitcase and unzip Courtney's. The shorter soldier paws through the bags, pushing aside clothing, hiking boots, scarves, hats, rainwear, and a dog-eared guidebook. He holds up Courtney's camera and tape recorder.

"Put them back," the tall soldier says.

They close the suitcases and push them toward me.

"How long are you staying?" the first soldier asks Courtney.

"Two weeks."

He holds out his hand. "Return tickets."

Courtney taps my arm. "He wants the tickets."

I take them from my jacket pocket. He looks them over and hands them back with our passports. "Welcome," he says, waving us on.

* * *

Courtney has booked us into a triple room in a cheap hotel near the center of town. The few other people staying there speak Spanish; I can tell from their accents they're visiting from somewhere else in Chile or have come from other countries in Latin America. Although it's midmorning when we get there, we're exhausted. We check in, dump our stuff, pick up bread and pastries for breakfast, eat, and crash. The mattresses on the three twin beds are lumpy and sag, but I don't notice, and I don't think Papá and Courtney do either.

I awaken at five. It's already getting dark. Courtney sits next to the window, reading the paperback she started on the plane—*Pet Sematary* by Stephen King. I watch her for a while as she turns the pages. Sometimes she stops reading and stares out the window at the mountains that rise far above the city.

"We should go out tonight," she says in Spanish. "I was looking at the guidebook, and there's this cute neighborhood with clubs and—"

"Bellavista," Papá mumbles into the pillow. I didn't know he was awake. "You two have a good time. I'm going to lie low."

"Do you want us to bring you anything?" she asks him.

"No. We still have pastries left over."

The night is chilly and damp, though it's not raining. It's a long walk to where we're going, but we want to see the city.

With her finger, Courtney traces the map in the guidebook. "We have to be back before curfew." She flips to the previous page and says, "It's kind of like the government is our mother."

"Yeah. Except she doesn't ground you when you miss it. She shoots you."

Courtney gawks at centuries-old Spanish buildings, illuminated by streetlight. On the next block are modern office towers, more than I remember from before, and a bit farther in the distance, high-rise apartment buildings. Once we leave the downtown area, the buildings are mostly two stories high, built of stucco or wood with tile roofs. I wonder where the neighborhood is where I grew up. I remember the apartments were in two- and three-story buildings, made of cement with tin roofs, and even though they were fairly new, you could see rust and water stains running down from the roof and windows.

I can tell we're getting closer by the jewelry and clothing stores, all closed for the night, and the posters announcing concerts, just like at home. I don't know any of the bands. Mamá has records of a lot of Chilean musicians, but they're either dead, like Violeta Parra or Victor Jara, or in exile in Europe, like Inti-Illimani or Quilapayún. Papá once told me that soldiers dragged Victor Jara to the Estadio Chile after the coup and murdered him by crushing his fingers, making him sing with his hands bleeding, and then machine-gunning him.

We find a couple of bands playing tonight and look for a street map. They're usually by metro stations, but on our way, we see a disturbance outside a building. Soldiers are standing in front of doors, blocking a lot of people from entering. We watch from across the street.

"By order of the Metropolitan Police, this building has been condemned," one of the soldiers announces with a bullhorn.

The people on the street boo him. He pays them no attention but proceeds to padlock the door.

There's a couple standing next to us. The man is swearing.

"What's going on?" Courtney asks him.

"They've banned the concert, but they don't want to

say it, so they condemn the building," he answers. The two of them cross the street.

The crowd shouts insults at the soldiers, who wave their machine guns menacingly but don't shoot. When they're done—I assume they're padlocking all the building's other doors—they get into a truck and leave.

A man climbs the couple of steps in front of the doors. He has a bullhorn too. "We don't care what they say. We're going to play outside, so everyone can hear us. There's a small park around the corner. We'll set up our equipment there." He points to his right—our left. People start heading in that direction. Courtney grabs my hand. We cross the street and follow along with them.

At the park, someone pushes through the crowd, asking for volunteers to help move equipment. "Hey, I've done this before," I say to Courtney. I leave her and follow the man to a pickup truck parked at the end of the street.

Two guys are firing up a generator in the back of the truck, as if they're used to this sort of thing happening. I wiggle my fingers, itching to get them onto the equipment and hear the band play.

There isn't a lot of stuff—a couple of large speakers, two microphones, a small soundboard—because the band is just a duo with guitars and if the *milicos* return, we'll have to pack up quickly. Someone on the truck lowers the speakers to me and another guy, and together we carry them into the park. I run wires to the soundboard and duct tape them to the sidewalk.

A floodlight is turned on, and I feel a hand on my shoulder. "Thanks, kid." I turn to see the guy who'd announced the change of venue. He's shorter than I am, with a thin, pale face, light brown hair, and a straggly goatee. He wears dirt-streaked khaki pants and a sweater and holds a guitar case.

"I know all about this equipment. I play in a band," I tell him.

"Which one?"

"Not here. I'm visiting from the United States, from…Michigan."

He opens the case and takes out an acoustic guitar. I suck in my breath.

"You want to try it?"

"Sure."

He hands it to me. I sit atop one of the speakers and pick at the strings. This is one sweet instrument. I don't know what inspired me to choose it, but I start to play Bob Marley's "Redemption Song," and I sing it with a passion that I've never in my life felt when playing. My whole heart goes into that song. And when I get to the third verse, I hear another guitar strumming along with mine. It's the second person in the duo, a taller man with darker skin, clean shaven, with curly black hair.

The musician with the goatee nods and smiles. "*Súperbien*. Great dreadlocks, too. We should call you Rasta." The way he rolls the *r* makes the name sound awesome.

"You should play with us," his dark-haired partner says.

"Would you like to play your Marley for the final song? We could introduce you as our long-lost gringo friend, Rasta." The one with the goatee pauses. "Though you speak Spanish like a *chileno*."

Would I like to play with them? Is the Pope Catholic? But this is a banned concert, and I'd be putting Papá and

Courtney in danger if I did anything to call attention to myself. "Sorry," I tell them. "I'm not supposed to be here, and if my parents found out, they'd kill me."

"I understand. We had that problem too." The guy takes back his guitar and hands me a lead to connect to the soundboard. "Thanks for the help. I hope you enjoy the concert."

I run the wire back to the group's sound engineer. He's connecting the speakers, so I hold the lead until he's ready. Another man stands next to him. I recognize him as the one who lowered the equipment from the truck.

"You play well and have a nice voice, too," the engineer says.

"Thanks."

He can't seem to take his eyes off me. I wonder if it's my dreads, which they've probably never seen. But then the engineer turns to his friend and says, "He looks familiar."

"I don't think so. I just got here today. *Soy norteamericano, de Michigan.*"

He waves his hand. "No, not you. You're too young. It's the red hair. And the face." He mouths something to his friend. I thought I heard "Nino," but I may have only imagined it. A smile crosses my face anyway.

The friend shoves his hands into the pockets of his baggy corduroy pants. "I heard they killed him last year. Tortured him to death."

CHAPTER TWENTY-EIGHT
August 4, 1986
Santiago

I haven't told Courtney or Papá what that guy at the concert said. I want to believe they were talking about someone else. I'm not sure the sound engineer actually said "Nino." So many people have died in prison that I've got to look like more than one of them.

The next day, Sunday, is cold and drizzly. We can't even see the mountains on account of the fog. Courtney and I stay close to the hotel, and Papá doesn't go out at all. When he's not sleeping, he works out. For a while we throw his little exercise ball back and forth and bounce it off the walls, and I tell myself if the weather doesn't clear up soon, I'm going to be bouncing off the walls too.

Monday the sun slices through the gap in the curtains and wakes me. I shower and get dressed. I want to go outside and see in the bright sunlight the city where I used to live. All night long, I dreamed of playing soccer, first in my old neighborhood and then in a big stadium, where I was about to score the winning goal when someone crashed into me. Blindsided me.

Courtney's still in bed, which surprises me. She usually wakes up with the sunrise. I squeeze her shoulder, nuzzle my face into her silky hair. "Hey, beautiful," I whisper in English.

"Let me sleep," she mumbles. "Papá had a bad night."

"I didn't hear anything."

"You must be deaf."

"Or dreaming of soccer fame."

While she's getting ready, Papá awakens with a moan. His left arm is twisted, and he holds the blue rubber ball in a death grip.

"Do you want a muscle relaxer?" Expecting an affirmative, I bring over a bottle of water so he can take the pill.

"Not if I can avoid it. I want to show you around, not sleep all day." The pain makes his voice brittle. My elbow and hand ache in sympathy.

I stretch and massage Papá's bony arm and pry his fingers from the ball, one by one. After I get his splint on, I stretch his leg muscles. Tightness spreads from my chest to my throat as I realize I may be doing this for the last time. We're dropping him off tonight. He said he wasn't going to risk traveling around the country with us for the next ten days.

"How are you going to do this when you're underground?" I ask him.

"You're almost never alone. We help each other out."

It's a mild day. Courtney, who's lived in the Midwest all her life, can't believe we're in the middle of winter. After breakfast, Papá leads us to the wide Alameda and points out three centuries' worth of buildings.

"The city's original name was Santiago del Nuevo Extremo," he tells Courtney. "It was a frontier outpost of the Spanish empire in Peru." He points to the mountains that rise from the eastern edge of the city. "Our country is less than two hundred kilometers from mountains to ocean, and more than four thousand from the desert north to the southernmost tip of the inhabited world. Any farther south is Antarctica." While giving her the basic geography-and-history lecture, he raises his weak arm to her shoulder, which is about as high as it's going today. I can tell he's still sore from the muscle spasms he had during the night. "So you see," he concludes, "we *chilenos* carry with us the consciousness that we inhabit the ends of the earth. It's why we create so much poetry."

"It's a special place to be," I add. "Unless, of course, we get an earthquake that knocks us right off the edge." I slice my hand horizontally through the air, and with a "boom" mimic a vertical drop.

"Shut up, you...engineer." Papá gives me a good-natured tug on the ear. "I'll take my chances."

I shake my head and mutter, "Addicted to risk," though I know the probability of all of us ends-of-the-earth-dwelling people being wiped out by an earthquake are infinitely more remote than Papá getting himself killed by the government.

Papá stops to rest on a bench in a small park. I gaze up at the trees, dark green and brown against the clear blue sky. The sun warms my face and the top of my head. It feels like home today, like the place where I want to live the rest of my life.

We eat *la comida*, the main meal of the day, not far from where Courtney and I saw the concert two nights ago. Papá has a meeting with Pato afterward. He told us yesterday that Pato made contact with the *Vicaría de la Solidaridad*, the Catholic Church's human rights office, for Papá to testify about his own experiences and work on some other investigations the church is conducting.

Courtney and I visit a couple of museums, and at a

jewelry shop she buys a silver-and-lapis necklace that matches her eyes. I check out a record store. The person working there shows me all the Bob Marley stuff, and I pretend not to speak any Spanish. I'm really getting into the Brian Shepherd Rastafarian thing. Maybe I should go out for Drama Club next year. I imagine how I'd list my experience: *International disguise artist. Smuggler of freedom fighters.*

It's four in the afternoon, and the sun is getting low by the time we meet Papá again in front of the café where we ate earlier.

"We're going to do this in two hours," he whispers. "We need to pack."

Back in the hotel, I rebandage his shaved head and check his medication bottles to make sure that the labels have the name of Thomas Shepherd and that the pills match the labels. We expect to be searched. Carefully.

Stay busy and you won't cry, I tell myself as I sort through his stuff. My hands shake.

Papá wears several layers of clothing. We can't exactly bring a suitcase. Courtney carries his meds in her bag. I hold his glasses. He carries the cane.

We're going to the cathedral on the plaza next to all the police and military buildings. It's a sanctuary building, which means the soldiers can't enter unless they want to pray. But they can stop us at the door.

And they do. Two men with machine guns, who call a third and a fourth over. The place is filled with military people. I see them under the streetlights as we wait to be searched: men in green camo visible among the palm trees, the stone buildings, and the civilians crossing the plaza. There are even a few officers, their medals and ribbons spots of color on their dark uniforms.

"Identification." One of the people who joins the soldiers is a metropolitan police officer, a *carabinero*. He holds out his hand.

Courtney takes our passports out of her bag. I'm sweating under my jean jacket, which I reclaimed from Papá this afternoon. I hope these guys don't notice something the immigration police missed.

"Your wallet." The *carabinero* points to me. I stare at him openmouthed.

"Give him the wallet," Courtney says. I hand over Brian Shepherd's wallet—driver's license, cash, a ticket stub for the Museo del Arte Precolombiano.

"Take off your jacket."

After Courtney translates, I remove my jacket. One of the soldiers rifles through the pockets, inside and out. He pulls out an empty pack of cigarettes and the cap from a whiskey bottle.

I reach for Papá's hand, as if I were six years old and crossing the street with him. He squeezes my fingers.

The *carabinero* throws me the jacket and takes Courtney's bag. One by one, he pulls things from it and hands them to the soldiers. They read the labels on the pill bottles.

"They're for our father. He has a brain tumor."

Out come the tape recorder and blank cassettes, and the camera. My insides tense when it looks like they might confiscate these. We haven't taken any pictures or made any recordings yet. With a grunt, the *carabinero* hands them to me. I shove them into the inside pocket of the jacket.

"What is your business in the cathedral?" His tone is

hostile. I'm glad Courtney's doing all the talking, because my insides are liquefying right now.

"Our father wants to pray."

"There are many other churches. Why do you want this one?"

"It's the biggest one. We don't really know where the other ones are, and he can't walk very far." She puts her hand on Papá's back. "He's almost blind, and he's paralyzed on his left side."

The soldiers with machine guns walk around us. I wonder how heartless these bastards can be, though I've heard enough of Papá and Courtney's tapes to know the answer.

"*Bueno. Pase,*" the *carabinero* finally tells Courtney.

We go inside. The sanctuary of the eighteenth-century cathedral is dimly lit and cavernous. Courtney takes our hands and leads us to the rows of votive candles that people have lit to offer prayers or remember the dead. She drops money into the box and lights a single candle. She prays silently. I pull my wallet from my back pocket, remove a bill, and slide it into the slot.

I glance at Papá. He gives me an amused smile—maybe because Courtney told the authorities he wanted to pray here and he's the only one not praying, maybe because he can't believe his own son would pray in a church. I shrug and smile back at him.

I light the candle and set it next to Courtney's. I feel the warmth of dozens of lighted candles—the hopes and the memories of people who have come here before us. My people. The warmth of the candles spreads through me. I close my eyes and breathe in, and when I open my eyes again, I'm surrounded by light. I pray in Spanish, the language of my childhood, but not as a Catholic because I was never raised that way. I pray the way I did the night Papá was taken away, but this time I ask God to protect Papá and help him make our homeland a safe place, a place without soldiers. A place where every human being is valued and respected.

I sense Papá's gaze on me, and when I step back, I notice he's holding out his wallet. He nods. I take a bill from his wallet and hand it to him. He lights his candle, limps to the altar, sets the candle next to mine.

He gazes up at the ceiling, takes a deep breath, and says, "It's time."

Chapter Twenty-nine
August 4-5, 1986
La Vicaría de la Solidaridad

A priest meets us in the corridor next to the sanctuary and walks us to a smaller, plain-looking building behind the cathedral. He takes Papá into an office on the first floor. We wait outside.

A woman offers us coffee and cakes. She's wearing a business suit, and her dark hair is pulled up in a bun on top of her head.

"Your father's a courageous man," she says, adding, "Thank you for bringing him home."

"*De nada*," I answer.

"I brought you some copies of *Justicia* so you can see what he did."

She hands one to each of us. It's a crudely printed extra-wide page, folded over. The paper is browned with age and rough, almost crumbly. I start with the lead story, dated May 21, 1979.

> **The body of Emilio Larranaga Hébert, 51, was found at 22 h, on Thursday, May 17, in an alleyway behind El Condor, a bar in Pudahuel. He had been severely beaten and his throat slit. The photographer El Gato Negro witnessed the body being taken out by police and saw them remove Larranaga's wallet**

> and gold watch and a clip holding a moderate amount of money. El Gato Negro took the photo below, of a *carabinero* holding the wallet and watch.

I look to the bottom of the page, and there's a grainy photo of a *carabinero*'s torso and arm. He's wearing the same uniform the one in front of the cathedral wore, and there's a wallet and a wristwatch in his hand. Beside it is another photo of his face. I guess El Gato Negro, whoever he was, had a telephoto lens. I read on.

> The official police version stated that Larranaga was the victim of a robbery in a crime-infested zone and that the thief or thieves stole his valuables. Why, then, were his wallet, watch, and money clip on his person at the time of his death? Why were the police holding them, as shown in the photo?
>
> Larranaga was last seen on the street near his home in the Providencia neighborhood, 12 km away, two hours before his body was discovered by a bar patron, who had stepped outside. Larranaga's widow told us that he had gone to the store at 20 h to buy bread. Several witnesses on the street claimed that a 1977 Mercury with no license plate pulled up alongside the university economics professor around that time. Two men with masks jumped out and pushed him into the car.

One of Larranaga's students reported that the economist had criticized the government's free market policies in a class two weeks earlier, on Thursday, May 3. His widow said someone had called her with a death threat that same evening.

From the second photo taken by El Gato Negro, below, the *carabinero* has been identified as Ramiro Gaston Velasco Cárdenas, a captain from the Pudahuel barracks. We are trying to identify the masked men—presumably the actual killers—and the other *carabineros* who were present when the body was recovered. We would also like to know what Captain Velasco and his wallet-stealing fellow gangsters—who are supposed to protect the citizens of Santiago from crime rather than committing crimes themselves—did with the money they took from the fallen Professor Larranaga.

Nino, Cándido, & El Gato Negro

* * *

I run my finger over the byline "Nino" and repeat Papá's nickname, along with those of the two other reporters. Was Cándido the printer they'd tortured to death? And whatever happened to the brave photographer known simply as El Gato Negro, the Black Cat?

When I'm done reading other articles, which announce demonstrations and name police and military people identified in earlier murders, I hand the paper to Courtney. She hands me hers.

"What was yours about?" she asks.

"A murder of a professor that was made to look like a street crime. The police even took his stuff for themselves."

"Jerks," she mutters in English, then switches to Spanish. "This one's about a nineteen-year-old woman who died in prison. Her mother had an autopsy done, and it turned out she was poisoned. She was also pregnant, and it had to be one of the guards because she'd been there nine months and was four months along."

My face burns. "So they killed a mother *and* her baby?"

Courtney squeezes my hand, which calms me down a little. She pushes the hair from her face, but several strands have caught on her eyelids and cheeks.

The article is titled "The Body Doesn't Lie." I check the date and byline. It's from 1977, and "Nino" is the only name listed.

I was eight or nine years old then, and this is what Papá did, what he saw, while he was raising Tina and me. *How could he live with this, and still take care of us?*

After a while, Papá comes out, looking paler than usual, followed by a man in a suit. "You three should spend some time together," the man says. He brings us to another office on the first floor, one with a sofa and a couple of chairs as well as a desk. He switches on some lamps because it's been night for hours. "Take as long as you want. We'll bring you supper." The man shuts the door softly.

The first thing we do is hug, all three of us. It's like we're holding each other up for the longest time. Nobody says a word. Papá's bandage is gone, replaced with a navy wool cap he must have gotten from the church.

Papá drops to the sofa. He's shivering despite layers of clothes and the cap. He lights a cigarette. We sit on the wood floor in front of him.

"They told me what happened to Jaime." He inhales and blows out a stream of smoke. "Pneumonia."

"Like what you had," I say.

"Except I survived and he died. I got out and he stayed …inside."

He stands, looking for an ashtray. He finds one on the desk and flicks the cigarette.

"I got decent medical care, and he was left to rot in that dungeon."

Papá sits at the desk, opens drawers, closes them again. "I need a drink," I hear him mumble. In the ashtray, the cigarette slowly burns down.

Courtney taps my shoulder. "Do you have the tape recorder?" she whispers in English.

I pat my jacket, over the inside pocket. Courtney reaches out her hand.

"No, Courtney. Let him be, this time," I say softly, all the while watching Papá feel inside each drawer of the tall file cabinet.

He opens the top drawer of a low cabinet underneath a paper shredder and comes out with a half-full bottle of whiskey. I wonder how he knew the guy would have something stashed away.

"Do you know the person in this office?" I ask him.

He shakes his head. "It was a good guess. It's difficult

work, what these people are doing."

He takes a swallow, wipes his mouth with the sleeve of his canvas coat, and hands me the bottle. I hesitate.

He nods. "Go ahead."

I drink. The whiskey stings the inside of my mouth and burns going down. Courtney takes a small sip.

Papá and I take another turn. My lips feel numb, and where there was an aching around my heart, now there's nothing—just a warm feeling in my stomach. Papá talks about Jaime again. He tells us that Jaime had been a medical student until they arrested him for running a safe house and treating wounded guerrillas. He was the one who taught Papá to talk and walk again and worked his arm and hand so they wouldn't become totally useless.

Papá wiggles his fingers. "I almost had full use of this hand, until I fell and broke my wrist last November. If Jaime hadn't set it and badgered them to put a cast on, the nerve damage would have been even worse." He shakes his head slowly. "I owe my life to him, but I was sitting up there in Gringolandia. I let him die."

"Could you have really done anything here?" Courtney asks. She seemed to bristle when he said "Gringolandia." I did too, back in February when he first arrived. Now I don't care.

"I would have been closer to him. I could have gotten information about his condition out of the country and into the hands of someone who could have helped him. People did it for me. That's how I got out alive."

A priest brings us sandwiches and tea. Papá hides the bottle under the sofa. About a quarter of it is left, and I know he's going to finish it before the night is done. Courtney and I eat our sandwiches, but Papá doesn't touch his. Eventually, when he's all talked out, he pushes the plate toward me with his foot.

The aching near my heart that vanished a while ago comes back in waves as I remember those months in Madison when Papá ate almost nothing and drank himself senseless every night. Will the same thing happen here when Courtney and I leave in two weeks? Who will take care of Papá, the way Jaime did in prison and Courtney and I have for the past few months?

I push the plate back. "You need to eat something," I say.

He shakes his head.

My throat is tight when I speak up again. "It won't do anyone any good if you end up like Jaime. You're not in prison now. You have a choice."

His glare turns me to ice. "Don't lecture me. You have no idea how much it hurts. Not just physically." He raises his arm, then lets it drop to his knees. "Everything."

I look over to Courtney, who appears engrossed in a magazine she found on the desk. I remember the way she touched her chest that night, her words: *Everything they did to him in that prison...It's all in here now.*

I'm waiting for her to tell me what to say, to do. *Come on, Courtney, how fascinating can that magazine be?*

But she doesn't even glance up. The next thing I hear is sobbing, loud and harsh. It hits me like an Arctic blast, the fact that I've never actually seen my father cry. Not when I was a kid and he worked on that newspaper, describing those terrible crimes against his people. Not in the months he stayed with us in Madison, separated from his country and knowing he would never be the same.

"Go to him. He needs you," Courtney whispers in

English. "It's hard for him to show his weakness to you."

I sit on the sofa beside him and lay my hand on his back. He puts his arm around my shoulders, pulls me closer. I feel myself trembling against him, because he was always so strong when I was a kid and I don't know if he's going to survive this. His sobs grow softer, interrupted by hiccups.

"A woman showed Courtney and me your newspaper," I say as soon as he's quieted enough to listen.

"Yes."

"Was Cándido the printer?"

He nods.

"And El Gato Negro?"

"A young muralist from Pudahuel. They shot him in March of '80." Papá clears his throat. "Which issues did you see?"

"One with corpse-robbing cops."

"A big story. They transferred that captain—the one holding the wallet—up north. They said it was punishment." Papá pauses. "But it was for his protection, too."

I shudder. "You wouldn't have killed him?"

Papá shakes his head. "Not me. But we had friends in the militant parties who watched our back. And they read the paper, of course. Because of them we got accused of publishing a hit list, but that wasn't our purpose."

He lets go of me, reaches for the bottle on the floor, and takes a drink. It's almost empty, maybe a shot left, when he hands it over.

"Finish it," he tells me, his voice thick. I do. Afterward, he says, "Whoever has this office is going to be surprised when he comes in tomorrow morning to find his secret stash empty and me on his sofa. Half the country thinks

Nino's dead." He hiccups again. "A lot of the time, I think I am too."

Papá scoots to the edge of the sofa, picks the bread from the sandwich, and bites off a chunk. I tell him what I heard at the concert.

"Yes, that's the official story," he says. "We're not denying it."

"Why not?"

"The fewer people know I'm back, the better. Less chance of someone betraying me."

I nod, realizing that we can trust almost no one here. No wonder Papá acted so suspicious of the people in Madison.

Papá takes another bite of bread, chews it slowly. With an expression of disgust, he drops the rest onto the plate and lays his arm across my shoulders again. "Look, you've been with me at a very dark time. I know you're worried about me, what'll happen after you two go."

"I wish I could stay—"

Papá cuts me off. "It's not going to be easy. I won't lie to you. I've lost too much. Too many people, too much of myself. I need to mourn, but at the same time, I need to fight. And I can't guarantee I'll live to see our victory."

I blink back tears. I really do want a guarantee from him.

"My job is to make our country safe and free. Your job—and I want you to be a man about this…" He pats my shoulder. "You're going back to Gringolandia. You're going to finish high school and university, so that you can be that engineer you always wanted to be. And if I and everybody else here…" He sweeps his weak arm in front of him. "If we win, you return and make your country a better place." He turns to face me. His lips glisten. His smile is crooked. Behind his glasses, his left eye wanders, but his right eye remains dark and focused. "*M'ijo*, when I do what I have to do, your return will be my hope."

Chapter Thirty
August 5, 1986
Santiago

Papá crashes on the sofa. Courtney and I miss curfew and end up sleeping in the chairs. I awaken to someone's hand on my shoulder, shaking me gently.

"Dan, it's me," Courtney whispers.

I turn away from her and glance out the window. Through a crack in the curtains, I see nothing but dull gray. Either the sun isn't up yet, or it's another rainy day.

"What time is it?" I ask.

"Six. Curfew's over. We should get out of here." Standing over me, Courtney squirms like she needs to pee. I pull my legs up to my chest and cover my face with my forearm. She tugs my wrist. "Come on."

I unfold myself from the chair. I'm a little stiff but not tired despite having slept less than four hours. Courtney's face looks drawn in the dim light, and there are dark circles under her eyes. Her hair is poofed up on one side. Even before she tells me about her horrible night in the chair, I know she didn't sleep well.

I shake out my dreads and fumble for my glasses on the desk. The first pair I grab are Papá's; they make everything around me appear huge and blurry. I put them back and find mine.

Papá is sprawled facedown on the sofa, the empty bottle lying on the floor next to his hand. He reeks of stale liquor. I pinch my nose and elbow Courtney.

She glares at me. "It's not funny, Dan. He pulled this stunt at my brother's place, and Matt still hasn't let me forget it."

"What are you saying about me in a language I don't understand?" Papá mumbles. There's a wet spot on the gray cloth next to his face. He wiggles his fingers, which make a faint pinging sound when they tap the bottle.

"Nothing, Papá. Courtney's just tired," I answer.

She shows her back and slips out the door, I guess to the bathroom. It's her huffy move, and I hope that once she's washed her face and fixed her hair a little, she'll be less cranky.

Papá tries to sit up, but falls back to the sofa with a grunt. "When are you two leaving?" he asks.

"As soon as Courtney gets back from washing up."

"No. The country."

"Next Friday." *He's already forgotten*, I think.

"Let's meet next Thursday. On Wednesday, I'll leave a piece of paper with the time and place"—He pauses for a few moments—"inside the flowerpot in front of the restaurant where we ate yesterday."

I make a mental note, though I doubt Papá's going to remember. He drank enough last night to still be trashed this morning, and we have more than a week for something to happen or him to forget.

"Don't worry. This is the way we always left messages for each other," Papá says. He closes his eyes, grimaces as if his head hurts, and waves me closer.

I crouch next to him, holding my breath. I hope the guy with the office has some mouthwash and air freshener hidden away too. "Thanks for last night, *m'ijo*." He reaches blindly for my hand, catches a couple of fingers, and holds on. "Now you two get out of here and let me do my job."

I expect him to at least try to hug me, but he doesn't. He's still hanging on to my fingers. I figure he wants to avoid any more teary scenes on his part or mine.

"*Chao, Papá.*" I squeeze his hand. "*Cúidate*, okay?" It's useless telling him to be careful, and right now his only job seems to be sleeping off last night. But it's about as much of a good-bye as we're going to have for the next ten days. Another squeeze, and I let go.

Courtney and I find a side door out of the building and wait for an army patrol to pass in the other direction. We speed-walk down a street that leads away from the well-guarded plaza. It's already the beginning of rush hour. She's complaining in English about people seeing her in her disheveled state. I'm worried about Papá, if I'll ever see him again, and if he's going to survive long enough to see our country free.

A block from the hotel, she picks up a piece of paper from the ground and stuffs it into her shoulder bag. When we get back to the room, she hands it to me.

It's some sort of flyer. I set it on the nightstand next to my twin bed. I pull her onto the bed and press my lips to hers. The image of my father sprawled on the sofa dissolves from my mind. The room is cold, but warmth spreads throughout my body from my hips, my belly, my face.

Ten days. We have ten days for nothing but this.

Our mouths separate with a pop. "I'll show you how good you look," I say.

I lie on my side and grab her wrist, urging her to slide her body next to mine. Instead she reaches for the flyer and holds it out for me to read.

We have clean hands: Women's march for human rights.

"You know how I was reading that magazine last night," Courtney says.

While Papá was falling apart and I didn't know what the hell to do. "Yeah, it must have been really interesting."

Courtney misses my sarcasm. "It was. It talked about how women are leading the way to democracy."

"So?" I suspect where she's going with this, but I wait for her to tell me.

"I want to see for myself. Today. Three in the afternoon."

I flip my arm to glance at my watch. "It's seven in the morning."

"I need to rest. I got zero sleep on account of your father passing out on the sofa."

"You could have rolled him off. He wouldn't have noticed." My groin feels hot and achy. I can't believe she's leaving me like this over a women's march and her beauty sleep.

Okay, so I'm cranky too, I tell myself. Four hours of sleep isn't really enough. Besides, there's the postmarch celebration and nine more days before we have to leave for home.

I stand and strip to take a cold shower. I can feel her eyes on me, but I don't see the naughty look in them that's always turned me on—the look of a preacher's kid about to do something really bad. I wonder if there's more behind it—maybe that we've played the role of brother and sister so long it would seem like incest. Maybe she's as upset as I am about saying good-bye to Papá and not knowing if we'll ever see him alive again.

I know she wants to talk, but I wait until after my shower. It's just too painful otherwise.

The minute I step into the room, towel around my waist, she ambushes me. "I can't believe you're thinking about sex after we've left your father in that place."

I shrug. At least I guessed right—she didn't blindside me. "It's a sanctuary church. He's safer there than a lot of places." I add, "Like a women's march in a slum."

"Is it a really bad neighborhood?" Her voice is hushed. I reach for a sleeveless undershirt and a pair of boxers. I notice that she's already changed into a thick flannel nightgown—definitely not sexy.

"Well, I haven't lived here in five years, but..." I put on my pajama bottoms and a sweatshirt to stall for time. I could scare her, tell her she'd get herself mugged or worse going out there, but it would make our country look like crap and besides, it probably isn't true, especially in daytime. She'd have more to worry about with the soldiers, who burned those kids alive. Still, I helped set up that illegal concert, and nothing happened to me. And we dropped Papá off with no problems.

Besides, there's probably nothing I can say that will stop Courtney from doing whatever she wants to do.

"But what?" Courtney presses on.

"You should be okay if the military doesn't try to break up the march. Anyway, I'm going with you."

"You don't have to. It's a women's march."

I sigh. "Did you think I'd let you go out there alone?"

"Don't be so macho. I don't need you to protect me."

With my already damp towel, I squeeze the water out of my dreads. "Courtney, this isn't Wisconsin. Women don't travel to unknown places by themselves. I'll go with you and wait for you there."

Courtney crawls into her bed and pulls the sheet and blankets over her. "I'd hate living here," she moans.

"You probably would." My voice is as cold as the room.

"You're not planning to come back after college, are you?"

I drop into a chair, wrap my arms around my legs, and rest my chin on my raised knees. "That's five years away. Assuming there's democracy." My chest is tight. *There has to be. Papá won't last that long if there isn't.*

Courtney pokes her head out from under the covers. "What about your U.S. citizenship?"

"I'm not getting it this year. Probation, remember?"

"You *are* coming back here. I can feel it." She blows out her breath. "Our days are numbered."

"So? You're going to UW." I think of what Willie said months ago. "You could fall in love with a college guy the first week and ditch me."

"You know I wouldn't do that." There's hurt in her voice. "Don't you trust me?"

I say nothing.

"Do you *want* me to go out with someone else?" she presses.

"No, but if Papá wants me back here and it's safe…" I stop there.

Courtney jumps into the silence. "Your father's a great man, Dan. He's just not the kind of person you should arrange your life around."

I get her point. A father I hadn't seen in five years until February tells me what to do for the next five years of my life—while he leaves his family to go back to the place where they imprisoned and tortured him and turned him into a cripple. I shiver, recalling how broken he seemed last night and how it would devastate him if he thought I had no intention of returning. *Take away a man's son and you take away his future*, he told me once in Madison.

"You heard him. He's counting on me," I say.

"You don't have to tell him anything now. He'll be so happy if the dictatorship falls, he might not care."

My fists are clenched, my fingernails digging into my palms. "I'm not going to lie to him. He's been through too much already."

I turn away from her and look out the window, at the gray sky and dingy buildings.

"I don't want to talk about it anymore," I say. "Let's get some sleep."

Courtney sets her alarm clock for one in the afternoon. She has to do her hair and put her makeup on—for a women's march. She wears her nicest peasant skirt, too. I tell her that wearing fancy clothes to a demonstration is not a good idea, but she says it shows respect when you don't look like a slob.

The clouds have thickened while we were sleeping, and dense smog envelops the city. I'm gasping the minute I step outside, but it may just be nerves. Courtney seems excited, while I'm going to have to worry about her.

Taking a bus, we get to the market where the march is supposed to begin. Right away, Courtney spots a group of women carrying signs. A few are young, but most look like mothers or grandmothers. As I approach them with Courtney, I read what they're carrying. Many signs have pictures of the two teens who were set on fire. Other signs have pictures of the women's own family members who've disappeared at the hands of the dictatorship—their names handwritten and the question "*¿Dónde están?*" A few signs have handprints with the words, "*Tenemos las manos limpias.*"

Courtney reaches skyward to show her clean hands—her peaceful hands—and joins the group. Five hours of sleep and another hour of primping have paid off. She looks radiant—her hair loose and freshly washed, with four skinny braids. She wears a long-sleeved dark green peasant blouse and green print skirt, boots, and a leather necklace with a wooden cross.

The problem is, she really stands out—not a good idea. I call her over.

"You're too blond," I tell her. "It's blinding." I hold out my cap. The guys at the record store yesterday talked me into buying it. It's reggae colors—red, yellow, black, and green. She shakes her head and gives me a thumbs-down.

"Meet me here in two," she calls out in English.

The women parade off in a thick crooked line that reminds me of an alligator's tail. I duck into the market. There are fresh food stands with meat and vegetables, but late in the day, the pickings are slim and some of the seafood has gone rank. In another part of the market are stands with T-shirts of characters from old Disney movies, cheap plastic toys, rubber soccer balls, cassettes from Brazilian pop groups, bestsellers translated from English. Many of the people working there are children younger than Tina.

The skinny, ragged kids depress me. I leave, cross the street, and make my way to a traffic circle. The stiff breeze lifts the dreads sticking out from under my cap, blows them in my face, slaps them against my glasses. A group of men are dragging what look like cardboard boxes and wood scraps into one of the streets off the circle.

I watch for a few minutes. The crowd of men grows. They're rolling tires toward the pile.

Three boys, maybe twelve or thirteen years old, run past me, calling, "*¡Ven acá!*"

In an instant, I switch off my English-speaking brain. Leaving Brian Shepherd behind, I pull alongside them. "*¿Qui'ubo, cabros?*" I ask.

"The *milicos* are going to attack the march. Help us."

Attack the march—where Courtney is. Where the mothers and grandmothers are.

There's a hole in a fence. I rush through it into a *población* of cardboard and plywood houses with tin roofs. My feet slide in the mud. It rained a little while Courtney and I were sleeping, and it looks like it's going to rain again.

"Here, take this," a man tells me. He has long, stringy, gray hair that reminds me of Papá's before I shaved it off.

I raise a warped and rotting sheet of plywood over my head, carry it past the fence and into the street. I haul out more plywood, cardboard, pieces of cement, rocks. The barricade grows. It's already over my head by the time I hear the roar of trucks in the distance.

"You!"

I glance up. A bearded man sitting atop the barricade nods in my direction. There are several people around me, but I'm pretty sure he's gesturing at me. "You got a name?"

I don't hesitate. "Rasta."

"You have strong arms, Rasta. Throw me the rocks."

I toss the rocks and cement chunks, one by one, to the man, who calls himself El Tigre. Behind him, a group of kids are soaking the barricade in gasoline. The first drops of rain hit the cobblestone street. The roar of vehicles grows louder.

I can't see how close the army trucks are because of the giant wall in front of me. El Tigre flings rocks. Another man climbs up as well, his sneakers slipping on the gasoline-soaked boards. Raindrops bead on the surface of the wood.

I step farther back. Three men now throw the chunks I pass them. A smoking canister flies over the barricade. Tear gas. I pull my scarf over my face like the others do. El Tigre tells us to stay upwind. I hear shots.

"Get down!" someone calls.

The men slide down the barricade. From behind the fence, boys run out holding bottles filled with clear liquid and stuffed with cloths. A man tapes the mouths of the bottles.

"Hurry!" El Tigre calls.

"I'm getting them!" the man cries. His hands shake as he cuts the duct tape with a small knife.

"I've got it," I tell him. I take the roll from him and tear off pieces of tape. He goes back to sealing the bottles.

We've got three Molotov cocktails lined up.

Four.

Five.

Six.

"Okay. Let them go."

El Tigre takes out a plastic lighter. I pick up the first bottle. My muscles are tight. *This is for Papá, for what they did to him. This is for the soldiers, who dragged me* out to watch. *This is for Jaime and the professor, for Cándido and El Gato Negro.*

This is what Rodrigo Rojas saw on the day the soldiers burned him to death.

"Don't screw it up, Rasta. We only have a few."

He lights the rag taped to the bottle's mouth. I wait for the rag to burn, good and strong.

I wind up, let the bottle fly. My arm hangs in the air.

I hear the crash, then the explosion as the barricade ignites. Like the opening chord, igniting the crowd. "Yahhhh!" I yell. I leap into the air, my arm raised, my fist clenched.

More bottles fly. More explosions. The barricade is engulfed in flames. The blast of hot air blows away the chill inside me. Sweat mixed with rainwater rolls down my face and neck. Tear gas canisters fly overhead. A couple of them hit the flaming pile and blow high into the air, above the black smoke.

We run. Some of the men scatter into the *población*; others dash up the street to warn the women still in transit. I join a bunch racing toward the market where the march is supposed to end. We have to make sure the women get home safely.

I realize that my reggae cap is gone. My mouth feels parched. I buy a pop, chug it, buy another. This one I drink more slowly as I drift from stall to stall, replaying in my mind the image of the flaming pile that separated the soldiers from the women. We were men and boys with a common purpose—to protect mothers, grandmothers, wives, girlfriends. I wish I could have talked to some of the others in the marketplace, but we're all wandering around alone because two or more together would be considered a conspiracy. I avoid the eyes of the soldiers who I now notice standing at the entrances to the market or walking among us.

I check outside to see if Courtney is back from the march. It's stopped raining, so I take my bottle and stand at the curb, watching the clouds break up. A few rays of sun filter through. A couple of military vehicles pass.

Then I see them—a smaller group of perhaps two dozen women—in a vacant lot across the street from me. The trucks slow, make U-turns. Soldiers with guns pour out. Right away, the women take off running.

Soldiers fan out, chasing the women across the lot. Some of the women fall. Soldiers jump on them, clubs swinging. The marchers are a herd of goats—the old, sick, weak ones have fallen behind the pack, and wolves have pounced on them to feast. There's not a thing I can do to stop it.

And then there's the baby goat, separated from mother and pack—too young to know how much danger she's really in. Courtney. I think she can't believe these guys will do anything to her—like her pale skin and blond hair are a Plexiglas bubble around her, keeping all the bad things away.

From my side of the street a soldier runs toward her. "*¡Manos arriba!*" he shouts.

She doesn't put her hands up. Her eyes grow wide. Her mouth gapes. She takes off toward the market, but her long skirt catches in her legs, and she stumbles. I hear a single scream. I'm not sure she sees me.

Holding my glass bottle, staring at the lot where the women are being chased and beaten, I step forward into the soldier's path to block him from hurting Courtney. I plant my feet, bend my knees, put my shoulder down, and at the last moment look into his sweaty light brown face and murderous eyes before pain explodes in my collarbone and everything goes black.

Chapter Thirty-one
August 14, 1986
Santiago

I end up with a separated shoulder, and the doctor says I might have a torn rotator cuff. The soldier who collided with me wasn't hurt, probably because he had about thirty pounds on me with all his equipment and was running at full speed. I'm lucky I remembered not to speak Spanish when I went down; I played the gringo tourist perfectly. The soldiers found a *carabinero* who spoke some English, and they drove Courtney and me to a hospital in an army truck.

At the hospital I overhear them talking about the goofy kid who went to that market because he misread the guidebook, wandered away from his sister, and wound up standing in the wrong place at the wrong time. A couple of them want to touch my dreads. They have to use hand signals to ask me, because they have no idea I speak *castellano* as well as they do.

"I can't believe how nice those soldiers were," Courtney says when we get back to the hotel.

"Yeah, I think they were worried on account of that *norteamericano* kid they burned alive." A muscle spasm silences me. I clench my teeth and adjust the ice pack I'm holding on my shoulder.

The pain in my shoulder, arm, and collarbone is intense, especially after the ice pack melts. Courtney scores a bag of ice from a bar around the corner from the hotel, but by midnight that ice melts too, and it's not safe for a woman to walk into a bar alone at that hour. The doctor gave me some major painkillers, but I can't keep them down.

I lean over the sink, my left arm pressed against my body, my stomach turning itself inside out to get rid of the pills and what little else I've eaten today. Every heave tears at my mangled shoulder. I feel Courtney's hands on my forehead and around my waist and the softness of her cheek against the back of my neck. I try to relax in her grip.

"I'm sorry, Dan," she says for the hundredth time.

"Now I know what Papá deals with every fucking day of his life," I rasp before spitting a gob of mucus into the sink. "If it were me, I'd go crazy."

Courtney wipes my face with a wet bandana, and it makes me shiver. Through the bandages and the pain, I feel her rubbing my back. "You were so brave."

And you were so stupid. You could have gotten both of us killed—and Papá captured. I push her away and stumble to my bed. When I drop to the mattress, it's like a knife through my body. I bite my lip to keep from screaming. I wish I could pass out, but it doesn't happen.

Even my hair hurts.

"Get the scissors. They're with the gauze and stuff," I tell Courtney.

"You're not touching your shoulder." Courtney doesn't say it as a question.

"No. You're cutting off my dreads."

"It's one in the morning," she protests.

"So what? Do you see me sleeping?"

She steps backward, a hurt expression on her face. "I've gotten to like them. They're cute, like you have a palm tree on your head."

I burp up acid and wipe my mouth on the front of my undershirt.

"Why do you want to get rid of them now?" she asks.

She probably thinks it's a Samson and Delilah thing. I've lost my strength. I've been reduced to a curled-up, shivering, pain-crazed shell of myself that smells like puke.

If that's what she's thinking, she couldn't be further from the truth. I haven't lost my strength—I've found it.

"*Porque soy chileno. Chilenos* don't have dreadlocks," I tell her.

She blows her breath out. "I knew it."

"Knew what? That one day I'd grow up and quit being your Latin boy-toy?"

"That's not what I meant."

"Then what did you mean?"

She turns away from me. "It's your father telling you what to do. I can't believe *you'd* want to come back to this place."

That was yesterday's argument, and I don't want to go over it again. "You know, Courtney," I begin, "it wasn't my idea to go to that march. If I had my way, the only thing we'd have to worry about is you getting pregnant—and I brought protection for that." Ten days of what I wanted to do are out of the question now. I'm breathing hard, sweating and freezing at the same time. "I think of things like that. Protection. Not wearing church clothes to a demonstration. Avoiding thugs with guns."

"I dressed to show respect," she repeats. "The soldiers

were wrong to attack us."

I struggle to sit up. "Like it makes a difference to them? This isn't Radical Disneyland. People get shot, burned alive, beaten into a coma," I say, my voice hoarse. "You saw what they did to Papá. You *wrote* the damn article. And he almost killed himself because of what you wrote."

"It wasn't the article. He was already suicidal, if you remember. He said it on the tape." She hesitates. "I told your mother about it at my graduation party."

Something else I knew nothing about. "Super. What else did you two discuss?"

"That he won't get the help he needs because he's too macho. That he self-medicates, so now he's an alcoholic. And that he hurts everyone around him because he's been hurt."

"That's obvious. We didn't need you to tell us." Still, her words leave a pain far deeper than my separated shoulder, as I think about how a person I love and admire more than anyone in the world has ended up at the point where he has zero chance of a decent life. "Besides, what he does makes a lot more sense than what you do. You get an idea into your head, you act on it without thinking, and nothing ever happens to you, but someone else gets hurt on account of you." I squeeze my eyes shut against the pain and suck in air. "You're trouble, Courtney. I can't deal with it anymore."

She's sobbing now, tears streaming down her face. "I want to do the right thing. I really do."

"I know. But you do it all wrong."

* * *

Courtney does a really crappy job with my hair. In some places, she's chopped almost to my scalp; in other places, there's about an inch left. I should probably shave it all off, but it looks as ragged as I feel, so I keep it. Neither of us gets any sleep that night. Toward daybreak, I hear her crying softly across the room.

I let her cry. I'm turning the last twenty-four hours over and over in my mind, the way I imagine Papá must have done so many nights in prison.

I'm not sorry I made Courtney cut off my dreads. I'm not sorry I broke up with her. But I *am* sorry about the way I spoke to her. The pain is no excuse. And that's what I tell her.

"Thank you." She snuffs and blows her nose. Her eyelids are puffy and pink. "It gives me hope that you'll be different."

"Different how?" That I'll love her again?

"From your father."

"You can't compare us," I say. I touch the sling, and even that causes my shoulder and back muscles to spasm. "This is going to heal. He never will."

Courtney nods. "Maybe when you're better, we can start over."

That'll be October at least. She'll be well into her freshman year. I hate problems that go on and on.

I'm sitting up in bed. I lean against the wall, but it doesn't give me any support. "We have to be together nine more days. Let's just try to be friends," I tell her.

* * *

Even though I'm in a lot of pain and Courtney's teary over our breakup, we go out that afternoon and buy a bootleg tape of the duo that I helped set up the other night. The street vendor suggests some other groups, so I buy their cassettes too. He says I'm lucky I found his cart, because the music is banned and most record stores won't sell it.

I take the tapes back to the room and play them on Courtney's recorder. The sound quality sucks, but I start to figure out some of the chords for whenever I can hold a guitar again. The next day I buy a little Chilean flag, which I'm going to hang on the inside of my locker at school because I don't have a cool car to hang a flag from the rearview mirror like Gregorio does.

By the fourth day after my injury, the pain in my shoulder settles into a constant dull ache. Courtney and I decide to do the tourist thing. We take the bus to Valparaíso and Viña del Mar and walk up and down the nearly deserted beach. Although there's a raw, salty chill, she chases the waves out into the ocean and lets them chase her back to dry land. She falls a few times, so her peasant skirt ends up wet and full of sand. We stay in a little inn by the ocean, and for the first time in many days I fall into a deep sleep.

* * *

Papá has left the note in the flowerpot like he promised. The paper looks like a piece of wadded-up trash that nobody's paid any attention to—the perfect post office box for a clandestine freedom fighter. He's scrawled the name and address of a restaurant in Bellavista and "14h"—

two in the afternoon.

Courtney and I arrive first. It's a small place, maybe six tables, all brightly painted in combinations of blue, purple, red, yellow, and orange. The walls are pink.

Four of the tables are taken. I wonder about government spies eavesdropping. A few of the men wear business suits, but there are also men and women in jeans who look like students. A beggar with a hooded overcoat, dark glasses, and a white cane stands next to one of the larger tables, talking to a man in a suit—hitting him up for money, I guess. It doesn't surprise me. The streets are filled with beggars of all ages, children too, who often come up to people sitting in cafés. The dictatorship has created a lot of very poor, desperate people.

The hostess shows us to a small table set for three. Courtney and I sit across from each other.

"Cute place," Courtney whispers in English. "I can see Frida Kahlo walking in here right now."

"Yeah, except she's been dead for thirty years," I mutter.

"Stop being so literal."

I notice the artwork on the walls. The pictures remind me of the posters in Courtney's bedroom. I pick up my menu.

I hear a tapping behind me and to my left but am too stiff to turn around. Courtney has already reached for her bag and is pulling out a bill. The blind beggar slides into the seat between us. He shakes himself free from his overcoat, and the first thing I notice is the navy wool cap.

"Papá!" I whisper. "You had me fooled."

Papá signals to the table he came from. The man in the suit appears alongside us. "Oscar, man, pay up. I told you

I could even fool the kids."

We meet Oscar, who Papá will be teaming with on human rights cases. He's the one with the office where we crashed. Papá leans his cane against the table and switches the sunglasses for his round wire-rims. With his teeth, he yanks off the fingerless glove on his right hand, then pulls off the left one, revealing the splint on his wrist. There's gray and brown stubble on his chin, and his overcoat smells of cigarettes and rancid wine.

As soon as Oscar returns to his table, I lean toward Papá. "Are you sure we can talk?"

"This place is safe. It's affiliated with the church."

"So what's with the stinky blind beggar act?"

"It's my cover. Being a cripple, I don't have a lot of options." He pulls a pack of cigarettes from his overcoat pocket. "As long as I'm in the country illegally, I might as well do fieldwork undercover. Oscar"—Papá glances sideways—"meets with the dignitaries, and I'm his dirtbag partner. We're writing reports together. I'm fact-checking them. We're going to smuggle them out of the country." He taps a book of matches lying on the table. Courtney strikes a match and lights his cigarette for him. He takes a long drag and leaves the cigarette in the ashtray. "These reports have to be accurate. We don't want to be sending bullshit abroad."

Papá pushes his chair back and ducks under the table. He seems to be adjusting his leg brace, but when he resurfaces, he's holding a stack of papers.

"Which reminds me," he continues, "these need to go to your mother."

I take the pages—about thirty of them—from him. *Divorce proceedings?*

"They're reports on some disappeared persons. For the Madison committee," he says, as if to answer my unspoken question. "And when you go back," he adds, "be decent to her. She's still your mother, and she's doing a good job. It's not her fault what happened."

Courtney nods to me, thinking, I'm sure, about her secret conversations with Mamá. Even though all of what they said is true, I have to defend Papá. "Don't think it was your fault either."

"It's the places she and I ended up, and that's all I'm going to say about it." He takes another drag from his cigarette. "She'll explain the rest if you ask her."

I stuff the papers into the inside pocket of my jacket. The arm of the jacket hangs loose. My arm is still taped and in a sling underneath.

Papá peels my jacket back. He gives me a questioning look with the half of his face that he can control.

"I had an accident," I say.

"A real accident?"

"No," Courtney cuts in. "He took a hit to save my life." She tells Papá what happened at the end of the women's march.

"Nice work, but I don't think dumb gringo tourist is a long-term plan, *m'ijo*." He pats me on the back gently and laughs. "What happened to those silly dreadlocks?"

"I had Courtney cut them off after I got hurt."

"Too hard to manage with one arm?"

I play with one of my shirt buttons to avoid speaking. I don't want to rehash any part of our fight and breakup with Courtney sitting there.

"It's not that bad once you figure out how to do it," he says. I recall how nasty his hair looked most of the time in

Madison, but I now suspect depression rather than disability as the cause.

The waitress drops off a bottle of wine—the payoff from Oscar—and takes our order.

"So was your shoulder dislocated or separated?"

"Separated."

He motions with his bad hand. "Let me see."

I lift off my jacket and unbutton the rest of my shirt, where the sleeve also hangs. He asks Courtney to light another cigarette for him.

"The doctor said I might need surgery when I get home," I tell him.

"Which your mother will blame me for."

"I'll tell her," Courtney says. "If she blames anyone, it should be me."

With his good hand Papá feels my shoulder and collarbone. They're still tender and achy, and I try not to pull away. He raises his weak arm to the front of my shoulder and from the back gently pushes the joint against his curled fingers.

"It's not stable. You'll need surgery all right," he mumbles, the cigarette still in his mouth. A few ashes drop off and fall between us.

This is not the news I wanted to hear. "How do you know?"

"One of the *compañeros* with Jaime and me, the interrogators wrecked both his shoulders. One was badly separated and never fixed. The other was a posterior dislocation, which you only get with a seizure or electric shock." Somehow he gets my shirt buttoned again. "Jaime wanted to document it when he got out, but it looks like that's my job now."

Papá drapes my jacket over my shoulders again. He pours three glasses of wine, clinks his glass against ours, and raises it. "*Hasta la victoria siempre*," he toasts. He drinks about half of his wine in one gulp. "So what else did you do while you were here?" he asks.

"Traveled around." I tell him where we went, though I leave out the part about helping to build the barricade and setting it on fire. I haven't even told Courtney. I feel like it's such a small thing—there were so many of us, and the real heroes were the three men sitting on top of the barricade chucking rocks at the tanks. I don't want either Courtney or Papá to think I did anything special.

Courtney seems unusually quiet. I know she doesn't want to say anything about us breaking up. I guess this must be hard for her, being so far away from home and things not turning out the way she expected. When our food comes, she picks at it.

Papá looks up from his grilled fish. "What's wrong, *m'ija*?" he asks her.

For a long while she says nothing. Then she slides a brown flask out of his overcoat. She must have been rifling his pockets while he and I were talking.

"Oh, that." He takes it from her, unscrews the top. "It's a prop, mostly water. See for yourself."

Courtney sniffs, then takes a sip. She passes it to me, and I try it. It's about three-quarters water, maybe more.

"I'm not an idiot," Papá says. "I have to be able to do my job."

I replace the top and hand him the flask. He drops it into his pocket.

Courtney frowns. I know she's still worried about his drinking. I've heard it from her all week. And I've told her there's nothing she or I can do about it, except love him the way he is—without expecting that he'll change.

"It's all right, Courtney," I whisper.

It's all right, but it's not all right. I want to have the same feelings for Courtney that I had before we left Madison. I want my parents to be back together. I want Papá to be strong and whole and free from pain. I want this beautiful country of my birth, where I have spent the past two weeks, to be a safe place for people to live.

After we finish eating, we walk out into the garden. Even though it's winter, the grass is green, some of the trees have leaves, and today, the sun shines. A group of students, who'd also eaten in the restaurant, stroll past us and leave through a metal gate.

Papá walks along the brick path, identifying some of the plants. "I'd like to have a garden like this one day," he says.

He pauses and leans against a cast-iron bench. I stop next to him. Courtney, who was checking out some of the birds, doesn't see us stop. When she crashes into my back, knocking me forward, pain wrenches my shoulder. I swear at her in two languages.

"I'm sorry. I wasn't paying attention." She pushes her braids out of her face. "I guess I shouldn't have had that second glass of wine."

I rub my upper arm, wondering what else I may have torn that will need surgery on account of her. Papá places his hand on the back of my neck and presses his thumb on a sore spot above my collarbone. I feel his hot breath on my ear. My muscles unclench, and the pain dissolves.

"That better?" he asks.

"How did you...?"

"The *compañero* in prison."

"Whatever happened to him?" I ask.

"He's still there. We're trying to get him out."

Courtney's gone silent again. Papá puts his arm around my uninjured shoulder and pulls her closer. I wish I could stay with him like this forever.

With her free hand, Courtney digs in her shoulder bag. She takes out the tape recorder and drops it into the pocket of Papá's overcoat. Then she stuffs in a handful of blank cassettes. "When it's safe for you," she says, "I'd like you to record more tapes."

He pats his pocket. "But don't get them published unless I ask you. Agreed?"

I take in the faint odor of wine, sweat, ashes, and Courtney's perfume—that's how close the three of us are standing. It makes me think of animals that huddle together for warmth and protection. Papá is in the middle of us and he hasn't panicked. A word escapes me. "Amazing."

"What?" Papá and Courtney say at the same time—he in Spanish, she in English.

"In Madison, you wouldn't let us get so near you."

"This is good for me," he says as he wraps us tighter around him. The warmth from his body spreads through my shoulder, and I imagine it healing without surgery—bones and tendons and ligaments knitting themselves together.

"I'm sorry we have to go tomorrow," I say.

"Me too, *m'ijos*. But I'm doing what I was meant to do, and you two helped me get here. So thanks for saving my fucked-up life. Both of you."

He squeezes my shoulder.

"And promise you'll come back to see me once in a

while, *m'ijo*. You're my kid. I know you'll find a way."

"And if you win…," I say.

"*When* we win," he corrects. "Come back for good."

I bet Courtney wishes she'd recorded what Papá said, but it doesn't matter. I'm going to remember it for the rest of my life.

Part Five
A Bird Named Pablo: A Metaphor

CHAPTER THIRTY-TWO
Atlanta and Santiago
October 5, 1988 and after

"It's official, *m'ijo*. We won. We're free." Over the phone, Papá sounds hoarse, exhausted. He's worked sixteen-hour days without a vacation for more than two years, writing articles and radio scripts and speaking to groups—all the things he tried to do when he lived with us, but this time with people who understand him.

I've spent all night in my dorm room at Georgia Tech listening to the results on my roommate's shortwave radio—he and I an island outpost of two people who care about a plebiscite in a country more than five thousand miles away. The next day I skip class to wait for my father's call.

"The General accepted it?" I can't resist adding, "That he ran as the only candidate and lost?"

"He didn't have a choice. The vote wasn't even close, and we made sure he couldn't steal it."

I hear someone talking to Papá in the background, partly drowned out by the static of the long-distance phone line.

"Listen, I have to go," he says after a moment. "They need me to cover a show—live interview with three organizers." He sighs. "Three women who think all us *machos* were in prison, drunk, or hiding under the bed when the revolution came. Wish me luck."

The bitterness of his tone tells me he hasn't gotten over what happened between him and Mamá. He hasn't seen her since the day he left for Chile, but they've stayed in touch. He knows that she'll get her doctorate in the spring and plans to marry a gringo architect as soon as the divorce is finalized. My future stepfather—Papá calls him the perfect antithesis of the *macho*—has offered to move anywhere in the United States that Mamá finds a teaching job.

"Good luck, Papá. And get some sleep when the show's over."

After he hangs up, I realize that despite having given so much to this victory, he sounded more weary than overjoyed. And he didn't ask if I was coming back. This past summer I worked with him at the radio station where he got a job after he emerged from hiding. Then I took advanced standing to graduate a year and a half from now so I could get back to him. But Papá doesn't seem to be thinking about the future the way I am. I'm worried that he thinks his work is finished now that there's democracy, and he's tired of dealing with the pain and what he can no longer do.

I'm still worried the next day, so after classes I call Papá at the station. They tell me he's taken some time off. "Nino was so fried, we told him to go to up north and sit on the beach until the end of the month," his producer says.

"He didn't go alone?" I ask.

"No, we're not fools. His sister took him. And a couple of us are going to drive up there to help her keep an eye on him."

"Thanks."

"And Rasta?"

"Yes?" I ask with a smile. I had the dreads a grand total of four days in Chile, but the nickname has stuck for two years and probably will forever.

"You concentrate on your classes. We're taking care of him for you."

It's the first of November when Papá calls me from work again. The victory must have sunk in, because he sounds much happier. He's thinking of buying a house, he tells me, even if for a good communist it feels like selling out.

"I asked Ileana, and she reminded me that Pablo Neruda was a communist and he had four houses," Papá says. "My one house would be nothing compared to that."

He asks me what I think.

"It's great," I answer.

"Why?" He knows I don't care about the details of left-wing politics.

"You've never owned a house. How long has it been since you even slept in your own bed?"

"You're the engineer. You tell me."

I write inside the front cover of my seismology notebook:

Prison: 64 months
Our place in Madison: 6
In hiding: 16
Crashing with Tía Ileana/living at the office: 10
Total: 96 months

"Eight years. One fifth of your life." I scribble over my calculations. "It's time you got a place of your own."

For a few seconds he doesn't respond, then he says, "I asked some of my friends in the Party, too."

"Do you need their approval?" I ask.

"No. I mentioned it when I asked them to get me a gun. For protection, you know, since I've pissed some people off over the years. They told me the house was a good idea." He pauses. "But they wouldn't give me the gun."

* * *

Four months later, I get a letter and some photos from him. He bought a house from a widow moving to the country. It's a semi-attached split-level—his side painted white, the other side beige. He says the backyard garden drew him to the place. I see that it's narrow and deep, with a variety of flowering plants, shrubs, and trees and a high wall covered with bushes and vines. It's almost like a small forest. I can see why he chose the place despite all those stairs.

His sister gave up her apartment and is moving in with him, but he says there's an extra bedroom for Tina or me. He got visitation rights for Tina as a condition for allowing the divorce to go through in Wisconsin. Since I'm an adult, I can choose where I want to live.

I graduate in 1990 and take a job in Santiago as an urban transportation engineer. I earn one-third the salary I'd earn for the same job in the United States. But the housing's free, I don't have to do my laundry, my new band gets gigs whenever we want thanks to the radio station, and I'm living with this crazy, crippled guy who's pretty much my best friend.

A few months after I return for good, Papá goes in for surgery to remove scar tissue and bone that are pressing on his brain. Over the past year and a half, he's rescued a half dozen Patagonian conures, and while he's recuperating, three chicks hatch. Every day, he sits outside, silently watching the little birds grow as their parents take care of them.

I want to tell him he didn't do such a bad job as a father, but I know he won't believe me. So I let it stay as one more thing he'll have to work through on his own.

I notice that his hand is steadier when he holds the birds, though. He still struggles with flashbacks, alcohol, and a lot of other things in his life, but most of the time now he seems stronger than what he's up against.

In January 1991—a few days after we release the young conures to the wild—he hands me photocopies of some handwritten pages. It's a cool summer morning. We're eating breakfast on the patio before I drive him to work and take the metro from there to my office.

"Are you going to send it out?" I ask. He's been promoted to news director of the radio station, but he also writes for several newspapers and magazines.

"Not here. It's not something I want the whole country to find out about me." He adds, "I'll mail it to Courtney, see what she can do with it." All along, he's been sending pieces to her to translate and publish in the United States. They've earned some decent money out of it, and her publication credits helped her get into graduate school in Spanish on full scholarship at UC-Berkeley.

"Don't let her do too much. We'll never recognize it," I say. Several years ago she won a prize for my account of the night the soldiers took Papá away, but I don't recall it having so much drama. And she totally made up the crying baby in the apartment next door.

Papá laughs. "If it's in English, I won't recognize it

anyway. But the essay is really for you." He runs his hand over his repaired head, where the hair has grown back—thick, wavy, and gray with a few brown streaks. Soon his hair will be long enough to fall over his bad eye, which, with his round gold-rimmed glasses and salt-and-cinnamon mustache, has come to be his preferred look. He says the hair and mustache help to hide the most visible of his wounds.

He turns from me toward the birds that are pecking at the pieces of toast he tossed to them. I wish he'd eaten the toast; he's still too thin. "It's not what you think, why I'm not publishing the essay here," he says without looking at me.

"So what line does this one cross?" I wonder how it could be more revealing than the story of his chance encounter with one of his torturers on a park bench, details about his battle with alcoholism, and his three-part series chronicling his unhappy months in Wisconsin. He jokes about becoming the national exhibitionist, a possibility given the huge audience for his articles and his daily radio show.

"The birds. I'm a writer, not a wildlife rehabilitator." He scrapes his chair back and collects his cigarettes and lighter from the table. "Read it and you'll see what I mean."

CHAPTER THIRTY-THREE
January 1991
Santiago

I stuff the pages into my backpack. On the way to work, the metro is less crowded than usual, because some people are still on summer vacation. I wedge myself into a corner of the train like it's my private world and slide the essay out of the pack. I scan the title several times: "*Un pájaro llamado Pablo: una metáfora.*" It feels like Papá's standing next to me, speaking to me, his breath hot on my face. I read.

A Bird Named Pablo: A Metaphor

Before Gringolandia devoured him, *compañero* Raúl suggested I stay there and get professional help. I told him I didn't need help, that going home to Chile would either cure me of my sickness or kill me, and I didn't care which. In fact, I expected to die before seeing democracy again. So many others had already died.

But things don't usually turn out the way one expects, and at our victory I found myself neither cured nor dead: forty years old, with a ruined body, a haunted mind, and half a lifetime ahead of me—if I chose to accept it.

So I bought a house.

I intended it as my claim to permanence on this earth.

After I moved in, my next-door neighbor, a man in his early fifties named Julián, invited me for supper. "Good luck with the parrot," he said.

"What parrot?"

"You didn't hear it?" Julián raised his voice as if I were deaf.

"I wasn't paying attention." It's one of the many peculiarities of my injury; if I focus hard on one thing—like trying to make sure my books and the furniture got into the right rooms that day—my other senses shut down.

Julián shook his head. "That bird screams all day long. Norma couldn't take it; that's the real reason she moved."

"Where does it live?"

"Behind us. Some of us went over there last winter, when he first got it."

"What happened?"

Julián glanced behind him and shrugged. "He listened, he apologized, and we thought he'd do something. But the parrot kept squawking."

At daybreak I heard the screams. At first I thought they were my own, or echoes from the depths of nightmares. Trembling and bathed in cold sweat, I assessed the rawness of my throat, the arch of my back, flattened my palm against the brand-new sheets to remind myself I was not in hell and no one had hurt me. I stumbled to the window and slammed it shut. The noise was gone, but my stomach churned and my mouth tasted like the oily rags with which they used to gag me.

As I splashed cold water on my face and rinsed my mouth, I thought, *I'm not going to be able to take this either.*

After work that evening, I followed the parrot's cries to a house on the next block and rang the doorbell.

A corpulent man, clean shaven with thinning gray hair, answered. He wore slacks and a dress shirt with the top buttons unbuttoned. A businessman or doctor, I guessed, for he had one of the larger homes in the neighborhood. I wondered what he would make of me, with my worn jeans, shaggy hair, and missing teeth.

"I'm your new neighbor, on the other side of the fence," I said. "I've come about the parrot."

"Yes. You bought Norma Guillén's house." He extended his right hand. "I'm Alfonso."

"Marcelo." No last names.

"Some of your neighbors already spoke with me. I'm sorry, but there's nothing I can do." Alfonso held up his empty hands in a gesture of surrender.

"You can bring the bird indoors."

"I do. Listen."

Alfonso was right. Inside, outside—I couldn't tell the difference. It was as if the walls were made of paper, or the bird's cries inhabited a surreal world unbound by wood, plaster, and clay tile.

"May I see it?"

"Certainly."

I followed Alfonso into the living room and saw the caged bird. It had plucked out almost all its feathers below its neck, and its ruffled down undercoat was dull gray with spots of dried blood.

I looked away, and in the next instant regretted it.

On the wall next to a sliding door was a large framed photo of my back-fence neighbor shaking hands with the dictator while smiling for the photographer.

Suddenly dizzy, I gripped the back of a chair. The bird's screams cut through me.

I forced myself to make eye contact with the creature. It quieted and tucked its wings to its body.

"How did you get the parrot?" I asked.

"Conure. A smaller cousin of a parrot," Alfonso explained. "At work. Then the office closed. I found a new job, but I couldn't keep it there."

In what kind of office does a parrot learn only to scream?

"Can you take it out?"

"It bites," Alfonso said. "It's a vicious bird."

"Then why do you keep it?"

"It's my cross to bear."

I stepped toward the cage. The little parrot held my gaze as if its instincts told it how much we shared. "Will it fly if you let it go?" I already suspected the answer—one of its wings dangled crookedly.

"No. You dislocate their wings when you catch them wild. Then you don't have to keep clipping them."

A spasm of rage seized me. "Maybe it screams because it's in constant pain from what you did to it."

"I don't know," the man stammered.

"You don't know," I repeated slowly. There was a long silence. Then I said, "I'll take it."

"I'm not giving it away."

I lifted the cage from its stand. "This is a very unhappy bird, Alfonso. It deserves a better life, and your neighbors deserve some quiet." On my way out, I added, "I'm sure you can find a cross to bear that doesn't involve hurting others."

At home, I set the cage on the kitchen table and slowly slid my left hand in, fingers curled under my wrist splint. "Hey, little friend. I know you don't look so good," I whispered. "You should have seen me when they let me out of my cage."

I waited. The bird hopped onto the black splint, pecked a few times, and perched on a strap. It stared at me with its yellow-white eyes while I welcomed it to my home and gave it the name Pablo, even though I had no idea if it was male or female.

I felt my sister's hand on my shoulder.

"What are you doing with that parrot, Chelo?" Ileana asked. I sensed her annoyance, as if I were a twelve-year-old and she the mother who'd have to take care of a pet I'd adopted on a whim. On hearing her voice, Pablo dug its claws into the strap and flapped its one good wing.

"We have a bird torturer living behind us," I murmured. "So I liberated it."

"What do you know about birds?"

"Nothing." I ran my finger along the creature's back. "But I know about *this* bird."

My friends brought in wood frames cast off from nearby vineyards, wire fencing, and large stones to build an outdoor aviary—not that Pablo could escape, but I wanted to protect it from predators that feasted on flightless birds. I hung a wooden ladder and strung insulated wire from the ground to the tree branches. Pablo's feathers grew back in brilliant hues of red, yellow, and green underneath and a dusky green on top that matched the Andean cliffs from where it came.

Pablo learned to accept my touch and often perched on my shoulder when I tended the garden or wrote articles in the backyard. It amazed me how quickly and completely the bird healed, and I envied the creature. One time when Julián and his wife came over for supper in the garden, he told me this wasn't usual—once a bird plucked its feathers, it would always pluck. "Maybe this one's trying to teach me something," I said.

Word spread through the neighborhood, and others brought their damaged and distressed parrots. I never figured out which ones were males or females, but the spring after Pinochet had finally given up power, three chicks hatched. Their crippled parents managed to build them a nest, take care of them, and somehow teach them to fly.

By then, my son had returned for good. When the chicks began to fly, we started looking for flocks in the city that they could join. Shortly after New Year's, we found about twenty conures in a park near our neighborhood.

"You know, they're a protected species," I told Daniel.

He grinned. "I see you're still saving the world—three birds at a time."

From the balcony outside his bedroom Daniel climbed onto the roof, crossed to the other side, and detached the netting. He squatted on the shingles, waiting for the conures to start squawking in advance of the sunset. Standing in the garden, cast in the evening's shadows, I handed up my cane.

The screeching started near the mountains. The birds in the city picked up the call. A small flock fluttered overhead.

"Let's do it, *m'ijo*," I shouted.

Daniel hooked one of the wire-crossed wood frames and pulled it away. In his other hand, he held a handful of crackers that he crushed and scattered along the roof. One after the other, the three birds hopped up and pecked at the crackers.

Daniel scooted to the top of the roof,

spreading more crackers. Parrots screeched from the tall trees. He threw the food in the air and raised his arms. "Go!" he shouted. "Be free!"

I watched the three siblings take off into the sunset. They circled, flew upward, high above the city, and vanished into the trees.

Daniel straddled the roof's peak, shading his eyes with his hand. The copper sunset painted his hair and the frames of his glasses. One side of his face glowed; the other was brown in the shadow.

I wondered if my son could see the birds better from his perch, or if he was merely enjoying the view of his new neighborhood. At my feet, half a dozen conures pecked at the sandy floor of their pen, among them the parents of the departed chicks.

"You don't care that your kids took off for good," I said to them.

I glanced up at Daniel, and the aching spread from my heart through the metal cage that was my body. I would never climb to the roof, never share airspace with the birds or watch my neighborhood from above.

From the yard next door I heard, "Good evening, Daniel."

"Good evening, don Julián," Daniel shouted back.

"You look like you're having fun up there."

"Papá and I were letting the young conures out. They can fly now."

"Are you taking good care of your *papá*?"

"Absolutely."

"He's a fine man, your father. If it weren't for him, those birds would have driven the whole neighborhood crazy."

"He does things like that, you know." Daniel stepped past the chimney to the roof on Julián's side. "If it weren't for him, I wouldn't be living here. I'd be a gringo."

Daniel stopped there, and Julián didn't ask him any more. It wasn't the kind of thing one shouted from the rooftop, especially with people like Alfonso nearby.

I inhaled the aroma of laurel carried on the evening breeze. *Hold on to this*, I told myself: the raw, sweet scent of the garden, the parrots calling to their *compañeros* at dusk, my son a free bird against the clear purple sky, the love of family and friends who watched over me.

The beauty of it all filled the hole inside, where torturers had tried to beat out or burn away every emotion except the fear and rage that they expected would eventually consume me.

Hold on to this. You need it.

I lowered myself to the ground next to the earthbound parrots. Pablo strutted up to me. I poked my fingers through the wire and stroked my little friend's head. "I'm healing too," I said. "Just give me time."

Glossary

Note: Spanish is the principal language of more than 350 million people living in Spain and the Americas. With some 20 Spanish-speaking countries and many regions within each of those countries, one finds enormous variations in spoken grammar, vocabulary, and slang expressions. Most of the words and phrases defined in this glossary represent standard Spanish, but I have also indicated those words and expressions that are uniquely Chilean.

amor—love

amigo/a—friend

apúrese—hurry up

botánica—a store that sells herbal and folk remedies, most common in the Spanish Caribbean and among Latinos of Caribbean origin

bienvenidos—welcome

buenas tardes—good afternoon

bueno—good, fine; also serves to indicate agreement or the end of a conversation

¿cachai?—"get it?", a popular Chilean expression

cállate—shut up

cálmate—calm down

carabineros—the police in Chile

castellano—Castilian, an alternate name for the Spanish language, acknowledging that even in Spain not all people speak Castilian Spanish as their first language

chao—in Chile, good-bye

Chelo—a nickname for Marcelo

chileno/a—Chilean

chuta—an expression of disappointment or displeasure, used in various countries in Latin America

colectivo—a Chilean taxi that generally takes several passengers and follows a set route rather than going door-to-door

la comida—in Chile, the main meal of the day, usually eaten around one or two in the afternoon

como el Che—like Che Guevara, the famous rebel leader of the 1950s and 1960s, who played a major role in the 1959 Cuban revolution and was killed in 1967 while trying to organize a guerrilla movement in Bolivia

¿Cómo estai?—a uniquely Chilean way of saying "How are you?" to a friend

compañero/a—companion, comrade

cueca—the Chilean national dance

cuídate—be careful, take care of yourself

¿De dónde son ustedes?—Where are you from?

de nada—you're welcome

el día de San Valentín—Valentine's Day

don/doña—a term of respect for an older person

¿Dónde están?—Where are they?, a reference to the thousands of persons who disappeared at the hands of South American dictatorships in the 1970s and 1980s; today, *los desaparecidos*, the Disappeared, are presumed dead but their bodies still haven't been found

empanadas—a meat-filled pastry popular in Chile and especially among Chileans living abroad

eso no es coraje—that isn't courage

¿Está aquí la Bruja?—Is the witch here?

flaco/a—literally "skinny" but an expression of friendship or affection in Chile fútbol—soccer

gracias—thank you

guerrilleros—warriors

jué—an exclamation of surprise, most often used by people from southern Chile

hasta la victoria siempre—always forward toward victory, a slogan often associated with Che Guevara

hijo del subversivo—son of the subversive

el hombre de la casa—the man of the house

el hueco—the hole

huevón—a common Chilean insult with a broad range of meanings, from idiot to asshole

justicia—justice

lo que no mata, engorda—what doesn't kill him makes him stronger (literally, "fattens him")

macho—literally, a male animal. In the United States, the adjective "macho" refers to someone who has a sexist attitude or shows extreme masculinity (*machismo*); in Latin America, the adjective *machista* would more likely be used 'mano (hermano)—buddy or friend, more commonly used in Mexico and Colombia

¡Manos arriba!—Hands up!

más o menos—more or less

medio cocido—totally wasted (stewed); *medio* usually means "half" in Spanish, but Chileans often use words as the opposite of their original meaning

Mierda. ¿Qué pasó?—Shit. What happened?

m'ijo/a—son, daughter

milico—a negative term for a person in the military

mira—look

no hay justicia—there is no justice

nombre de guerra—underground name (*nom de guerre*)

norteamericano/a—person from North America, especially the United States or Canada; this term lacks the negative connotations of gringo/a

otra vez me sacaron la cresta—a Chilean expression that means "they beat the crap out of me again"

oye—hey

pasaportes—passports

pase—go on, go ahead

pastel de choclo—a popular Chilean dish made of ground corn, meat, hard-boiled eggs, potatoes, black olives, and spices

permiso—excuse me

pisco—a liquor made from distilled grapes and a principal ingredient of the popular Chilean and Peruvian cocktail, the pisco sour

población—a shantytown in Chile

porque soy chileno—because I'm Chilean

puta—whore; used as an adjective, it is an expletive indicating annoyance or disgust

¿Quién es?—Who is it?

quiero morir—I want to die

¿Qui'ubo, cabros?—What's up, kids?

sí—yes

el submarino—literally, submarine, a common torture technique in Chile, Argentina, and Uruguay that involved dunking prisoners and holding them under water; in contrast to waterboarding, a torture technique that simulates drowning by forcing water into prisoners' mouths without submerging them

The cover image features a pool used for el submarino. *It was taken at Villa Grimaldi, an infamous torture center in Santiago, Chile.*

súperbien—excellent, often used in Chile

tenemos las manos limpias—we have clean hands; a popular slogan of the nonviolent resistance to the Pinochet dictatorship

testimonio—testimonial, witness

tetas—tits

tiene clases—s/he has classes (to teach)

tío/a—uncle/aunt

un trago—a drink, usually an alcoholic drink

ven aquí/acá—come, come here

¡vete!—get out, go away

ACKNOWLEDGEMENTS

I am grateful to the many people and organizations that supported this novel in its long journey to publication. Olga Tedías and the members of the Pablo Neruda Cultural Center in Madison, Wisconsin encouraged my initial efforts. In Chile, dozens of people shared their stories, and I would especially like to thank the Chileans who hosted me—Nelson Schwenke, Franca Monteverde, Marcelo Nilo, Manuela Bunster, Eduardo Peralta, and Jaime Barría. A generous grant from the Society of Children's Book Writers and Illustrators not only allowed me to travel to Chile to witness the remarkable, peaceful transition from dictatorship to democracy but also gave me a reason not to give up on the manuscript after I lost a contract for an earlier draft.

I could not have revived this project without my critique group at Professor Java's—Gene Damm, Eric Luper, Mary Nicotera, Robyn Ringler, and Leonora Scotti—or readers Lily Ringler, Beth Janicek, Renee Rude, Kathryn Mora, Jane Gangi, and Beverly Slapin. The late Alexander Taylor and the editorial committee at Curbstone Press, including Jim Coleman, Janet Dauphin, and Bruce Clements, offered the manuscript a new home and valuable suggestions. Mario Nelson helped me with the Chilean Spanish or found someone else who could. I am forever grateful to my longtime *MultiCultural Review* copyeditor, Valerie Shea, and to the folks at Curbstone—Jantje Tielken, Bob Smith, Judy Doyle, and the Board of Directors, who turned a bunch of typed, double-spaced pages into a finished book. Finally, I'd like to thank Guillermo Prado for his cover design, inspired by his own experience as a political prisoner in Pinochet's Chile and his return years later to see the former torture center of Villa Grimaldi converted into a park for peace and human rights.